MISSION TO THE MOON

Books by Mark Cheverton

The Gameknight999 Series
Invasion of the Overworld
Battle for the Nether
Confronting the Dragon

The Mystery of Herobrine Series: A Gameknight999 Adventure
Trouble in Zombie-town
The Jungle Temple Oracle
Last Stand on the Ocean Shore

Herobrine Reborn Series: A Gameknight999 Adventure
Saving Crafter
The Destruction of the Overworld
Gameknight999 vs. Herobrine

Herobrine's Revenge Series: A Gameknight999 Adventure
The Phantom Virus
Overworld in Flames
System Overload

The Birth of Herobrine: A Gameknight999 Adventure
The Great Zombie Invasion
Attack of the Shadow-Crafters
Herobrine's War

The Mystery of Entity303: A Gameknight999 Adventure
Terrors of the Forest
Monsters in the Mist
Mission to the Moon

The Gameknight999 Box Set
The Gameknight999 vs. Herobrine Box Set
The Gameknight999 Adventures Through Time Box Set (Coming Soon!)

The Rise of the Warlords: An Unofficial Interactive Minecrafter's Adventure
Zombies Attack! (Coming Soon)
The Bones of Doom (Coming Soon)
Into the Spiders' Lair (Coming Soon!)

The Algae Voices of Azule Series
Algae Voices of Azule
Finding Home
Finding the Lost

AN UNOFFICIAL NOVEL

MISSION TO THE MOON

THE MYSTERY OF ENTITY303

BOOK THREE

<<< A GAMEKNIGHT999 ADVENTURE >>>

AN UNOFFICIAL MINECRAFTER'S ADVENTURE

MARK CHEVERTON

SKY PONY PRESS
NEW YORK

Sky Pony Press books may be purchased in bulk at special discounts for sales promotion, corporate gifts, fund-raising, or educational purposes. Special editions can also be created to specifications. For details, contact the Special Sales Department, Sky Pony Press, 307 West 36th Street, 11th Floor, New York, NY 10018 or info@skyhorsepublishing.com.

Visit our website at www.skyponypress.com.

10 9 8 7 6 5 4 3 2 1

Library of Congress Cataloging-in-Publication Data is available on file.

Cover design by Owen Corrigan
Cover artwork by Thomas Frick
Technical consultant: *Gameknight999*

Print ISBN: 978-1-5107-1888-3
Ebook ISBN: 978-1-5107-1891-3

Printed in Canada

For my son, the strongest and bravest person that I know. You started this whole adventure with me, and look where we are now!

NOTE FROM AUTHOR

Well, here it is: my eighteenth Minecraft novel. Thinking back to the very first book, *Invasion of the Overworld*, I'm shocked that my characters have gone so far, and that all of you have really taken them into your lives. For that I will truly be forever grateful.

I can remember thinking up Erebus and his battle with Gameknight999 and old Crafter in the first book. I didn't really expect that book to be a success, so getting the opportunity to create Malacoda was really exciting. And then having the battle on the steps of the Source in the third book was such a great treat, for I never really expected all of you to accept my books as warmly as you did—too bad we didn't have the End Cities back then. I think my favorite villain, other than Herobrine, of course, was Xa-Tul. I really love Erebus, and there was always a spooky kind of feeling about him to me, but there was something about Xa-Tul that really resonated with me. My favorite moment with Xa-Tul was probably when Ba-Jin confronted the zombie king; that scene gave me chills, and I hope it did for all of you, too. I'm a little surprised when I say Xa-Tul was my favorite monster, because I thought all of the four horsemen (Xa-Tul, Reaper, Charybdis, and Feyd) were really cool, and at one time, I would have said they, collectively, were my favorites. I particularly love the imagery of them riding their monster horses, but still, I think Xa-Tul is my favorite of the monster kings; sorry, Erebus.

I had a ton of fun writing this series and diving into modded Minecraft. The Twilight Forest mod in Book One is fantastic, and I really enjoyed having Gameknight and his friends explore that world. Originally, I wasn't going to use Mystcraft as the mod for Book Two, because I didn't think it was a big enough change to the basic gameplay, but once I started messing around with it on my PC, I had a great time trying to build a stable Age. The different worlds Gameknight goes through in that book are the actual Ages I constructed when I was learning how to play that mod. I quickly realized there was much more to Mystcraft, and had to include it into the series.

But now, we bring ourselves to Book Three, Entity303, and outer space. If you haven't seen the Galacticraft mod—which enables Gameknight999 to fly into outer space—you should really check out some of the videos listed at the end of the book in the Minecraft Seeds sections. Playing it is super fun, and going to the other planets, especially Fronos, is super cool. I wish the bosses on the planets were different, though; I would have loved to see a space-wither boss. That would have been cool, but the mod is great nonetheless, and I hope many of you get the chance to download it (with your parents' permission, of course) and play it on your computers.

Through eighteen books, I've taken Gameknight999 through countless adventures, so after this one, I'm planning on giving him a little rest. In the next series, *The Rise of the Warlords*, I really want to bring you something new and exciting, and to do that, I think I need some new and exciting characters. There have been some new hero NPCs, with new skills and different characteristics, bouncing around in my head, and in *Zombies Attack!*, the first book of *The Rise of the Warlords*, you'll meet a few of the new characters: Watcher, Planter, and

Blaster. They all have some unique and surprising qualities that I think you will love as much as I do. (What's happening between Watcher and Planter, for instance?) I'm looking forward to using them to explore some new areas of Minecraft, as you'll see discussed at the end of this book.

I've been developing these new characters while writing the eighteen Gameknight novels, but they never seemed to fit into the existing storylines. I really have been thinking about these characters a lot, though, and have written a few short stories about them; for example, some of you have already met one of them, Watcher, on my website at www.gameknight999.com. But I think it's just about time to let all of the new characters get a little sunlight, and for all of you to meet them finally. So, sadly, after this book, we must let Gameknight999 and his friends take a little break while some new characters come out into the sun. I still have some great ideas for Gameknight, but they'll need to wait for a while as Watcher and his friends take the stage.

Thank you for taking Gameknight999, Crafter, Digger, Hunter, Stitcher, and now Weaver into your lives. The stories I've received from you on my website, www.markcheverton.com, have been fantastic. I love reading them all, and hope you keep sending them; it's wonderful to see what you create and bring into the world. Some of you are becoming quite accomplished writers, and that warms my heart.

Keep reading, keep writing, and watch out for creepers.
Mark

The choices you make will determine the trajectory of your life and the consequences you must face. Give thought to your choices and don't act rashly out of anger or jealousy. Instead, think carefully and make the choices that are necessary to get you to your goal. Sometimes, these choices will be extremely difficult and require hard work, but in the end, they will give you the life you seek.

CHAPTER 1
THE MOON

The cold vacuum of outer space wrapped around the rocket like a dark shroud. Stars sparkled in the distance, but they were so impossibly far away they seemed completely inaccessible. Gameknight999 couldn't believe how vast—and empty—space was.

Squawk, Tux, his pet penguin, said softly.

"I know, Tux," Gameknight replied. "I'm afraid too. I didn't think it would be this scary when we blasted off in this rocket ship into outer space. But we had to follow Entity303 into space. He's the only one that knows the location of the portal that'll send Weaver back into the past."

He leaned forward and peered through the window into the darkness. He was stunned by the immensity of it.

Squawk, squawk.

Gameknight patted the tiny animal on the head, but his gloved hand just slid across the penguin's square space helmet, doing little to reassure her.

"Don't worry, I've played this mod a hundred times and it—"

The rocket was suddenly buffeted back and forth for a moment, as if they'd gone through something like space-turbulence. Gameknight's heart thumped in his chest like a drum. It was terrifying.

"Wow, that was . . . scary."

Squawk. The penguin glanced up at Gameknight, a look of fear in her little eyes.

"Yeah, I'm afraid. Being inside the game, *really inside,* makes all this seem a little more dangerous than I thought. But if Entity303 can do it, then so can I."

Squawk.

"I hope that means you have faith in me," Gameknight said.

Squawk, squawk! Tux replied.

"If I remember correctly, soon the rocket should—"

Their rocket shuddered again, as if some great space-beast had grabbed hold of it and was shaking it around. The ship then broke apart, the top and bottom flying out into space, leaving Gameknight and his companion in a square box he now remembered was called the Eagle. It was named after the landing craft from the Apollo 11 mission that actually put two astronauts, Neil Armstrong and Buzz Aldrin, on the Moon's surface for the first time. And now, he and Tux were in Galacticraft's version of the famous spacecraft.

Squawk! Tux warned.

"I know, I can see the speed indicator," Gameknight said. "We're falling faster. . . . How do I slow down? When I played this before, I just hit the space bar, but now, the controls seem totally different."

Tux jumped up, floating through the microgravity until she landed on the Eagle's control panel. Waddling across the console, she started pecking randomly at buttons and lights. Her beak struck a large yellow button, and instantly a thruster fired, pushing upward on the craft.

"Ok, I see it."

He pressed on the button as the little penguin floated back to the ground. With each touch, they slowed down just a little.

Squawk, squawk.

"I can't just press it all the time," Gameknight explained to the tiny penguin. "We have a limited amount of fuel. It needs to be used in spurts."

Over and over, he pressed the button, slowing their descent, then released it, allowing the speed to increase a little, then repeated the process. They sped up, then slowed down, then sped up again as they drew closer to the lunar surface. Gameknight knew that if they hit the ground too hard, they would not survive, but if they ran out of fuel, then they would likely perish as well. It was a tricky balancing act. He watched the fuel indicator as he activated the thrusters, doing the delicate dance between accelerating and decelerating.

The ground was now visible. The surface of the moon was a gray expanse, devoid of any color. Nothing grew here, for there was no air, but he could see countless monsters moving about on the lunar surface. Craters covered the landscape, and although they seemed small and inconsequential from far away, Gameknight realized as the craft drew closer just how huge they actually were.

Soon the ground completely filled the view out the window of the craft, the horizon and space no longer visible. Monsters moved about on the lunar surface, their space helmets occasionally reflecting the light of the sun like shining mirrors. He hit the thruster again and again, slowing the craft's descent. Their landing site was now in view; the base of a small hill. A group of zombies shuffled nearby, but were moving away. Maybe they wouldn't see the ship landing.

Gameknight used the thruster again . . . and again . . . and . . . it stopped working. A red light indicating their fuel level was shining a bright warning; they'd run out. The Eagle drifted down, the gentle tugs of the one-sixth gravity pulling the lander closer and closer, its speed rising until . . . it landed with a rough jolt, kicking up a large puff of dust into the dark sky.

Glancing out the window, Gameknight couldn't see any monsters nearby . . . yet. Opening the hatch, he stepped out of the spacecraft and floated gently to the ground, Tux following close behind. He yanked open a side compartment to access the lander's inventory and pulled out the landing pad and his rocket for the return trip. They also had the oxygen generation equipment and blocks of leaves given to them by King Iago back on the floating island in Mystcraft.

"Come on, Tux," Gameknight said, then stepped toward a small hill nearby. "We need to get our base set up."

As he stepped, he was instantly propelled into the air, his legs churning as he soared across the landscape. Next to him, Tux floated gracefully, flapping her little wings to control her motion. Gameknight reached out and did the same, flapping his arms like an awkward, featherless bird, but of course it did nothing. They floated higher and higher, drifting over a group of black space spiders, each wearing a space helmet and carrying oxygen tanks, their eyes colored a bright, angry green. The fuzzy monsters stared hungrily up at them, and as they floated back to the ground, Gameknight drew his diamond sword with his right hand, the iron blade with his left. As they touched down, the monsters attacked.

Tux moved behind Gameknight, squawking in fear. A spider lunged at the little animal, but the User-that-is-not-a-user was there, ready. His diamond blade came down on the monster, tearing into its HP. The spider screamed in pain, its voice muffled by the space helmet. Spinning, the monster tried to face Gameknight, but it was too late—before it could turn to counterattack, he moved forward, slashing with both swords. The creature disappeared with a pop.

Pain exploded across Gameknight's back. Rolling to the side, he turned and swung his iron sword, blocking the wicked, curved claw that was heading toward his head. Two spiders were trying to attack, one in the way of the other. Gameknight shifted to the side, keeping one spider in front of the other, then attacked the closest. The monster swung with two legs, one from the right and one from the left, dark claws shining in the harsh sunlight. Gameknight deflected both away, then brought his blades down upon the creature. She screeched in agony and backed up. He glanced around and found the second spider gone . . . good. Advancing, the User-that-is-not-a-user attacked with a flurry of strikes, and though the monster tried to deflect them, she was not fast enough. His blade found her flesh over and over again, causing the creature to flash red as she took damage. And then finally, with a look of despair on her hideous, green-eyed face, the spider disappeared, leaving behind three glowing balls of XP.

Tux screeched. Gameknight spun around. A spider was approaching from behind, ready to strike his exposed back, but Tux was attacking it with her little yellow beak. She pecked and pecked at the spider while she screeched and squawked. The spider stopped her advance and turned towards its irritant; that was its first mistake. Tux pecked at the monster's leg again and again, but her beak did no harm to the fuzzy creature. Annoyed, the spider raised a curved claw and swung it at the penguin; that was its second mistake.

"Oh no, you don't!" Gameknight screamed as loud as he could, then launched himself at the spider, barreling into the creature with his body. The spider was knocked aside, but quickly stood and attacked again. But the User-that-is-not-a-user was ready. He blocked an attack from the right, then two claws came at him from the left. Gameknight deflected the claws, his swords ringing with each impact. The creature tried to retreat, but he pressed the attack, his blades everywhere at once. He hit the beast on the side, then the head, then the legs, each time causing the monster to flash red and take damage. The spider looked around desperately, hoping for help from another monster, but there were none nearby.

Making a carefully controlled jump, Gameknight came down on the creature, driving both blades at the monster and taking the last of her HP, finally causing the fuzzy giant to disappear.

With a sigh of relief, Gameknight put away a sword and reached up to wipe his brow with a sleeve. His arm bumped up against his glass space helmet as beads of sweat trickled down his face, one of them tumbling to the edge of his mouth; it tasted salty.

He turned toward his companion. "I guess we need to remember that monsters on the moon are just as dangerous as in the Overworld, Tux."

Squawk, squawk.

Gameknight glanced around, making sure there were no other monsters nearby. There were none. *Good.* He motioned Tux to follow, and moved to a large crater. Jumping from the rim, he floated to the bottom of the recession.

"This will be a perfect place for our base, Tux. Monsters won't be able to see us from far away."

Squawk, squawk!

The penguin moved to the rim of the crater and scanned the terrain while Gameknight pulled more equipment from his inventory. The oxygen collector was placed on a flat section of moon rock, followed by the coal generator. Around the collector, he started placing blocks of leaves, keeping them as close to the mechanical cubes as possible. Pulling a stack of coal from his inventory, he placed it in the generator. Small sparkles floated from the leaves to the collector as oxygen was collected from the leafy blocks.

"Okay, we're making oxygen; now we need to make a large bubble so we can take off these space suits."

He picked up a gray cube that looked like a furnace, but this one had multi-bladed fans on each side: an oxygen distributor. He placed it on the ground just a few blocks away, then ran glass pipes between it and the collector.

Nothing happened.

"Where's the bubble?" Gameknight said to himself, confused. He checked to make sure the pipe was connected on the correct side of the distributor; it all seemed good.

Squawk, Tux called out. She had jumped off the hill of moon rock and was now standing on the coal generator.

"Oh, of course . . . we need power."

Gameknight pulled a second coal generator out of his inventory and placed it next to the bubble distributor. Opening the top, he placed pieces of coal inside, then closed the lid. Instantly, a bubble of air formed around the distributor, slowly growing bigger and bigger.

"Now we're talkin'," the User-that-is-not-a-user said. "What do you think, Tux?"

Squawk, squawk, squawk.

"OK, come stand next to me. When I remove your helmet, you must stay inside the bubble. . . . You got it?"

The penguin jumped up and down in affirmation. Gameknight waited until the bubble grew to full size, then grabbed the glass cube on the creature's head and removed her helmet. Then he did the same for himself.

Air never smelled so sweet. He took a deep slow breath and just enjoyed the oaky aroma and the freshness of the atmosphere; the leaves must have been from an oak tree. He glanced down and saw the penguin taking a deep breath and almost smiling with her yellow beak.

"OK, now we bring our friends."

Gameknight pulled out the magical ring he'd been given by one of their allies in Mystcraft, a demon named Kahn. The ring sparkled in the light from the square sun that blazed overhead. A single blood-red gem sat in the center of the ring, ornate runes scrawled across the top. He put it on his finger.

"Okay, I hope this works."

He reached for the ring, but paused. Gameknight struggled with the thought of bringing all of his friends to this incredibly inhospitable place. Being on the moon was dangerous, incredibly dangerous. Chasing their enemy, Entity303, had been a fatal mission for some of their friends already, and he knew the worst of it was yet to come. If he brought his friends on this pursuit through outer space, some of them might get hurt . . . or worse.

"I'm just a kid, and Entity303 always seems to be a step ahead of us. How could just the two of us be expected to stop him?"

He stared down at Tux. Her dark eyes seemed to agree with him, but there was also a shadow of confidence there as well that Gameknight didn't share.

"I wish the Oracle were here. She'd tell me the right thing to do."

The Oracle was an anti-virus program sent into Minecraft to defeat a virus, Herobrine. Her presence was always there in the game, noticeable by the music that floated through Minecraft. But since Entity303 had reprogrammed the game with mods, the Oracle had been strangely silent.

Suddenly, a bright, jagged gash appeared in the sky overhead. It wasn't a lightning bolt or light from another spacecraft; no, it wasn't an object at all. What it looked like, in fact, was a rip in the sky, as if someone had just tried to tear apart the universe. But as quickly as it had appeared, it sealed itself up, mending the rift and healing the Minecraft universe.

"You see that, Tux?"

Squawk! the penguin replied, sounding just as concerned.

"I think all the mods Entity303 loaded into Minecraft are starting to cause glitches in the servers. We need to hurry." Gameknight turned and faced his penguin friend. "I have no choice, Tux. I know I can't do this on my own. If I try, I'll just mess it up, and then *everything* could be destroyed." He glanced up at the spot where the tear in the fabric of Minecraft had been and shuddered. "My friends will help keep me from messing this up and failing. I need them here with me, regardless of the danger."

He sighed, then pressed the crimson gem. A flash of light momentarily blinded him, but when his vision cleared, he found all of his friends clustered together in front of him. At the center was the stocky form of Digger, taller than the rest of the NPCs. Herder, his long black hair tucked under his helmet, quickly checked the helmets on each of his wolves, then sent them out to form a protective circle. The animals had a difficult time moving across the moon at first without flying up into the air, but they quickly adapted.

Crafter moved to his side and gazed up at the blue and green cube that hung high above them in the dark sky. It was the Overworld, their home. His blue eyes were bright with wonder.

"Being the oldest villager in Minecraft, I thought I'd seen it all," Crafter said, his bright blue eyes glowing from behind his square space helmet. "But I never imagined I'd see something like this."

"It's beautiful," Stitcher said, her red hair almost shining with a crimson halo in the bright sunlight.

The young girl already had her enchanted bow out and an arrow notched, ready for battle.

"Yeah, I'm not one to talk about things being pretty and all that," her older sister, Hunter, said. Her curly red hair was just as magnificent as her younger sibling's. "But that is pretty cool."

"We must hurry, yes, yes," Empech said. The gray skinned gnome adjusted the huge backpack that he always wore; it didn't fit well over his oxygen tanks. "The enemy, Entity303, must be found."

"Hmmm . . . Empech is correct," Forpech, the other gnome in their party, and a new addition to the group, added. His dark eyes seemed filled with fear. "We must return Weaver to the past before it is too late."

"I agree," Crafter said. "Maybe we should go out and scout around until we find some sign of Entity303. He must have—"

"I can see his base from here," a voice shouted.

They all turned to see Weaver standing atop a large hill of moon rocks about two dozen blocks away. The young boy pointed off into the distance.

"Let's go!" Weaver yelled, then took off running.

"Wait!" Gameknight shouted, but the boy was already gone. "Herder, send your wolves with him. If Weaver is killed, we'll never be able to send him back into the past and repair the timeline."

Herder nodded, then whistled and pointed toward the hill. The wolves instantly responded, loping across the dusty landscape after the boy. Gameknight put on his helmet, then replaced the glass cube over Tux's head. He glanced around at the makeshift base he'd constructed, then sighed.

"We can't just leave this here," Gameknight said. He pulled out his pickaxe. "Digger, can you help me?"

"I'll do it," the stocky NPC said. "You go, and I'll be right behind you." Not waiting for a response, he started shattering the blocks of leaves and oxygen generation equipment with his pickaxe, storing everything away in his inventory.

Gameknight turned and sprinted after Weaver and the wolves, the rest of the party following. They bounced across the gray landscape, everyone struggling to keep their feet on the ground, except the pechs—somehow, the small, gray-skinned gnomes were able to run across the dusty landscape without any problems; maybe it was because of the oversized backpacks that each wore, weighing them down.

Cresting the hill, they saw Weaver approaching a collection of leaves. The wolves were already within the bubble of air Entity303 had constructed around them. As he neared, Weaver entered the bubble and removed his helmet, then waved at the others, his blue eyes, identical to Crafter's, shining in the bright light. It was no surprise his eyes were the same as Crafter's, since they were related; Weaver was Crafter's great uncle, taken from the past and brought into this time.

Finally, Gameknight reached Entity303's base. A pile of tree leaves was positioned around his oxygen collector, the bubble distributor nearby. Inside the base, they found equipment: pieces of dark metal, nose cones, large rocket engines . . . all of the things necessary to build a rocket. But by the size of the parts, the new rocket would be much larger than the one that had brought Entity303 to the moon.

"Gameknight, look at this," Crafter said.

Trying not to bounce, Gameknight moved to the young NPC's side. On a wall of cobblestone was a map. It was almost entirely black, with concentric circles drawn around a yellow spot. Outside of the first rings was another spot, with smaller concentric circles.

"What is it?" Digger asked, his voice sounding weak and afraid, far from its normally booming volume and confident tone.

"It's a map of Galacticraft," Gameknight said. "This first set of circles is our solar system. The third planet is the Overworld, and the little dot next to it is the Moon; that's where we are now."

"What are those circles near the edge of the solar system?" Digger asked.

"It's another solar system," Gameknight explained. "If you have a large enough rocket, then you can go way out there and explore those planets."

"There's something written next to the moon," Stitcher said. "What does it say?"

Crafter moved closer. He took off his helmet so he could get closer; the bubble of air around them allowed him to breathe. "It says, 'Minecraft's core, that is where the destruction will start.' I wonder what that means."

"I think there's more writing near the other solar systems, but I can't quite make it out," Stitcher said, pulling out a torch and placing it on the ground. The flame cast a wide circle of flickering light. "I think it says, 'The cake is a lie.' What's that mean?" She moved closer to the map, trying to read some even smaller letters. "It also says, 'All paths through space go through the Moon boss. That's where the destruction of Minecraft will begin.' This is kinda creepy."

Just then, the sorrowful moan of a zombie floated across the lunar surface. The wolves instantly growled, their proud voices muted inside their space helmets. The animals moved to one side of the base, their fur sticking out and eyes bright red. Gameknight drew his sword. At first, he'd planned to choose the yellow-glowing infused blade given to him by King Iago, but, after a second thought, he put away that weapon and instead drew his diamond blade.

Who knows how long the energy in the infused-sword will last? Gameknight thought. *I'll save it until it's necessary.*

He took a step toward the monster sounds. Far away, he could see a zombie shuffling aimlessly about. The creatures hadn't noticed them . . . not yet.

"We need to catch Entity303 before all the moon monsters find us," Weaver said.

"And before he escapes, yes, yes," Empech added .

"But where do we search for him?" Stitcher asked. Her enchanted bow was in her hand, magical power flowing across the weapon, casting an iridescent blue glow on the surroundings. She glanced anxiously in the direction of the zombie moans, then looked back at Gameknignt999. "We could go off in any direction and completely miss him."

"Then which way do we go?" Gameknight turned to Crafter. "What do you think?"

"Well, I . . ."

"Hmmm . . . we should go to the moon village," Forpech said, his deep, scratchy voice sounding like distant thunder.

"Moon village?" Crafter asked, confused.

The pech pointed off into the distance with an enchanted wand, its tip capped with a dull green crystal. "Yes, Forpech senses a village. Hmmm . . . it is just over that hill."

"Hunter, Stitcher . . . go check," Gameknight commanded.

The sisters took off running, almost hopping through the faint gravitational field. When they reached the top of the hill, Hunter turned and waved her bow, signaling that the little gray gnome was correct.

"OK," Gameknight said, glad to have a place to start their search. "Let's get to that village and see if they can help. Entity303's map says his path leads through the Moon boss, so let's get there first and surprise him."

"Alright!" Weaver exclaimed and took off running, the rest of them following close behind.

Gameknight checked Tux's helmet, then lifted the penguin and held her under his arm.

"I hope it wasn't a mistake bringing all my friends here, Tux," he said in a soft voice.

Squawk, she replied, her squeaky reply almost a whisper.

"This might be too dangerous for us, and I may have sentenced at least one of them to death, maybe more," Gameknight said.

Squawk, squawk.

He sighed, then took off running as needles of doubt pierced his every nerve.

CHAPTER 2
ENTITY303

Entity303 stepped into the Moon Boss chamber, his blue and white Alpha Yeti armor sparkling with magical enchantments. Instantly, the Moon Boss appeared at the center of the chamber, materializing out of the dark. The evil user knew what the huge skeleton would try to do, though, and he wasn't going to give the monster the chance.

The Moon Boss reached down, trying to grab the intruder and toss him into the columns of lava that flowed from ceiling to floor in the corners, but Entity303 had used a potion of Swiftness before entering the room; the monster couldn't touch him.

Streaking past the creature, he slashed at its bony legs, his yellow-glowing sword tearing into its HP. The Moon Boss bellowed in pain, then turned and fired a string of arrows. Entity303 leapt high, shooting his body toward the wall. Flipping around, the user landed with his feet against the gray brick wall, then pushed off hard, launching himself as if he were an armored missile. When he collided with the massive skeleton, Entity303 slashed repeatedly at the monster, scoring hit after hit. The giant creature flashed red as it took damage.

More arrows streaked through the lunar atmosphere, but Entity303 was too close for the creature to get a good shot.

"Ha ha . . . is that the best you got?" the user laughed cruelly.

"No one mocks the Moon Boss." The skeleton tried again to reach out and grab Entity303, but missed. "I will make you pay."

"We'll see who pays."

Entity303 pushed away from the monster. He slowly settled to the ground, slashing with his blade as he descended. The monster screamed again, agony filling its voice.

The Moon Boss fell to one knee. He dropped one of his bows, but still fired with the other one. Entity303 danced around the projectiles, moving in for another attack, and then struck the monster, his glowing blade digging in deep.

Dropping his remaining bow, the Moon Boss fell to the floor.

"You are defeated, skeleton," Entity303 said. "All I want is the tier-two key. Give it to me, and you will live another day." He moved close, his sword pointed at the creature's pale head. "Don't make me destroy you."

The monster glared up at the user, an expression of fear on his bony face. With a sigh, he pulled out the key and tossed it onto the ground.

"You should remember my name, skeleton. It's Entity303, and I'm going to destroy all of Minecraft."

The Moon Boss mumbled something, but in his weakened state, he could barely speak.

"I'm gonna take what you have in your treasure room, and go to the farthest reaches of outer space," Entity303 bent down and picked up the key. "No one will suspect what I'm going to do until it's too late. Enjoy your last few hours of life, Moon Boss."

The monster mumbled something again. Entity303 couldn't understand him, so he just kicked him hard, causing the creature to groan in pain. The evil user laughed.

"Those fools who fired me from the Minecraft programming team will rue the day they messed with Entity303." He moved to the passage opening that led to the treasure room, then turned and glared at the collapsed monster on the ground. "I will destroy their creation from within, then laugh as they try to salvage anything."

He glanced one more time around the gray chamber. Columns of lava flowed down the corners of the room, with iron bars lining the edges of the boiling stone. They cast an orange glow across the room, making the chamber unusually bright compared to the rest of the dungeon. The boss lay crumpled on the ground, barely alive and whimpering . . . pathetic.

Turning, he strode out of the room and into the next passage. As soon as he left the chamber, the Moon Boss disappeared. He would respawn the next time someone entered.

"I hope the Moon Boss takes his vengeance on whomever comes next," Entity303 said to the cold brick walls.

Entity303 walked majestically through the side passage that led to the treasure room. The narrow hallway turned once to the left, then to the right, blocking out any of the orange glow from the boss chamber. Now, cloaked in darkness, the passage seemed to have a hint of danger to it; was there something hiding just out of reach? Entity303 took out his blazing yellow sword. Instantly, the infused blade filled the corridor with light, showing the gray brick walls.

Normally, he wouldn't be afraid of any monster in Minecraft, for the hostile mobs were insignificant compared to Entity303's skill in the game. But, in this case, he wasn't just playing the game; he was really *in* the game. After stealing Gameknight's father's invention, the Digitizer, from the company it had been sold to, Entity303 had used it to bring his entire being into the game, just like Gameknight999. He was a user, but he was also something more. He could call himself a User-that-is-not-a-user, but he knew that was the title his enemy, Gameknight999, used. It was a title for a pathetically weak player he'd left trapped in a previous mod, Mystcraft.

"Without Gameknight999 chasing me, I can do whatever I want," he said to the cold walls.

The passage turned again, then opened to a bright room: the treasure room. Tall columns of glowstone stood in the corners of the chamber, bathing the small room in a golden-yellow light. With no monsters nearby, he put away his sword, then pulled out the key he'd taken from the Moon Boss. At the center of the room sat a wooden chest. It looked ancient, as if it hadn't been opened in centuries. He knelt before the chest and inserted the gold key. Turning it, he heard a satisfying click. He knew he shouldn't be able to hear the locking mechanism disengage, for there was no air to transmit the sound waves, but Minecraft didn't necessarily follow the same rules of physics as the outside world.

Carefully, he opened the chest and peered inside. Before him lay what he was searching for: the designs for the next rocket. He breathed a sigh of relief.

"This rocket will let me get even deeper into the cosmos," Entity303 said; he loved the sound of his own voice. "And the closer I get to the edge of Minecraft, the more destruction I can cause."

He reached into the chest and withdrew the plans, the parchment crackling as if it were ancient. Stuffing it into his inventory, he slammed the lid shut, dust rising from the chest. He chuckled a maniacal laugh that echoed off the stone walls and reflected back to him from all sides. It made it seem almost as if he were at the center of a huge party, though only he was in attendance.

"Those programmers destroyed my reputation by firing me from the Minecraft development team," Entity303 said. "I lost all my friends and associates. I lost everything. Now, I'm going to teach them what that feels like. Soon, those who fired me will feel my pain."

Moving to a corner of the room, Entity303 put away his sword and pulled out a diamond pickaxe. It sparkled with enchantments, casting a glow on his yeti armor. He removed his chest plate and stuffed it into his inventory, then pulled out a jetpack and quickly put his arms through the straps.

"It's time to get out of here," he said.

Stuffing the piece of paper in his inventory, he activated his rocket pack. With tongues of flame shooting out behind him, he floated to the ceiling. Swinging the pickaxe with all his strength, he dug straight up. Normally, in Minecraft, that was a bad thing to do, digging straight up, but on the Moon there was no gravel or sand or lava, making it completely safe. He carved his way upward until he finally pierced the last layers of moon dirt and moon stone, and shot up into the star-speckled dark sky.

Turning off the jet pack, he slowly settled to the ground. As he descended, Entity303 gave himself the smallest of nudges with the jet pack, carrying him back toward his hastily constructed base. But as he approached, he could see footsteps leading to his base, then heading away toward the distant village of aliens.

"Huh . . . it seems that the pathetic User-that-is-not-a-user, Gameknight999, survived Iago and the monsters in Mystcraft after all," Entity303 said to the empty landscape. "He must have followed me here into space. But where did he get his own rocket ship?" And then he realized who must have helped him. "Iago," he said, then laughed it off. "So what? All the better. Let him watch the destruction of Minecraft from the cold emptiness of outer space."

Turning off his jetpack, he landed on the ground and moved to his NASA workbench. Long, gangly arms stuck up out of the bench, apparently designed to hold the device being constructed. He placed the tier-two rocket schematic on the bench. Instantly, the space ship was unlocked, allowing him to begin crafting.

"Now I'm glad I didn't destroy all the monster spawners down in that dungeon," Entity303 said as he fitted the rocket fins and hull plating to the rocket. "When the Moon Boss respawns, I bet he'll be especially angry after he realizes I looted his chest . . . good. Maybe he'll take it out on Gameknight and his annoying friends."

He put the last touches on the rocket, then moved his new ship from the workbench to the launch pad that sat outside his bubble of air. Quickly, he put his oxygen tanks in the compressor and topped them off, filling them to the brim with life-sustaining air. Putting the oxygen gear back on, he used his pickaxe on the compressor, bubble distributor, and oxygen collector, breaking them down so he could place them back into his inventory. He then took all the pipes and leaves, too.

"No sense leaving anything behind that'll help my adversaries," he said with a sneer. "Though, maybe I can leave behind one little present."

Entity303 reached into his inventory and pulled out a spawner he'd been holding onto for a while. It was a creeper spawner: a dark cage able to bring the explosive creatures to life, complete with space helmets and oxygen gear.

He placed it on the ground, then backed away. Instantly, a tiny green figure began to spin within the spawner. The monster slowly grew in size, but would take a while before it was ready to come forth and wreak havoc. Moving to his ship, the evil user climbed in and closed the hatch.

"I hope you have enough air, Gameknight999," Entity303 said with a laugh, then climbed into his ship. "See you on Mars, User-that-is-not-a-user. That is, if you manage to get off the moon . . . alive."

And with that thought, he pressed the large red button on the control panel and blasted off into the inky black sky.

CHAPTER 3

ALIENS

They crossed the dull gray wasteland in leaps and bounds. With the reduced gravity, a jump into the air caused each of them to soar six times higher. It was fun at first, but Gameknight quickly became frustrated.

"I just want to sprint, not fly," the User-that-is-not-a-user complained.

"When you had Elytra wings, all you wanted to do was fly," Hunter chided. "Now you can fly anytime you want, and you want to stay on the ground. Sometimes, I think you like suffering."

She cast him a sarcastic smile as she soared over his head. Gameknight watched as she did a few graceful flips, then landed delicately on the dusty ground. He moved up next to her, loping along in lock step.

"Did you see any monsters while you were up there?" he asked.

She nodded. "Yep, they're all over the place, but fortunately, none are nearby . . . for now."

"I hope it stays that way," Gameknight replied .

"Not likely." Hunter replied lightly as she leapt into the air again, her joyous giggles muffled slightly by her glass helmet.

Gameknight looked up at his friend and smiled. Her long, curly red hair was trapped inside the space helmet; the curls were pressed up against the transparent cube, piling up around her ears and the back of her head as if they were trying to break free. The crimson locks bounced about when she ran, but floated, weightless, as she soared through the air. It reminded him of the box of springs his dad kept in their basement, which at the moment was probably just a few feet from his unconscious body in the physical world.

"Gameknight, Weaver said something," Herder said, glancing over his shoulder. "You listening? Are you awake?"

"Sorry, I was just thinking," the User-that-is-not-a-user replied, chagrined. "What did he say?"

"I said, 'The village is just over this hill,'" Weaver shouted from atop a huge mound of moon rocks.

Gameknight ran to the top of the hill and gazed down at the village. He was shocked at what he found. Instead of a collection of square homes with pointed roofs, it was a group of pale domes, each identical in size and shape. They were clearly made from the same material as the landscape, pale gray moonstone. The curved buildings merged in with the land around them, making them difficult to see from a distance. However, the farms were easy to spot. The brown soil and green stalks of wheat stood out in sharp contrast to the mundane background. It was almost as if the color in the plants was somehow amplified, the greens and yellows and browns incredibly bright in comparison to the pallid, lunar landscape.

"Come on, let's go talk to them," Gameknight said.

Herder stepped to the User-that-is-not-a-user's side and put a restraining hand on his arm, stopping him from running down the hill. Gameknight turned and looked at his friend just as the boy whistled. The shrill sound was muffled by the space helmet on his head, but it still carried. The wolves barked and ran to his side. He pointed to the distant village, signaling the wolves to go check it out first. The furry white protectors bounded down the hill and into the village, searching the community for threats. A minute later, the pack leader let out a majestic howl, signaling it was safe. With a nod, Herder ran down the hill, followed by Weaver; the two were now inseparable friends. Gameknight smiled and followed, the rest of the party close behind him.

When they reached the domed structures, the place seemed deserted. The crops were well-tended and the walkways swept, but no villagers could be seen.

"They're inside the buildings," Stitcher said, seeing the expression of confusion on his face.

"What?"

"Inside their domes," the young girl answered, her crimson curls glowing bright in the sunlight.

Gameknight moved to one door, but Digger got there before him. The big NPC peered through the inset window, then slowly opened the door.

"It's OK, we won't hurt you," the stocky NPC said reassuringly. "We're friends."

A villager with blue skin stepped out of the building, his arms linked across his chest. He wore a brown smock with a dark brown stripe running down the center. The stripe didn't seem to identify their job, for all of the villagers in the building were dressed identically. Digger stepped out of the way and allowed the NPC to pass. Another adult, likely the first villager's wife, moved past, her dark red eyes glowing on either side of her bulbous nose. They mumbled something, but neither Digger or Gameknight could understand anything.

"We need your help," Gameknight said to the mother. "Have you seen any other people like us?"

Crafter approached and tried to talk with the father. The villager mumbled something unintelligible, then glanced back at the open door. Just then, two alien children emerged, a boy and a girl.

"Children," Digger moaned. "They have a girl and a . . ."

The big NPC looked down at the kids and became very quiet. Gameknight knew Digger was thinking about his lost son, Topper. He turned away, moving into a dark section of the curved home, lost in the sudden despair. After a moment, he returned, square splotches of moisture stuck to the inside of his space helmet.

"You seem about the same age as my Topper," Digger said, his voice choked with grief. Kneeling, he gazed at the boy with sad eyes. "He was probably your age when he . . . died."

Gameknight moved to his friend's side and put a reassuring hand on his shoulder. The stocky villager reached into his inventory and pulled out a loaf of bread. He extended it to the boy, then proffered an apple to the girl. The children took the food and instantly sat on the dusty ground to eat.

Crafter moved behind his friend to add his support to the grieving villager.

"Digger, maybe you should tell us what occurred," Crafter said. "You've never spoken about what happened to Topper. Unburdening yourself and leaning on your friends will help."

"Nothing will help. This is my failure . . . a parent's failure," Digger said in a soft voice, almost a whisper. "I must bear it alone."

The stocky villager stood, then turned and stared at Gameknight999. He was just about to say something more, his eyes filled momentarily with hope, but then his perpetual expression of sadness washed across his square face again and he turned away.

Gameknight sighed. He had to help his friend somehow; but how do you help someone with the loss of a child? Long ago, before the User-that-is-not-a-user had used his father's Digitizer to go inside the game, he'd been a griefer, and back then he wouldn't have thought twice about casually destroying a village. Back then, he'd assumed the villagers were just lines of mindless code, not living beings with hopes and dreams.

Back then, in his arrogance, he'd caused the death of Digger's wife, who was Topper's and Filler's mother. When he entered the game as the User-that-is-not-a-user, Digger had hated him, and rightfully so. But when Gameknight had saved the village from a monster attack, with the help of his friend Shawny, Digger had finally forgiven him for his stupid and careless act. Since then, Gameknight had been brought in as part of their family, fully accepted by Digger and his children. And now, here was his friend, the kind and forgiving Digger, suffering such overwhelming grief. It made Gameknight's heart ache to see him like this. He had to do something for him, but what? If only he could . . .

"Zombies! A lot of them!" Stitcher suddenly shouted from the watch tower. "And they're heading straight for us!"

Gameknight would have to worry about Digger later. Right now, it was time to fight.

CHAPTER 4

MOON ZOMBIES

A chill ran down Gameknight's spine as the sorrowful moans from the zombie horde floated across the lunar landscape. They moved across the gray surface effortlessly from a lifetime of experience.

An arrow flew across the sky, followed by another. Gameknight glanced up at the village watch tower and saw Hunter had climbed up there with her sister and was now firing at the monsters. The arrows leapt from her bow, their points wreathed with magical flames. But the fiery tips were immediately extinguished due to the lack of oxygen. At first, most of the arrows flew well beyond the zombies, completely missing. Hunter yelled in frustration, but then she corrected her aim, adjusting for the reduced gravity, and fired again. The arrows now fell amongst the advancing horde. The zombies moaned in pain, the pointed shafts finding green zombie flesh. They flashed red, taking damage.

Gameknight pulled out his own bow and fired at an approaching monster. The arrow sailed over the monster's head, completely missing.

"You have to aim lower than normal because of the moon's gravity," Crafter said, reminding him.

The young NPC was at his side, his own bow humming as he fired arrow after arrow at the monsters. Gameknight tried again, this time aiming almost directly at the nearest of the creatures. It was a tricky thing to get used to, having aimed a certain way in Minecraft for so long, but this time the arrow struck the monster in the leg, causing it to stumble for just an instant. Herder's wolves immediately dashed out to attack the fallen monster, but their space helmets prevented the canines' sharp teeth from hurting the zombie. Instead, the wolves were now defenseless. One of the animals yelped in pain as a zombie's claws raked across its side.

"I don't think so!" Herder yelled as he drew his iron sword and charged at the offending monster. "Nobody hurts my wolves!"

"Herder, wait!" Gameknight shouted, but the lanky boy didn't listen.

Herder attacked the zombie. But he lunged with too much force, and rocketed up into the air, flying high over the monster. While the creature stared up at the would-be attacker bouncing over his head, Gameknight leapt forward, keeping his body low to the ground, and smashed into the zombie with his enchanted diamond blade. Loud cries of pain came from the creature as the User-that-is-not-a-user hit it repeatedly. Before it ever had a chance to flee, the monster disappeared with a pop. Colorfully glowing balls of XP glittered on the ground where the zombie had stood.

Herder slowly settled back to the ground. He moved to Gameknight's side, a crazed look on his square face.

"Herder, send your wolves back to the village," he said. "They'll only get hurt out here."

The boy nodded, then whistled and pointed to the village. Moving silently, the animals sprinted to the village, then formed a defensive line, ready to protect the blue NPCs if the zombies decided to advance in that direction.

"Come on, Herder," Gameknight said.

Nearby, he saw Weaver running toward a group of zombies. The boy was completely outnumbered, but did not hesitate. The User-that-is-not-a-user ran straight toward him, Herder right on his heels.

"Weaver, run toward us," Gameknight shouted.

But the boy ignored him. Instead, he slashed at one zombie, then jumped high in the air. As he soared overhead, Weaver twisted in the air, turning himself upside down. As he floated over the zombie's heads, he struck at them with his sword, hitting each and making them flash red. When he landed on the ground again, the zombies turned and charged. But now, Gameknight and Herder were there, attacking the monsters from behind. They tore into the monsters, destroying one, then the next, and the next, until the entire group was eliminated.

"They're attacking the farms," Hunter yelled from the watch tower behind them.

Arrows soared across the dark lunar sky, seeking zombie flesh. Hunter and Stitcher were firing toward the fields of wheat and beetroot, trying to push the monsters back. Gameknight ran toward the farms. He could see zombies approaching, their angry moans floating through the vacuum. The unbridled anger in their decaying voices was easy to hear. This rage was something unusual, though—not the typical zombie violence. There was something else happening here.

The companions reached the fields at the same time as the monsters. Swords met zombie claws as the two sides clashed. Gameknight blocked an attack heading for Weaver just as another creature slashed at his shoulder. The claws scratched across his diamond armor, and one razor-sharp nail made its way through a small gap, finding soft flesh. Pain flowed down his arm as if it were on fire, causing him to flash red as he took damage.

Meanwhile, Herder and Weaver were fighting shoulder-to-shoulder, their attacks completely synchronized as each watched out for the other. They were like a dual-bladed machine of destruction.

Crafter suddenly appeared at the User-that-is-not-a-user's side, the young villager's enchanted iron sword landing critical hits. Digger moved into the line, but the expression on the big NPC's face told Gameknight he was terrified, his courage still a distant memory.

The friends pushed the monsters back, destroying one after another. Their orchestrated attacks, one person attacking while the other defended, were devastating. The zombies didn't stand a chance and fell under their blades until just a single monster remained.

"Don't destroy the last one," Gameknight said. "We need to understand what's going on here. This wasn't a normal attack." He turned to Digger. "Make a hole for our green friend here."

Digger dug a hole two blocks deep. Herder and Weaver, with the sharp tips of their swords scratching at the monster's neck, slowly pushed the zombie backward until the creature fell in the narrow pit.

"This zombie is put in a hole so that the villagers can do murder?" the monster asked, its growling voice muffled by its space helmet.

"We don't murder," Gameknight replied. "But we will defend ourselves and our friends from attack at all costs. Now, if you answer my questions, we will allow you to live. If not, then balls of XP will be all that remain after you are destroyed."

"Why should this zombie believe you?" The zombie glared up at them.

"I'm Gameknight999," the User-that-is-not-a-user said. "I always keep my word."

The zombie glanced up at the NPCs that surrounded him, then glanced at the blue-skinned moon villagers peeking out of windows and from behind doors.

"Alright. Since no other choice is available, this zombie will answer your questions," the creature moaned.

"Tell me, why did you attack this village?"

"A pale-skinned villager attacked and murdered zombies not far from here," the monster said. "We avenge our own, whether they be zombies, or skeletons, or spiders. The mobs on the moon will not tolerate senseless violence."

"What are you talking about?" Crafter asked. "We didn't hurt any monsters until you attacked this village."

"A pale-skinned villager attacked zombies for no reason. It looked like that one." The zombie pointed a dark claw at Gameknight999. "Letters floated over its head. It used a glowing sword, destroying many. The attack was for no reason. And worst yet, the criminal laughed as it slayed zombie after zombie. Revenge is sought."

"That sounds like Entity303," Gameknight said.

"Destroying zombies for no reason sounds like something he would do," Crafter said.

"Absolutely," Weaver added. "After he captured me, taking me out of the past and into the future, he killed things all the time for no reason, just because he could."

"Your enemy is our enemy," Gameknight said to the zombie. "The murderer is named Entity303 and he seeks to destroy everything in Minecraft. He's taken this boy, Weaver, from past, altering Minecraft's timeline. This allowed Entity303, somehow, to add modifications to Minecraft which are slowly tearing the fabric of this universe apart. We're on a quest to capture him so we can return Weaver back to the past and repair all this damage."

Just then, another tear formed high overhead, splitting open the pitch-black sky. It looked as if someone had slashed the heavens with a jagged blade. But just as quickly as it appeared, it disappeared again.

"What was that?" Stitcher asked in shock.

"The fabric of Minecraft is strained, yes, yes," Empech said.

Everyone remained silent, the zombie included, as they all stared up at the star-filled sky.

"That's the second time that's happened." Gameknight moved closer to the monster and knelt.

"We need to hurry up. Did you see where our enemy, Entity303, went?"

"Yes," the decaying creature replied.

"Will you show us?" Gameknight asked.

"Why should this zombie help?" the creature growled. "You are likely to show me to my death no matter what I do."

"No," the User-that-is-not-a-user replied. "You have answered our questions, and we will honor our deal. Now you can go free."

"Gameknight . . . no," Hunter whispered.

The User-that-is-not-a-user cast her an angry glare, then pulled out a shovel and dug a set of steps into the hole, allowing the zombie to step out.

"All of you, back up so our friend here can leave." Gameknight turned his gaze to the zombie. "You have a choice: leave, or help us stop our common enemy. If Entity303 can continue, he'll destroy everything, including all the monsters on the moon. Come with us and help stop him. You have my word: no harm will come to you, regardless of your choice."

He took a step backward, then motioned for his friends to do the same. They all moved away from the zombie, allowing the creature to run away, if it chose.

The zombie stared up at Gameknight999, then smiled a malicious smile, as if the creature knew some terrible secret. "Yes, this zombie will help you and show you where the murderer went."

"Great," the User-that-is-not-a-user replied.

The green moon monster stepped out of the hole.

"That user went to the Moon Boss," it said. "This is the way."

The creature shuffled off to the east, the rest of the party following.

"Why would Entity303 go to the Moon Boss?" Gameknight asked the decaying creature.

"This zombie doesn't know and doesn't care," the monster replied. "Likely, the Moon Boss destroyed him.

It will be a treat to watch all of you go into that dungeon, knowing full well that few will survive. My brothers and sisters down there will destroy every intruder, and then they will feast on your XP."

"Just say it walking, zombie," Hunter growled, pointing an arrow at the monster.

"How does this zombie know the redheaded one will not commit murder as soon as the entrance to the Moon Boss' dungeon is shown?" the zombie asked.

"Would you rather I shot you now?" Hunter asked.

The zombie shook his head.

"Hunter, be nice," Stitcher chided. She turned to the monster as they walked across the lunar landscape. "We have no argument with you or your kind, but we will defend ourselves if we must. You will not be harmed; Gameknight999 has given his word, and all of us respect that promise. We just need to speak with the Moon Boss and find out how he helped our enemy."

"Help . . . the Moon Boss, what a laugh," the zombie growled. "None who have gone searching for what lies in the treasure room have ever survived the Moon Boss's wrath. The Moon Boss would never help an NPC, especially one who looked as foolish as all of you, with your pale skin and tiny, tiny heads." The zombie turned and glared at Gameknight999. "The Moon Boss destroys all enemies."

"We'll see," Gameknight replied.

Squawk! Tux added.

"Lead us where we need to go, zombie," Crafter said. "Then, your obligation to us will be complete."

The zombie growled, then gave them all a terrifying toothy grin. The animal-like sound of the growl passed through the emptiness of space, echoing within Gameknight's helmet, making little square goose bumps form on his arms and neck.

He had a bad feeling about this Moon Boss, but he knew they had no choice; they had to follow the path Entity303 laid out for them, for good or for ill . . .

He was betting on the latter.

CHAPTER 5

DUNGEONS OF DARKNESS

The zombie led them across the empty lunar surface, traveling in a straight line through the gray wasteland to some distant location where the entrance to the dungeon lay. With only the occasional growl or moan, the creature said little else. It glared suspiciously at Hunter, as if it expected to get an arrow in the back at any second.

"Where are you taking us?" Hunter asked, distrustful of everything the zombie did.

"To the Moon Boss, of course," the creature replied.

"I don't see any structures out here," she replied. "Everything seems completely deserted."

"The pale-skinned villagers are ignorant," the monster said.

"Hey, who are you calling ignorant?" Hunter snapped.

The zombie laughed.

"Now let's just relax for a moment," Crafter said. "But I agree with Hunter. This does seem a little strange."

"The Moon Boss is underground, yes, yes," Empech said.

Gameknight glanced at the small gnome. His gray skin almost merged with the pale moon rocks that covered the ground. The huge pack on the creature's back jingled about as it jostled back and forth with every step.

“Hmmm . . . Forpech agrees. The Boss can be felt deep under the surface of the moon,” Forpech said. “But there are dangers near the Moon Boss . . . hmmm . . . great dangers indeed.”

“Are you leading us into some kind of trap?” Hunter growled.

“This zombie already said the Moon Boss destroys all intruders,” the monster said. “Was that difficult to understand? Are the heads of these pale villagers too small to hold any brains?”

“You watch your rotten mouth,” Hunter said with a glare. “When we’re done, I’m gonna . . .”

The monster held up a clawed hand, silencing Hunter’s threat. “The entrance is here.”

Before them sat a huge crater, a scar on the face of the moon from some ancient meteor impact. The walls of the crater were rough but easily scalable. Herder sent the wolves forward to investigate. The furry white animals stood out against the gray moonrock, their fur nearly glowing in the light of the sun. They spread across the crater, searching for threats, then converged to the center of the recession, howling to signify that it was safe.

Gameknight moved forward, leaping into the air, then slowly falling into the depression, landing softly. He approached the hole with caution, careful not to lean too far over and fall in.

The walls of the hole were roughhewn, blocks sticking out here and there, creating an easy parkour course that would get them to the bottom without taking any damage. Only the top of the vertical shaft was lit by the sun; the deeper portions were bathed in darkness.

“This leads to the Moon Boss?” Crafter asked.

“Of course not,” the zombie replied, as if it were obvious. “This is the entrance to the Moon dungeon. Those that wish to steal the Moon Boss’s treasure must first go through the dungeon. If any make it through the dungeon’s passages, then the Moon Boss can be challenged. But none here will survive.”

The monster laughed a croaking, growling laugh, then turned to face Hunter.

"This zombie is ready for death. Fire your arrows."

Hunter glared at the zombie, then glanced at Gameknight999.

"You have met your obligation," the User-that-is-not-a-user said to the zombie. "Go in peace. If we meet again, I hope it is under better circumstances."

The zombie seemed shocked. He stared at Hunter, then turned his monstrous gaze toward the pechs, expecting one of them to attack when his back was turned.

"You heard him—get moving." Hunter put her bow back in her inventory and waved the monster away.

The creature glanced one more time at Gameknight, then left the companions staring down into the deep hole before them.

Leaning out into the opening, Gameknight peered through the darkness. There were no lights in the dungeon, but a faint yellow glow seemed to flicker far below, lighting the way. The dim outline of bricks was visible across the floor, but then a dark presence moved past the opening; something—or maybe even some*things*—were moving down there.

"What was that?" Stitcher asked, alarmed.

"I can't tell, but I bet it isn't kittens," Gameknight said.

"Kittens? Why would there be kittens down there?" Hunter said.

"It was a joke."

"Was it supposed to be funny?" the older sister asked in disbelief.

Gameknight scowled, but then Hunter started to laugh.

"Ha ha . . . you should have seen your face," she said. "You seemed pretty confused for a minute."

"Enough," Crafter snapped. "We need to get down into that dungeon. How are we going to do it?"

"Just follow Hunter," Gameknight said, then laughed when it was Hunter who looked confused.

"Come on, it's time for some parkour," the User-that-is-not-a-user said.

He moved closer to the edge, then jumped. Slowly he floated downward, descending six blocks before landing on a rocky outcropping. He jumped out and descended to the next block, the low gravity of the moon allowing him to fall without taking damage. But he was sure if he dropped the whole distance in one jump, he would get hurt . . . or worse.

Slowly, the party snaked their way down the sides of the vertical shaft, leaping from block to block until they reached the opening to the dark chamber below.

"As soon as we jump into that room, we need light," Gameknight said. "I wouldn't want to end up fighting a bunch of monsters in complete darkness."

He glanced at his comrades as they stood perched on blocks of moonrock that lined the passage. They all appeared nervous. None of them seemed very excited about jumping into this strange dungeon without knowing what waited for them.

I hope I did the right thing, bringing them into space with me, Gameknight thought. *Maybe if I were alone, I could have slipped through undetected.*

The clicking of a spider floated up from the chamber below. It was followed by the clattering of bones and the angry growls of zombies, each sound muffled slightly by space helmets.

Gameknight sighed as fingers of dread kneaded his soul.

"All of you ready?" the User-that-is-not-a-user asked.

They nodded.

Squawk, Tux added.

"OK . . . jump."

The friends leapt out into the opening and slowly floated down to the floor of the shadowy dungeon. Instantly, Gameknight sensed movement all around.

The light from his enchanted sword gave off the smallest bit of illumination, allowing him to see the monsters around him. A giant spider lunged, the wicked curved claws at the end of its fuzzy legs just missing his helmet. Gameknight ducked, then counterattacked, swinging his sword with all his might. He slashed at the creature, scoring hit after hit as he brought his iron sword out to add to the attack. The dark creature screamed out in pain and surprise. He blocked the spider's attacks with one sword, then tore into its HP with the other. With a pop, the fuzzy monster finally disappeared.

Something materialized into existence off to the left, in the corner of the chamber. The sorrowful moans of a zombie now drifted through the vacuum; there must be a spawner over there, the User-that-is-not-a-user realized.

"Digger, I need you," Gameknight shouted.

He charged forward, engaging the zombie before it could move much farther forward. His swords clashed against razor-sharp claws, blocking every attack. The monster snarled and slashed at his armor, its claws scraping against Gameknight's diamond coating but doing no damage.

Suddenly, Digger was at his side, his two big pickaxes in his hands. The NPC hesitated for just an instant, though, and the monster saw the pause and attacked, slashing at the big villager with his dark claws. They scraped against his iron armor, one of the points finding soft flesh, and Digger yelled in pain. Gameknight kicked the monster hard in the chest, sending it flying backward, smashing into the wall. Before it could move, he slashed at it with his swords, landing hit after hit until its HP was consumed. When the monster disappeared, Gameknight saw the spawner under its feet. Another zombie was spinning about inside the metallic cage, slowly growing larger.

"Digger, destroy it," Gameknight said.

The stocky NPC finally snapped into action, smashing the device with his pickaxe, hitting it with his left, then his right. It shattered in seconds, leaving behind only an empty hole.

"We need to search the room for more spawners." Gameknight peered into the darkness, searching for the telltale sparks that always accompanied the magical cubes. "Follow me."

Gameknight sprinted through the room. He pulled a torch out of his inventory and placed it on the wall. The torch flared briefly, then went dark, the yellow flame extinguished immediately. He pulled out another torch and stuck it into the ground. It, too, went dark instantly; torches cannot burn without oxygen. They had no choice but to run through the darkness, using the light from Gameknight's enchanted weapon to illuminate the way. The sound of his friends fighting in the darkness behind them echoed off the walls. Zombies shouted out in pain as skeleton bones clattered and spilled onto the dungeon floor.

I hope they're all okay, Gameknight thought. *If any of them get hurt, I'll just . . .*

"Here's another one," Digger said.

A skeleton burst into life over the sparkling cage-like block.

"Skeleton!" the big NPC shouted, his voice filled with fear.

The User-that-is-not-a-user moved in front of him, slashing at the monster with his sword. The skeleton notched an arrow to its string and tried to fire, but Gameknight's iron sword was already there, chopping at the monster's weapon. It clattered to the ground, lost to the darkness. The monster looked up and stared at Gameknight with venomous hatred. Before it could move, an arrow sliced through the vacuum and struck the monster, taking the last of its HP. It disappeared with an expression of confusion and despair on its pale face.

"Digger, the spawner!" Gameknight shouted.

The stocky NPC just stood there, still overwhelmed with fear.

"Digger!"

The villager seemed immobile, a terrified look carved into his square face.

Gameknight put away his swords and snatched the pickaxe from Digger's hand. He smashed the iron tool into the dark cage, tearing into it. Thin cracks began to spread across its surface until it shattered into a million pieces.

He turned and tossed the pick back to the stocky NPC. It floated slowly through the air until it landed in Digger's hands.

"Come on, we need to help the others." Gameknight reached out and grabbed Digger's arm. The big NPC didn't move. "Digger!" He shook the villager, finally getting his attention. "Follow me."

Gameknight moved toward the sounds of battle. Darkness cloaked the figures, but the sound was easy to follow. They crossed the chamber until they reached Weaver and Herder. The two boys were fighting side-by-side again, one blocking while the other attacked. They finished off the spider, then turned and scanned for more enemies. The chamber was now silent.

"Check the corners for any more spawners," Gameknight said.

Herder whistled and waved his sword over his head. The wolves instantly moved throughout the chamber, searching for threats. When they returned without making any sound, Gameknight knew they were safe . . . for now.

"That was fun," Hunter said. "Nothing like fighting against an unknown adversary in the dark. Great plan, Gameknight999."

Stitcher punched her older sister in the arm.

"Ouch," Hunter said, rubbing her shoulder.

"Well, what do you expect?" Stitcher asked, shaking her head.

Hunter just shrugged.

Gameknight reached into his inventory and pulled out another torch. He placed it on the ground, and like the others, it instantly went dark.

"No oxygen," Crafter confirmed.

"What do we do?" Gameknight asked. "We can't go blundering around through this dungeon without any light."

"Hmmm . . . Forpech has something to help," the dark-eyed gnome said.

He set his huge backpack on the ground and rummaged through it for a moment, then pulled out a stack of things that resembled torches, but their ends glowed as if yellow lightbulbs were mounted to the tip. He took one from the stack and placed it on the wall. Instantly, the light source filled the room with illumination, pushing back the shadows to reveal even the cobwebs high up on the walls.

"Glowstone torches, yes, yes," Empech said.

Forpech nodded his oversized head and smiled.

"Glowstone torches . . . I've never heard of them," Crafter said in wonder.

Gameknight took a handful from the pech and stuffed them into his inventory. The rest of the party did the same.

"OK, let's find us this Moon Boss," Gameknight said as he put away his iron sword and pulled out his steeleaf shield. "I want to know what he discussed with Entity303, and what our enemy wanted from that treasure room."

"Hopefully, we can just talk with him and not fight," Crafter said.

"Unlikely," Hunter said.

Stitcher gave her sister a warning glare.

"Weaver, come up here with me," Gameknight said. "I want you to help me by placing torches while I hold my shield and cover you, ready for arrows or anything else." The boy moved to his side and smiled, his bright blue eyes seeming brighter than usual. "Come on, everyone, let's find us a Moon Boss."

And into the dark, terrifying dungeon they ran.

CHAPTER 6

MARTIAN MOBS

Entity303 stepped out of the strange craft that had deposited him onto the surface of Mars. He didn't enjoy the rolling and tumbling necessary to land on the red planet, but he didn't have a choice.

"Whoever programmed that landing sequence should be shot," he growled to the empty landscape.

Turning to inspect his craft, the user wondered why anyone thought this would be a good way to land on Mars . . . strange. Reaching into the cargo compartment, Entity303 took out his rocket and landing pad. Without that rocket, he'd be stranded on the planet forever, so it was always critical to collect those supplies and keep them safe. The idea of living out his life on Mars was not very attractive, though he knew of an easy way to get back to the Overworld. Only a master of modded Minecraft would realize how easy it would be to get back, rocket or no rocket. But he doubted that fool Gameknight999 had any idea what to do.

Sprinting across the red planet, the user found a nice flat place atop a large hill for his base.

This will give me a good view of the surroundings, he thought. *I'll be able to see monsters coming . . . as well as my enemies.*

Quickly, Entity303 pulled out leaves and the other equipment necessary for him to survive for a while. Placing the green leafy blocks in the shape of a wall, he knocked a block out of the center and placed the oxygen collector right into the middle. Using glass pipes, he ran the oxygen to the bubble distributor, then placed a magmatic engine near each. After connecting the engines with gold piping, he poured a bucket of lava into each. Instantly, boiling stone powered the magmatic engines and started pumping, generating electricity for the oxygen generator and bubble distributor. A blue hemisphere of air slowly expanded outward, encompassing the leaves and engines. It spread in size until it reached a radius of ten blocks, then stabilized.

Entity303 took off his helmet and took a clean breath of air.

"Ahhh . . . that's some good-tasting air," he said to himself.

He pulled an oxygen compressor out of his inventory and hooked it up to the system, then filled his air tanks, which were getting low. Reaching into his inventory one last time, he produced a piece of meef he had left over from the Twilight Forest mod and ate it quickly, reducing his hunger to zero.

"Okay, now I'm ready to find me a Boss."

Replacing his air tanks and helmet, Entity303 then pulled out his jet pack and put it on.

"It's time to fly," he said with a smile, pleased with himself. His arrogance was just as strong on any planet.

The jetpack lifted him high into the air and across the red surface of Mars.

"First," he said to himself, "I need to find some monsters to question."

He scanned the landscape until he found a group of skeletons shuffling across the Martian surface. Soaring high overhead, he positioned himself directly over the group, then allowed the weak gravity to bring him to the ground. Just before he landed, Entity303 used the jetpack to slow his fall, landing lightly on the rusty soil without taking any damage.

Before the monsters could even react, he pulled out his yellow-glowing infused-sword and slashed at the creatures. He slew one after another, their pleas for mercy summarily ignored, until there was only one skeleton and a bony child left. The skeleton child held up his bow, pointing a tiny arrow at his armored chest.

Entity303 glared at the monsters, then gestured to the child.

"You, little skeleton, you can leave."

The young monster just stared up at the user with terror in its dark eyes.

"I have no need to destroy you, but if you stay here, you will fall victim to my blade."

The child looked up at the wounded skeleton adult. The older monster nodded his bony head.

"Go back to your parents," the skeleton said. "Tell them you fought bravely."

"I will not abandon a fellow skeleton," the child said.

"It's better you live to fight another day," the elder said, shaking its head.

"Listen to your bony friend," Entity303 said. "He is wise and knows what's what."

The pale child glanced one more time to the skeleton adult, then turned and ran for home somewhere across the Martian surface.

"Thank you for letting the little one go free," the monster said.

"I don't have an argument with children," the user said. "The adults who make Minecraft are the ones who wronged me. I have nothing against kids; that one I will allow to live the rest of their life, though it will be brief."

"What about me?" The skeleton glanced at his bow on the ground, it was cracked and chipped from Entity303's attack, but still looked functional. He casually leaned toward it.

Entity303 kicked the monster in the chest, knocking him to the ground, and held his sword to the skeleton's neck. Then he brought his heavy-booted foot down upon the skeleton's bow, shattering it to pieces.

"You're gonna tell me where I can find the Martian Boss," Entity303 said.

"Why should I tell you anything?" the skeleton snarled.

The user smacked the hilt of his sword on the monster's space helmet. A small crack formed on the front.

"How much do you enjoy breathing?"

"You won't get anything out of me," the skeleton said, its voice filled with confidence.

Entity303 laughed; he could see the fear in the creature's dark eyes. Banging the hilt on the helmet again, the user cracked the glass cube even more. Hitting it again and again, the cracks spread across the front and crept up the sides like deadly spider webs. A faint hissing sound came from the helmet as the air from the skeleton's oxygen gear leaked out.

"That's not a good sound," Entity303 said with a smile. "I have another helmet here." He reached into his inventory, pulled out a spare space helmet, and placed it on the ground, just out of reach from the skeleton. "You tell me what I want to know, and I'll give you the helmet. If you don't, then you'll slowly suffer until your HP is gone." The user moved the hilt of his sword closer to the monster's helmet. "What's it gonna be . . . life or death?"

The skeleton glanced at the space helmet on the ground, then up at his attacker.

"OK, I'll tell, just give me the helmet," the monster said.

"Information first . . . helmet second," Entity303 said as he banged on the skeleton's helmet again. The hissing grew louder.

"Alright! The entrance to the Martian Boss' dungeon is to the north, just over the line of hills." The skeleton pointed to a collection of red mounds that stood up tall against the red landscape. "You'll find it behind the mountain on the right. Now give me the helmet, quick."

Entity303 bent over and lifted the helmet off the ground. He held it out to the skeleton, but when the bony monster reached out to take it, the user turned on the jetpack and soared high up into the sky, leaving the skeleton with a look of shocked despair on his bony face.

"Ha ha ha . . . thanks for the info," Entity303 mocked the doomed creature. "Enjoy the time you have left, skeleton."

Leaning toward the north, he accelerated, soaring through the red Martian sky, slowly settling to the ground. He shoved the spare helmet back into his inventory and ran across the red sands, scanning the rusty planet below, searching for any sign of his enemy, Gameknight999.

"I hope the Moon Boss prepared a nice welcome for my old friend," he said with a laugh.

The evil user ran up the side of the mountain that blocked his view of the dungeon entrance. At its peak, he descended in great leaping bounds. On the way down, a huge crater came into view, likely the impact point of some massive meteor the thin Martian atmosphere could not burn up as it fell. At the bottom of the crater was a shadowy recession.

"That's probably it," Entity303 mused to himself. He really loved the sound of his own voice. "But I want to be cautious and make sure nothing is hiding around the crater, waiting to catch any unsuspecting visitors."

He ran closer to his goal, the many enchantments on the furry armor lighting the surroundings with a blue iridescent glow. He approached the edge of the crater and crouched behind a small hill of sand. There were holes and tunnels all throughout the crater, many opening into spaces underground. Likely, a fall through one of those holes would not be fatal, but it would probably trap the victim in a cave with some kind of ravenous creature. At the very bottom of the recession, a dark passage yawned like the gaping maw of a gigantic beast. The user knew that was the entrance to the Mars dungeon.

"I need to be careful here," Entity303 said to himself. "Getting surprised by a bunch of idiotic monsters would not be acceptable. I'll just take my time, and maybe destroy some mobs on the way to the bottom of this crater."

Gripping his glowing sword firmly in his hand, the evil user moved around the edge of the crater, looking for monsters to destroy as he planned his path down to the dungeon entrance.

CHAPTER 7
MOON BOSS

Gameknight and his companions moved through the dark passages with care. Blocks of spider webs were everywhere, foreshadowing the presence of the fuzzy monsters. The gray brick walls reflected sounds of monsters, making it seem as if there were an army waiting for them . . . which might be true, for all they knew. Weaver ran along next to Gameknight, placing glowstone torches on the walls as they moved forward and Gameknight held his shield in front of them.

Thump . . . thump . . . thump!

Three arrows thudded against Gameknight's shield.

"Skeletons ahead," Gameknight said in a hushed voice.

More arrows struck his shield, one of the sharp projectiles going all the way through and sticking out the other side. Gameknight broke the shaft off with the hilt of his sword.

"Another room coming up," Weaver whispered.

The growls of zombies echoed off the ancient walls, the clicking of spiders adding to the sounds.

"I'm pretty sure they know we're coming," Crafter said from behind Gameknight.

"Then let's do something to surprise them," Gameknight said. "Crafter, you and Digger should search for spawners. Hunter and Stitcher, your job is to get the skeletons. Herder, have your wolves run around, barking and causing a distraction. I know they can't really bite any of the monsters with their helmets on, but they can confuse them while we fight. Empech, Forpech, you two stay back and protect Tux." He glanced over his shoulder just as another arrow struck his shield. "Everyone ready?"

They nodded their heads.

"What are you gonna do?" Crafter asked.

"I'm the snow plow," Gameknight said. "Come on . . . FOR MINECRAFT!"

Then he charged ahead, hoping the others were following. The sound of their boots echoing off the cold passage walls was reassuring. When he reached the next chamber, he barreled straight through the room, using the shield as a battering ram. He smashed into skeletons and zombies, pushing them back with his shield until they were pinned against the opposite wall. Gameknight considered just holding them there, keeping the monsters out of the battle, but a hissing sound filled his hears. He'd heard that noise a thousand times in Minecraft and knew exactly what caused it.

Dropping his shield, Gameknight spun around and swung his blade at a creeper that was about to detonate. The mottled-green monster was glowing white. His diamond sword struck the monster, stopping the ignition process. The creeper staggered backward, its glow diminishing. The monster tried to detonate again, but Gameknight kept hitting the monster, tearing away at its HP until it disappeared with a pop.

He turned to face the monsters he'd pinned against the wall, only to find them battling Herder and Weaver. Gameknight scanned the rest of the chamber. The pechs were placing glowstone torches throughout the chamber, Tux following and squawking excitedly. Digger had destroyed the last of the spawners, eliminating the threat of reinforcements.

"Spawners are gone!" Digger boomed.

"Good," Gameknight answered as he charged toward a spider.

The fuzzy monster was hiding in the corner, likely waiting to jump out of the shadows and surprise the unwary, but the creature's green-glowing eyes gave her away. Gameknight leapt into the air and landed directly on the monster, striking her with his sword. The spider tried to knock him off with a claw, the sharp point scraping across one of his boots. Suddenly, a pair of arrows sprouted out of her side, and then another set of shafts streaked through the room and hit the monster, taking the last of her HP. She disappeared, leaving only Gameknight and his companions.

"Anyone hurt?" Gameknight asked, looking around at his companions.

"Nothing serious," Crafter replied. "Let's keep going."

They used this strategy again in the next room, Gameknight storming through the chamber with his shield held out before him while the rest of them flowed into the room after. They cleared room after room as they moved slowly through the dungeon. One thing that helped their progress was the fact that there were only two spawners in each room; if there had been more, then it would likely have been difficult to fight all the monsters and destroy the spawners at the same time.

After traversing four more rooms, they finally reached the boss chamber. Gameknight edged forward and peered inside. Tall columns of lava spilled down the corners, filling the chamber with an orange glow. A row of metal bars ran along the perimeter of the room at a height of four blocks, then another row at eight blocks, and the third row near the ceiling. Gameknight noticed the bars did not completely cover the lava. If someone climbing on the metallic ledge were not careful, they could fall into the flowing lava . . . and that would not be good.

"Okay Gameknight, what do we do?" Crafter asked.

"Well, the Moon Boss will spawn when we go into the room," the User-that-is-not-a-user said.

"And how do we beat it?" Hunter asked.

"Well . . . I don't know. I never really did this legit," Gameknight admitted.

"What do you mean, *'Never really did this legit?'*" Hunter took a step closer to him and stared straight into his eyes. "Are you telling me you've never fought this boss before?"

"Well . . . no, not really. When I did this, I was just playing the game, so I went into creative mode and destroyed him." Gameknight looked down, ashamed. "That was a long time ago, when I didn't know about things being . . . you know . . . alive."

"Great!" Hunter exclaimed.

"Be nice," Stitcher said, then pushed her older sister out of the way and stood before Gameknight999. "So, what *do* you know about this boss?"

"Well, I know it's a skeleton with dual bows," Gameknight explained.

"Dual bows?" Hunter asked. "This is great."

"Oh yeah, and the Moon Boss is also really, really big," he added. "Like, twice as tall as any of us, if not taller."

"It just gets better and better," Hunter groaned.

"Hunterrrr," Stitcher chided.

"So, do you have a plan?" Crafter asked.

Gameknight could feel all their eyes focused on him, every pair expecting him to come up with some kind of trick to make winning easy. But he knew from things he'd seen on the Internet that there was nothing easy about this battle. It would be dangerous and there was no way around it.

But then, an idea surfaced from the foggy uncertainty in his mind; Gameknight knew what he had to do.

"Yeah, I have a plan," the User-that-is-not-a-user said. "All of you stay here and let me take care of this."

"What?" Crafter asked, shocked.

"Don't be ridiculous," Hunter said, shaking her head in disbelief.

"I don't think so," Weaver added, sounding concerned.

But Gameknight didn't hear any of their complaints; he was already in motion. Sprinting as fast as he could, he shot into the boss chamber with his diamond sword in his right hand, steeleaf shield in his left. Instantly, a gigantic skeleton appeared at the center of the chamber, a bow in each hand. Gameknight had never really understood how it fired the bows if it didn't have a free hand to pull back the arrows, but logic and physics never seemed to stop Minecraft.

Suddenly, a dual *twang* filled the air. Rolling across the ground, Gameknight ducked under the pair of arrows. When he stood, he held his shield before him, ready for the next attack.

"I haven't come here to fight," the User-that-is-not-a-user said in a loud, clear voice. "I know a user like me was here earlier. You have to tell me what was discussed."

"I AM THE MOON BOSS!" the monster bellowed. It made the walls shake and some of the lava splatter out of the neat columns, falling on the ground. "You don't demand anything in my domain."

Then, the huge monster fired not just one or two arrows at him, but a steady stream of projectiles. Gameknight moved quickly to the side, knowing that skeletons tended to shoot right at where you were in that moment, not where you could be a moment later. The arrows streaked past harmlessly, some embedding themselves in the gray brick walls, some of them splashing into the lava and bursting into flame.

"I don't want to fight, I just want to talk!" Gameknight yelled as he dodged the projectiles.

"You're here for the same reason as the other one," the Moon Boss growled. "You want that which I keep in my treasure room. Well, you'll never get it."

"Did Entity303 get it?" Gameknight asked. "Where did he go?"

"The Moon Boss doesn't know where Entity303 went!" a voice shouted from the chamber entrance.

Hunter was just inside the chamber, standing behind a pair of cobblestone blocks she'd placed on the ground. The Moon Boss turned and fired a stream of arrows at her, but she ducked behind the stone, avoiding the pointed shafts.

"You see . . . this skeleton doesn't know anything," she shouted. "He doesn't even know where Entity303 went."

"I do so know," the Moon Boss growled. "He went deeper into outer space, and you'll never catch him."

"And why's that?" Gameknight asked.

The monster spun around and glared at the User-that-is-not-a-user.

"Because I will not give you the key to the treasure chest," the monster said. "I will take it to my grave before I give it away again."

"Listen, we don't want to fight with you, but we need—"

Gameknight couldn't finish the sentence, because the skeleton suddenly charged forward. The monster picked him up and tossed him through the air, directly at the lava flowing down one corner. Fortunately, he hit some of the metal bars and avoided touching the molten stone.

As Gameknight flew through the air toward the lava, Hunter opened fire, shooting as fast as she could. Stitcher stepped into the chamber and added her bow to the attack. Crafter and Weaver also stepped forward and opened fire, while Digger placed blocks of cobblestone down on the ground in front of the archers, giving them some protection from the Moon Boss's attacks.

A shrill whistle echoed off the walls, followed by proud, majestic howls. Herder's wolves charged into the chamber and ran around the monster, confusing it. The skeleton tried to shoot at the wolves, but they moved too fast. When he realized they weren't biting him, the massive creature turned his bow back on Hunter and the others.

Gameknight charged forward and slashed at the skeleton with his diamond sword. The blade bounced off the creature's bones as if they were made of iron. He saw tiny chips of bone fall off the monster's pale legs, but the sword didn't do very much damage.

The skeleton king turned and fired at Gameknight. He raised his shield just in time, blocking most of the arrows, but one of them slipped past the edge and found Gameknight's shoulder. He screamed in pain and fell to one knee.

Hunter shouted her battle cry and fired with reckless abandon, aiming for the monster's head. Her arrows bounced off the creature's pale skull, one in five sticking into the bone and making the creature flash red with damage.

The Moon Boss turned to fire back at Hunter. This gave Gameknight the chance to attack again. This time, he pulled out the weapon King Iago had given him back in Mystcraft. It was a yellow-glowing infused-sword identical to the one Entity303 carried. The User-that-is-not-a-user charged, slashing at the monster. The glowing blade bit deep into the creature, making the skeleton howl in pain. The Moon Boss quickly reached down and picked Gameknight up. Aiming for the lava, the monster started to throw his enemy again.

Suddenly, one of the wolves flipped off its space helmet and jumped into the air, grabbing the monster's arm with its sharp teeth. The other wolves did the same, casting aside their life-preserving helmets so they could bring their powerful jaws to bear. The monster dropped Gameknight as it screamed in pain.

"No!" Herder screamed, but the young boy could not do anything to help his wolves.

Gameknight stood and saw the wolves flashing red; they were taking damage because of the lack of air. He had to do something . . . fast. Glancing at the bars ringing the room, he ran and jumped as high as possible. He landed on the first row of bars, then leapt up through the diminished gravity and grabbed the next row. Turning, he pushed off and floated through the room.

Gameknight finally landed on the Moon Boss's back. With the infused-sword, he slashed at the monster, smashing the glowing blade against the pale bones. The monster flashed red as it took damage, but the wolves continued to flash as well.

"Empech, Forpech . . . healing potions for the wolves, quick," Gameknight shouted.

The pechs ran forward while the User-that-is-not-a-user continued his attacks. He struck harder and harder as Hunter and the others fired their bows. Their arrows were now finding weak points in the skeleton's bones, doing more damage. The creature fell to a knee, then collapsed to the ground.

Gameknight did not relent. He continued his attack until a strange laughter came from the monster.

"Everyone, get back," the User-that-is-not-a-user yelled.

He put away his sword and scooped up a wolf and a helmet. Shoving the glass block back on the creature's head, Gameknight placed the animal on the ground, then grabbed another.

The laughter from the Moon Boss grew louder as his HP slowly fell. Hunter and Stitcher kept firing while the others helped the wolves.

"You will never stop him," the monster croaked. "He's probably already there, and soon he will destroy . . ."

The last of the monster's HP finally disappeared. The Moon Boss exploded in a flash of light and smoke, throwing glowing balls of XP all across the room. When the room finally cleared, a shining gold key floated on the ground where the creature had perished.

"Is it over?" Hunter asked.

Gameknight nodded. He turned and glanced at Herder. "Are the wolves okay?"

"Yeah, the healing potions kept them alive until we got their helmets on," Herder said. He walked to the pechs and gave each a gigantic hug. "Thank you."

Empech and Forpech both bowed to the boy, then put the remaining healing potions back into their oversized backpacks.

"Come on, let's check the treasure room," Gameknight said.

He sprinted across the chamber and into a side passage. It turned a couple of times until it led them to a room with columns of glowstone in the corners. At the center of the room sat a wooden chest.

"Why is the chest still here?" Crafter asked. "If Entity303 had already been here, I'd think he would have taken everything."

"I think it's because he didn't destroy the Moon Boss completely," Gameknight replied.

"You think that evil user actually showed some compassion?" Stitcher asked.

"I'd never believe that," Hunter said. "Entity303 doesn't know the meaning of the word mercy."

"As I remember, if you don't destroy the boss and you leave the room, it respawns at full health when you enter again," Gameknight explained. "I bet because the boss respawned, so did the loot in the chest."

"Who cares?" Hunter said. "Let's just get whatever is needed and get out of here."

Gameknight knelt at the chest and inserted the gold key. Some internal mechanism clicked, and grabbed hold of the key, unlocking the chest. Lifting the lid, Gameknight and his friends peered inside.

"Well?" Hunter asked.

Gameknight reached in and pulled out some pieces of iron and a safari net.

"Well, is it there?" Hunter asked again, sounding impatient.

Gameknight withdrew some pieces of bread and a potion of swiftness.

"Well?" She bonked him on the glass helmet with her bow, causing him to turn. "Did you find what you needed?"

Gameknight just smiled, then held up a piece of paper. It had intricate drawings and equations scrawled across the white sheet.

"That's what we fought for, a piece of paper?" Hunter exclaimed, then turned and stormed to the other side of the room.

"This is exactly what we came for," Gameknight said. "These are the plans to a new space ship. It'll unlock the tier-two rocket designs. When we build this bigger ship, we'll be able to access planets farther away than the moon. I'm sure Entity303 is heading into the deepest parts of outer space, just like the Moon Boss said."

"But why do you think he's heading out there?" Digger asked.

"Because then he'll be near the edges of the Minecraft universe, in the Far Lands of outer space," Crafter said.

"What are the Far Lands?" Stitcher asked.

"It's the edge of the world, the border between the chunks of land that have been spawned, and the area where no one has ever set foot," replied Crafter.

"Exactly," Gameknight said.

"The Far Lands, yes, yes, that makes much sense," Empech said, nodding his head.

"Hmmm . . . our enemy plans on tearing the fabric of Minecraft open there," Forpech grumbled, his deep voice causing the glowstone blocks in the corner of the room to vibrate.

"But how is he gonna do it?" Gameknight asked the gnome.

"How indeed," the two pechs responded as if they were the same person.

"I think maybe we should go catch this user before he does any more damage," Digger said slowly, his deep voice filled with uncertainty.

"Absolutely," Gameknight said. "Let's go build us a rocket."

CHAPTER 8

LIFT OFF

"How do we get out of here?" Herder asked.

The lanky boy moved to the entrance of the treasure room and peered into the darkened corridor.

"With all the spawners destroyed, we could just go back the way we came in," Crafter suggested.

"But when we pass through the Boss chamber, the Moon Boss will respawn," Gameknight said. "I'd rather not take the chance of that skeleton hitting someone with an arrow or two."

"Well, what do you suggest?" Hunter asked.

Gameknight moved to one of the corners and found a hole that went straight up to the surface of the moon.

"I think we dig." Gameknight glanced at Digger. "Can you get us out of here?"

The stocky NPC smiled, then nodded, his warm green eyes brightening just a bit. He tossed one of his pickaxes to Gameknight999, then pulled out his other tool. The two companions started to dig, forming a set of stairs that led to the surface. The User-that-is-not-a-user sweated as he dug, the inside of his helmet fogging up a bit. As his arms grew weary, Gameknight handed off the pick to Weaver, but Digger never relinquished his tool. In fact, none of them could keep up with him; the big villager outpaced them all.

In a short time, they made it to the surface of the moon.

"Herder, have your wolves scout for our footprints," Gameknight said. "They should be able to find them quickly enough, and then we can follow those back to Entity303's base."

With a series of whistles and gestures, the boy commanded the wolves to do as instructed. Within minutes, one of them was howling victoriously.

"Come on," Gameknight said.

They ran across the desolate surface, following their footprints. Soon they saw the moon village, the blue-skinned NPCs shuffling about.

"Entity303's camp should be off to the right," Weaver said. "I remember it's right behind that big hill. Follow me."

He took off at an angle, veering away from the village and back toward Entity303's base.

They climbed the hill in huge bounds, the reduced gravity on the moon allowing them to make three- and four-block jumps, something that would have been impossible in the Overworld.

When he reached the top of the hill, Weaver stopped, his posture slumping ever so slightly, as if he were defeated. Gameknight reached his side.

"What is it?" the User-that-is-not-a-user asked, concerned.

Weaver pointed.

Where Entity303's base had once stood was now just a collection of a few blocks of leaves and the shattered remains of his tier-one rocket. All of the supplies, all of the equipment, and all of the oxygen generation gear was gone.

"It's all gone . . . he took it all," Hunter growled.

"That's okay, we have our own stuff," Gameknight said. "Let's get moving."

Gameknight jumped down the hill, soaring high in the air, only to land on the ground and leap up again. When he reached the base, he quickly began placing blocks of leaves on the ground, rebuilding his original moon base. Placing the oxygen collector near the leaves, he ran the glass pipes to the bubble distributor, then attached the coal generators. Instantly, oxygen began flowing from the collector to the distributor. A bubble of air grew from the distributor, becoming wider and taller until it stretched out a distance of ten blocks in each direction.

"You see," Gameknight said. "We don't need his stuff. We have our own . . ."

A hissing sound filled his helmet. Was something leaking? Was a pipe broken? The hissing grew louder and louder until . . .

"CREEPER!" Digger shouted.

The stocky NPC threw one of his pickaxes toward Gameknight999. It brushed his shoulder as it shot past, then hit something behind him with a thud. Gameknight turned and found he was face-to-face with an evolved creeper, complete with space helmet and oxygen gear. He quickly drew his diamond sword and attacked, hitting the monster hard on the shoulder, then kicked it backward, away from his friends. Before the User-that-is-not-a-user could advance to finish the job, Herder and Weaver charged at the beast, slashing at it with their swords until its HP was consumed and it vanished, leaving behind three balls of XP and a pile of gunpowder.

"Digger, check for a spawner," Gameknight said. "That creeper had to come from somewhere."

"I found it," the stocky NPC said. He smashed the cube with his pickaxe, destroying it just as another creeper was about to spawn.

"Now, let's get building."

Gameknight pulled out his NASA workbench, courtesy of King Iago in Mystcraft, and set it on the ground. It was a dark box with long, spindly arms that stuck up into the air like the legs of an upturned spider. The specialized crafting bench was necessary to build a rocket in the Galacticraft mod.

Placing the plans for the tier-two rocket in the bench, the User-that-is-not-a-user unlocked the next space ship, making it possible to build. Pulling pieces of heavy duty hull plating, fins, and nose cone from his inventory—items that had been given to him back in Mystcraft by King Iago,—he slowly assembled their next space ship.

"Iago must have had a suspicion about Entity303's plans in space," Crafter said. "He gave us everything we need to build this ship."

"And probably parts to build the next one as well," Gameknight said, nodding.

"You mean this isn't the last rocket?" Hunter asked.

"Nope."

She rolled her eyes.

In minutes, he had the rocket complete and on the launch pad.

Crafter approached the rocket and ran a hand along its smooth metallic side. "Gameknight, do you have any idea where Entity303 went?"

"There's only one place he's likely to go," the user-that-is-not-a-user replied.

"Where's that?" the young NPC asked.

"Mars," Gameknight said.

Hunter moved to Crafter's side and stared up at the space ship. "I suppose there are Mars monsters, as well as a Mars Boss, there?"

"Yep."

She rolled her eyes again. "Great."

Gameknight shrugged.

"When I get to Mars, I'll use the teleportation ring and bring you all there," Gameknight said.

"You need to set up the base first," Crafter said.

"No, I'd rather leave this stuff here, to make sure you'll have air," the User-that-is-not-a-user said. "We don't have two sets of oxygen generation equipment."

"Then you need to take this and get a safe place prepared for us," Crafter said.

"If you were to use the teleportation ring before we disassembled the base, then we'd be left with nothing," Stitcher said. "You have to take it with you."

"Are you sure?" Gameknight asked. "You have enough air?"

Crafter nodded his head, but didn't reply.

"OK, then all of you sit down and conserve your supplies."

They sat on the lunar surface as Gameknight and Digger broke down all of the equipment with their pickaxes. Once it was all taken apart, the User-that-is-not-a-user put the parts into his inventory, then moved to the door of the rocket.

"Tux," Gameknight said, extending a hand as if he expected her to take it.

The penguin waddled forward and climbed into the rocket, then stepped back, away from the door.

"I'll be quick, I promise," Gameknight said to his friends, a worried expression etched into his square face.

"Just hurry up, and don't be an idiot," Hunter replied.

With a nervous sigh, Gameknight slammed the door shut, then hit the red button that began the countdown. He knew it always started at twenty, but this time, the numbers scrolling through his head seemed to proceed with an aching slowness that chiseled away at his patience. Finally, the ship shuddered and began to climb into the air, leaving his friends to wait on the surface of the moon, their air slowly running out.

CHAPTER 9
ENTITY303'S CREATION

After destroying a nest of spiders, a large group of zombies, and a handful of creepers, Entity303 was now satisfied the crater was clear of threats. He moved into the recession, taking huge leaps in the reduced Martian gravity. With two mighty jumps, he landed next to the dark hole that extended downward into the darkness.

Peering down into the shaft, Entity303 thought he saw something moving through the gloom.

"More monsters . . . perfect," he said to the empty landscape.

Drawing his glowing yellow sword, he smiled as he thought of the creatures he was about to destroy.

"Get ready for Entity303!" he shouted into the the hole, then jumped down.

Using his jet pack, he slowed his descent, landing on a block of stone near the bottom of the passage. Reaching into his inventory, he pulled out a splash potion of night vision and shattered it at his feet. He then removed the jet pack and replaced it with the Alpha Yeti armor, the enchantments on the chest plate lighting the area. Below him, he could see spiders staring up at him, their green eyes glowing with excitement.

"Ready or not, here I come."

He stepped forward, drifting slowly to the ground. Even before he touched the ground, his sword was already flashing through monsters, tearing HP from their terrifying bodies. With a pair of spiders quickly destroyed, he moved toward a group of zombies. His blazing yellow sword tore through the creatures as if they were made of paper. They fell to the ground, then disappeared with *pop*s. A creeper tried to sneak up behind him, but the idiotic monster hissed like a leaky tire. Entity303 made short work of the green creature.

One last zombie shuffled forward. It was a small monster, probably younger than the others. He had just stood there in the corner, shaking as he watched the slaughter of the other monsters right before his eyes.

"You, zombie . . . are you going to attack me too?" The evil user pointed at the beast with his glowing sword.

The zombie shook his head.

"This zombie does not want to fight."

"You don't want to fight? Does that mean you want to help . . . and live?"

"Yes," the monster moaned.

"Very well," Entity303 said. "Stand there and don't move."

The user moved to the corners of the room, where the spawners were located. Keeping an eye on the zombie, he dug them up with a pickaxe. But instead of leaving them floating on the ground, to eventually disappear, he put the dark cages into his inventory.

"I have a little idea about how I can use these spawners to make a little surprise for anyone who might be following me."

"What?" the zombie asked.

"Nothing." Entity303 moved to the second spawner, broke it, and shoved it into his inventory.

"What's your name, zombie?"

"This zombie is called Da-Rir."

"Da-Rir, huh. That's a stupid name."

The zombie child said nothing.

"Very well, Da-Rir. You are my new scout. You're going to go into each room and tell the monsters there that I'm a friend . . . that is, if you wish to live."

Da-Rir shook ever so slightly as the evil user approached, the glow from the yellow sword pushing back the darkness.

"Now move it. Take me to the next room. If you are foolish enough to warn the monsters, you will be the first one I'll destroy. Do you understand?"

The zombie nodded his scarred head.

"Good . . . now go!"

The zombie shuffled off through the passage with Entity303 walking right behind. The passage was lined with strange green bricks, and torches were placed on the walls, but they were all extinguished. Entity303 smiled. He'd released his tainted virus here on Mars long ago. The self-replicating segment of code had spread across the planet, destroying the life that once flourished on Mars. The last thing to be destroyed was the atmosphere, forcing all the monsters to evolve and develop their own oxygen gear. Now Mars was a wasteland, all courtesy of Entity303 and his programming skills. He'd done this everywhere in the solar system with the exception of the Overworld, and now he needed to check on those planets.

"Why do you seek the Mars Boss?" Da-Rir asked.

"He has something I need and I'm going to take it from him."

"What could the Mars Boss have that a user needs?"

"A ticket to deep space, zombie. That's what I'm here for."

"But the Mars Boss has never been defeated. This zombie has seen many challengers try, but none have survived."

"Don't you worry your little decaying head. I can take care of myself." Entity303 stopped walking and whispered to Da-Rir. "Here's the next room. I want you to go in there and tell them I'm just passing through and won't hurt them. If what you say is true, then the Mars Boss will destroy me and none of your kind needs to get hurt. Agreed?"

"The user is just passing through the next room?"

"Of course . . . I wouldn't just destroy living things for no reason. Now go."

"Wait until Da-Rir calls."

The young zombie shuffled off down the passage. Entity303 watched with his enhanced night vision as the child moved into the next chamber and talked with the other monsters. He pointed into the passage as he explained, then let out a sad moan and waved for Entity303 to enter.

The user sprinted through the green, brick-lined tunnel and into the room. The monsters foolishly just stood there and waited as he approached, their claws withdrawn, their guard down.

Entity303 burst into action as soon as he entered the room. In seconds, he destroyed a cluster of spiders. Turning, he slashed at a group of skeletons, ignoring the confused and terrified expressions on their bony faces. The zombies growled and advanced, but they underestimated Entity303's skill with his sword. Kicking one aside, he brought his glowing blade down upon the largest of the monsters, striking it with a flurry of attacks. The creature cried out in terror as its demise approached, then vanished into oblivion. The vicious user destroyed more zombies with ease as if he were swatting away insignificant bugs, leaving Da-Rir in shock as a whirlwind of destruction flowed around him

"What is happening?" Da-Rir shouted in shock.

Entity303 ignored the zombie child and attacked another group of skeletons. Their arrows bounced harmlessly off his Alpha Yeti armor, the Projectile Protection enchantment on his chest plate making their shafts completely harmless. He tore through their pale bones with reckless abandon, shattering their HP in seconds. Turning, he dove at a group of zombies that were assembling near a spawner; they didn't last fifteen seconds. With the last of the monsters destroyed, he pulled out a pickaxe and dug up the spawners, sticking them into his inventory.

"The user told Da-Rir he would not kill for no reason."

"I told you the truth, fool. I destroyed those monsters for a reason . . . because they were in my way."

Entity303 hit the zombie child lightly on the arm. The glowing yellow blade dug deep, causing the monster to moan and flash red as it took damage.

"Now, if you want to stay alive, you'll put on the same act in the next room." He took a step closer. "If you don't play your role well, then I will make you suffer terribly before your HP is exhausted. Understand?"

The monster nodded, cringing.

"I like you, zombie. You have a good head on your shoulders," Entity303 said, his cruel voice barely a whisper. "Let's see if we can keep it that way. Now go."

Da-Rir shuffled off through the next passage. They repeated their little play until they'd destroyed all of the monsters in the dungeon, save for the Mars Boss.

In the last chamber, Entity303 used his pickaxe to dig into the wall, enlarging the chamber. He then dug up the brick floor and placed all the spawners in the ground. Using the brick from the floor, Entity303 built a wall, hiding the presence of the tiny metallic cages so they would be difficult to find, but also allowing the monsters to congregate without being seen. He then moved through the next passage and started building a wall of cobblestone behind him, sealing off any escape from the spawners.

"Why did the user place the spawners back in the ground?" the zombie asked.

"I have a little friend following me," the user explained. "This will be a surprise for him. Nothing like stumbling into a bunch of monsters when you don't expect it."

The zombie seemed confused.

"That fool, Gameknight999, will try to get through that room, see all the monsters, and just run away, but then they'll end up at this wall with a bunch of monsters at his back, and he'll have nowhere to go. I'm sure he'll survive, but how many of his friends will perish in the battle?" He sighed. "I'd love to be here to watch."

"This zombie doesn't understand. If it is a friend, won't the monsters attack them?"

"You don't really understand sarcasm, do you?"

The zombie appeared perplexed.

"Anyway, you said you'd get me to the boss chamber, and here we are."

"Then this zombie will be set free?"

"That's right, you are now a free zombie," Entity303 said with a malicious smile.

"But how does Da-Rir get out of the dungeon?" the zombie asked.

"Ha ha ha . . . that's not really my problem, is it?" the user said. "Now stay out of my way or I will change my mind and test my sword on you."

a-Rir stepped back until he bumped into the cobblestone wall the user had just built.

Entity303 turned his back on the zombie-child and moved to the edge of the Boss Chamber. The room had a few glowstone blocks around its edges that cast a yellow glow on the walls, but left the center of the room still cloaked in darkness.

When he stepped into the room, a sparkling thing materialized at the shadowy center; the Mars Boss had spawned. At the same moment, the evil user's night vision potion finally expired, leaving the darkness complete and impenetrable. The Mars Boss was barely visible. It was clearly massive, easily twice the evil user's size, but Entity303 knew that made no difference. Across the monster's skin, sheets of electricity danced and sparkled, giving only a hint to his shape. But Entity303 knew exactly what this creature was, and it made the vile user smile.

I can't wait until this creature meets Gameknight999, he thought.

"WHO DARES ENTER MY CHAMBER?" the Mars Boss boomed.

"It is your creator, Entity303."

"MY CREATOR?"

"Yes, I planted the self-replicating virus that spread its tainted evil across this world, destroying all life and causing the monsters to evolve so they could survive. The diseased virus flowed through your villages, destroying everyone, but leaving the last villager alive . . . you. My gift changed you into the creature you are now. You are my creation, and I am here to give you commands."

"I REMEMBER SOMETHING OF WHAT YOU SAY," the Martian said, his voice then becoming soft and uncertain. "There was a time, before, with a . . . family . . . and friends, but those memories are difficult to grasp in my mind."

"That's right, I freed you from your pathetic existence and made you the king of Mars. Now do as I command; give me the key to the chest."

"I WILL NOT," the Mars boss growled, his voice booming again. "MY TASK NOW IS TO PROTECT THAT CHEST."

"Of course it is, you fool—I programmed you to protect that chest until I returned. But now I am here, so give me the key."

The sheets of electricity pulsed around the monster like a blue curtain. It made the details of the creature's body hard to see, but Entity303 knew what stood before him.

"I AM THE BOSS OF MARS. I RULE HERE, AND I WILL NOT TAKE COMMANDS FROM THE LIKES OF YOU."

Entity303 sighed.

"You've just made this unnecessarily difficult, and you're delaying me. I have important things to do, and cannot be bothered with you anymore. This is your last chance. Give me the key, or I will take it from your cold remains."

"YOU WILL GET NOTHING FROM ME," the Mars Boss bellowed.

"Very well . . . prepare to meet your fate!"

Then Entity303 doused himself with a potion of swiftness and dashed toward the sparkling creature, his glowing infused sword streaking through the air like a bolt of yellow lightning.

CHAPTER 10

LEAVING THE SOLAR SYSTEM

The ground shook as if a nerve running through the flesh of Minecraft had just been electrocuted. It was more like a pained convulsion than an earthquake, as Mars reacted to the destruction of its Boss. Entity303 didn't care. All that mattered was that he had been successful again, and was now one step closer to his goal.

Glancing around the boss chamber, Entity303 smiled. Beads of sweat trickled down his forehead and under his armor. His breathing was heavy with exertion. The Boss of Mars had been stronger than he'd remembered, making the Lunar Boss seem pathetic by comparison. Checking the corners, the user made sure he'd destroyed the last of the Mars Boss's little minions, then finally breathed a sigh of relief; the room was clear.

The cruel user yanked his sword out of the ground, where he had plunged it after defeating his enemy. The ground shuddered again, as if withdrawing the blade hurt the world as much as it had going in . . . good. With a triumphant expression on his square face, he walked out of the chamber and into the connecting tunnel that led to the treasure room.

"I think maybe I made that boss a little too strong," he said to the empty room. "And I totally forgot about adding those little ones to the code, so they were a bit of a challenge; they're hard to see and really quiet. I hope the Loser-that-is-a-loser, Gameknight999, makes it to this chamber. I'd love to see what happens when the Boss respawns and sees another user like me. I don't think that Martian will be very happy. Ha ha ha."

The thought of Gameknight999 having to face the monster brought an evil smile to Entity303's square face.

"He doesn't stand a chance against my creation."

Entity303 laughed again, his hollow chuckles echoing through the empty passage.

"Now, for the treasure."

He ran through the brick-lined corridor, following the seemingly random turns until it ended at a chamber lined with cubes of glowstone. The glowing columns sat nestled in the corners of the room, filling the area with yellow light. At the center sat an ancient chest. Entity303 removed the key the Martian Boss had dropped and inserted it into the lock. A satisfying click sounded when he turned it, allowing the lid to flip open. Inside, he found what he'd stashed so long ago when he'd made the original changes to the Galacticraft mod.

Reaching in, Entity303 lifted out a single sheet of paper. There were mechanical drawings all across it, the black ink standing out against the white parchment. Carefully, he closed the lid, then stared down at the chest.

The evil user smiled, pleased with himself.

Glancing around the chamber, he made sure he was still alone, then removed his Alpha Yeti chest plate and donned the jet pack. Moving to the corner, he flew up to the ceiling, then used the pickaxe to tunnel his way to the surface, just as he had on the moon.

Flying across the rusty, red landscape, the user quickly found the entrance to the dungeon, then backtracked to his base. With the plans to the tier-four rocket in hand, he quickly constructed a new ship with the supplies he'd brought with him into Galacticraft. Once the fuel tanks were topped off, he broke down his base once again, storing the leaves and oxygen generation equipment in his inventory.

Entity303 glanced up into the sky. "I wish I knew which one was planet Diona, but I'll be there soon enough, hopefully without Gameknight999. I bet the Mars Boss is plenty angry at his defeat. Hopefully, when that monster respawns, he'll give those pests following me quite the violent reception."

He stepped into his ship and closed the hatch.

"Goodbye Sol, and hello Sirius solar system. Diona . . . here I come."

He laughed a wry, violent laugh as he soared into the sky and headed deeper into outer space, closer to the edge of the Far Lands, where the destruction of Minecraft was soon to begin.

CHAPTER 11
MARS

Gameknight slowly drifted through the cold reaches of outer space toward the red planet below. He held Tux tightly under one arm as they descended, but this time they did not see a lunar lander around them like they had on the moon. And they couldn't see a parachute slowing their descent, which is what happened when landing on most planets in Galacticraft. In fact, they couldn't see any stars around them at all, because they were now encased in what looked like a bunch of giant balloons.

As soon as the rocket neared Mars, the ship they were traveling in had disappeared, and in its place had appeared groups of massive, white balloons. Reaching out, Gameknight pressed against the wall of the container they were in. It now felt soft and bouncy, like being trapped in a huge ball of bubble-wrap. As they fell through the thin atmosphere of Mars, they tumbled and rolled, making it impossible to tell which way was up. In outer space, up was wherever your head was pointing; north, south, east, and west didn't matter. But near a gravitational body like Mars, up was as easy to identify as it was on the Overworld, and tumbling around as they descended was like being on a bad carnival ride.

Squawk, squawk! Tux shouted.

"I know, girl, I don't like it either, but soon it'll be over." Gameknight said reassuringly, hoping he was correct.

Squawk!

Just then, they landed with a thud against something solid. Gameknight assumed it was the Martian surface. Just as he was about to search for a door in the huge balloon-thing, they bounced back high into the air again, flipping and spinning. They hit the ground, then sprang back into the air and bounced several more times until finally coming to a rest. The User-that-is-not-a-user finally found a hatch and shoved it open. Instantly, the balloon thingy began to deflate, and he and Tux climbed out.

Looking back at the contraption, Gameknight realized he'd been right; they'd been surrounded by numerous white balloons which had cushioned the landing, and allowed them to bounce around harmlessly (though it had made him a little queasy) until finally coming to rest at the bottom of a crater.

"I think this is the same way the actual Mars Rover landed on the red planet in the physical world," Gameknight explained.

Squawk! Tux replied.

"I know, I figured you didn't care . . . but I think it's pretty cool that the designers of Galacticraft spent time researching how NASA landed the Rover on Mars, and then added it into the game."

Squawk, squawk!

"What's that, Tux?"

Squawk, squawk, squawk! She pointed behind Gameknight with one of her flippers.

Gameknight turned and found himself staring directly into the bright green eyes of a spider. The fuzzy black monster swiped at him with her curved claw. It scraped across his diamond armor, tearing a gouge in the protective coating. Drawing his diamond blade, he slashed at the monster, pushing it away from the penguin. With his left hand, he reached into his inventory again while he kicked at the hairy creature. He grabbed the hilt of a sword and pulled it from his inventory. It was the glowing yellow blade given to him by King Iago in Mystcraft. He quickly put the blade back. It wasn't clear how much energy that infused sword had left in it, and he wanted to save it until it was absolutely needed. Pulling his iron sword out with his left hand, he advanced toward the spider.

Gameknight could feel his pulse quicken. Beads of sweat trickled down the back of his neck. It felt like little insects crawling across his skin. The ground underfoot was rough, with deep holes extending into underground caverns. He had to be careful; if he fell he might—

The spider sprang forward suddenly, a pair of claws reaching for his head. Gameknight batted away the fuzzy legs, then slashed at the monster, scoring a hit. She screeched in pain as she flashed red. The User-that-is-not-a-user faked an attack with his right, then swung with his left, hitting the spider hard on the side. She flashed red again. The fuzzy creature backed up, but not fast enough. Gameknight sprang forward and landed on her back, then hit her again and again until the monster disappeared with a pop.

"You see any more, Tux?" he asked, looking around warily.

Suddenly, a zombie growled as it reached up out of a hole in the ground. The monster slashed at Gameknight's armor, slicing a set of parallel grooves into his diamond boot. The User-that-is-not-a-user stomped on the clawed hand, then knelt and shoved his sword in the hole. The monster moaned in pain and backed away. Putting away the sword, he pulled out his bow and fired at the decaying green creature. The monster tried to avoid the pointed shafts, but it had nowhere to hide. In a minute, it was gone.

Gameknight scanned the terrain, searching for any more threats.

"You see anything else?"

The penguin shook her head.

"Okay, let's get our base built, then."

He moved out of the crater and found an area without so many holes in the ground. It was on the side of a smooth hill of red Martian dirt. As before, Gameknight placed the blocks of leaves on the ground, then added the oxygen collector and bubble distributor. Connecting the two devices with glass pipes, he then added the coal generators next to each . . . but nothing happened. The User-that-is-not-a-user picked up the generators and made sure they were facing the correct direction, then put them down again . . . again, nothing.

"This isn't working. I need to hurry up; they must be getting low on oxygen. It took a long time for us to get to Mars."

Gameknight checked the connections again. It all seemed right.

Squawk, squawk, Tux said. She pecked at the top of the generator with her little yellow beak.

"Of course, the coal!"

Gameknight pulled out a stack of coal and stuffed it into one generator, then shoved another stack in the second.

Instantly, a bubble began to form around the bubble distributor. It grew slowly at first, but as the oxygen collector pulled in more of the life-preserving element, the bubble expanded at a greater rate until it stretched out, forming a large, gaseous hemisphere of air.

Gameknight reached into his inventory and pulled out the teleportation ring. He put it on his gloved finger and pressed the blood-red gem. There was a flash of blinding light. It was so intense, he had to look away, but when his vision cleared, and the purple teleportation cloud faded, he found his friends lying on the ground.

"Take off your helmets . . . quick!" Gameknight shouted.

He ran to Crafter and pulled off his helmet, then moved to Weaver and Herder and did the same. Stitcher pulled hers off and gasped and coughed. The others followed suit. Gameknight ran to the wolves, who were lying on their sides, panting heavily. He moved from animal to animal, pulling off the glass cubes from their furry heads. Their breathing slowly eased as the fresh air from the oxygen bubble filled their body.

"That was close," Crafter said. "I started taking damage."

"Sorry it took so long—there were monsters I had to get rid of," Gameknight explained.

"Are you telling me you stopped to play with some monsters before you used that crazy ring?" Hunter complained.

Stitcher crawled to her sister's side and punched her in the arm.

"Ouch," the older girl complained.

"I'm sure he did everything as fast as possible," Stitcher reprimanded, "so be nice."

Hunter was about to reply, likely with something sarcastic, when the ground shuddered in a strange and terrible way. The red sands writhed and shook as if Mars was recoiling from some kind of grievous wound.

"What was that?" Digger asked, his eyes wide with fear.

"Likely our enemy," Empech said, sounding worried. "Entity303 has been here a while, yes, yes. He has had time to do more harm."

"It felt like the planet had just been damaged by something," Herder said. "But how does someone hurt a planet?"

"Who knows," Hunter replied.

"Entity303 would know how," Gameknight said. "That frustrated user is so mad at the makers of Minecraft for firing him, he'll do as much damage as possible. I have no doubt he'll continue to hurt innocent bystanders on the way to wherever he's going."

"Hmmm . . . our enemy becomes bolder, striking at the heart of the planet," Forpech said in a deep voice. He pulled out his wand, the green crystal on the tip reflecting the light from the small square sun in the sky. "We must hurry and catch our enemy before . . ."

He didn't finish his statement. Instead, he lowered his gaze to the ground.

"Before what?" Crafter asked.

"We must hurry . . . hmmm . . . before we are too late." The pech raised his oversized head and stared into Gameknight's eyes. "We cannot fail."

"I know," the User-that-is-not-a-user replied. "We won't."

But will I fail my companions and let them suffer while I chase Entity303? Gameknight999 thought.

He shuddered, like the planet just had, when he thought of all the things that could happen to his friends.

I must protect them all, especially Weaver, if I want to repair the timeline and repair Minecraft. But will any of them be able to protect me?

Have faith, child, an ancient, scratchy voice said in the back of his head. He recognized the voice, but knew it was impossible. She wasn't here and neither was the music of Minecraft. There's no way that voice could have really been her. Maybe he was going crazy—maybe Minecraft was already starting to fall apart.

Maybe we're too late already, Gameknight thought, then started to shake as daggers of fear stabbed his soul.

CHAPTER 12

ACROSS THE RED SANDS

Gameknight installed the oxygen compressor to the collector, then placed everyone's tanks into the system, filling them to the brim. He was shocked at how low the levels were on all the tanks—his friends had almost run out of air. If he'd been any slower, some of them might not have survived . . . and it would all have been because of him.

When he finished refilling the last tank, the User-that-is-not-a-user sat on a pile of leaves and pulled out a piece of beef. He ate the meat, the nourishment eliminating his hunger, then glanced at Weaver and thought about the very last battle he'd fought in Minecraft's past. The villager army had stopped Herobrine and the Great Zombie Invasion on the shores of the massive lava ocean in the Nether.

Gameknight hoped all of his friends in the past were well, but in the back of his mind, he knew that it wouldn't matter unless he could return Weaver back to where he belonged on Minecraft's timeline. The young boy was the key to everything. Somehow, his absence in the past had allowed Entity303 to add these mods to Minecraft and destabilize the entire system. And now, that evil user was getting ready to finish the job he'd started a hundred years ago. Gameknight refused to let him win, but still wasn't sure how he was going to stop him.

The User-that-is-not-a-user stood up and paced back and forth, trying to hide his nervousness and fear, but not doing a very good job of it.

"Are we ready to go?" Crafter asked.

"Sure," Hunter replied. "But where are we going? We have an entire planet to search and no idea where our enemy might be."

"I'm sure he's heading to the dungeon here on Mars," Gameknight replied. "If he wants to get to the farthest reaches of the Far Lands, then he has to get as far from the Overworld as possible."

"You mean he'll want to get to the last planet in the solar system?" Herder asked.

"No, somewhere even further away," Gameknight explained. "There are other solar systems out there, even beyond Pluto—though Pluto isn't a planet anymore. I can remember two other solar systems. One of them . . . its name starts with a K, but I can't think of it right now. Anyway, that system has only one planet, so I can't imagine that's where Entity303 is heading."

"Why is that?" Stitcher asked.

"Because, as I recall, there's nothing there. It's just a big empty planet."

He gazed up at the sun. It was half the size he was used to. Off to the right, Gameknight could see a shining spot in the pale sky, brilliant enough to be visible in the daytime: the Overworld. It sparkled like the rarest gem, flashing green and blue and white. It seemed so fragile from here.

"No, he won't strike at an empty world," the User-that-is-not-a-user continued. "Entity303 will want to do the most destruction possible. That means he'll go to the other solar system, the Sirius solar system. There are multiple planets in that system, some very far away from the Overworld and near the edges of the Far Lands. That's where he'll strike."

"But which planet will he attack?" Digger asked.

"I don't know," the User-that-is-not-a-user replied. "We'll just have to get closer to that solar system and find out."

"That's all great, but which way do we go now?" Hunter asked, her loud voice sounding impatient.

"I know where to go!" a distant voice shouted.

They all turned and found Weaver standing atop a huge hill of red sand, the tiny mountain making him look miniscule as he stood on its peak.

"Come up here!" Weaver yelled to them, waving and beckoning them toward him.

Everyone checked their helmets, then ran to the hill. Gameknight waited until all of them had left the air bubble, then disassembled everything with his pickaxe and stuffed it into his inventory. Then, picking up Tux, the User-that-is-not-a-user followed his friends.

They climbed the small mountain, taking huge upward leaps in the reduced gravity. When they reached the summit, they gazed down across the surface of Mars. It was entirely featureless, with no plants or trees or rivers or anything . . . just rusty red sand everywhere. Gameknight thought there had been life on the hilly Martian landscape of Mars at one point, when Galacticraft had first been released. But then something had happened and it was all eradicated. Now, the surface was devoid of any living things other than the occasional monster, and giant, rolling hills of rusty red sand were all he could see. They were like massive swells on a red ocean, frozen in time to give a snapshot of the terrain.

But cutting across the featureless hills was a single set of footprints. It was clear they were made by a set of boots, not zombie feed or spider claws.

Gameknight knew that on the real Mars in the physical world, the planet had an incredibly thin atmosphere, but frequent dust storms could obscure the surface of the planet for days. Did the programmers add that kind of realism to the Galacticraft Mars? He wasn't sure, but in all likelihood, it meant these footsteps were recent, or they'd have been covered by dust.

They ran down the hill and approached the trail of prints. The wolves tried to smell the ground, to pick up the scent, but of course sensed nothing; their glass helmets were keeping them separated from the environment around them. They growled in frustration, then spread out and watched for monsters. In the distance, the faint moans of zombies could be heard, but they were far away. The wolves glanced in the direction of the sound and watched for threats.

"Come on, everyone," Gameknight said. "We gotta run."

He sprinted off across the sands, following the trail. A pair of wolves moved far out in front as the rest formed a wide protective circle around the party. Gameknight ran at the front, but was surprised as the two pechs moved up on either side of him. Even though they had short legs, they were easily able to keep up with him. In fact, their breathing never even seemed to become strained, while Gameknight was quickly panting heavily, his space helmet fogging up slightly. He even thought he heard one of the pechs humming some sort of melodic tune. If it weren't for their surroundings, the song might have been relaxing. But with the bleak, lifeless terrain around them, the soothing notes were unable to chip away at his trepidation.

"So Empech, Forpech, what part of Minecraft are you from?" Gameknight asked as he ran.

"Hmmm . . . Forpech remembers something about Thaumcraft," the pech said.

"Yes, yes, that name is familiar," Empech said.

"So both of you are from a modded version of Minecraft? From Thaumcraft?"

"Hmmm . . ." Forpech said, a look of confusion on his oversized gray face.

"What?" Gameknight asked.

"We have other memories, yes, yes," Empech said. "Things we do not understand."

"Like what?"

"Forpech remembers having a lair underground, with a great jeweled throne."

"And wolves . . . many wolves, yes, yes," Empech added.

"Underground home and wolves," Gameknight said. "It doesn't make any sense. Do you remember anything else?"

"Well . . . Forpech remembers something that is important somehow, it is not clear. But it's about . . . hmmm . . . leaves."

"Leaves?" Gameknight was confused. How could a memory of leaves be important? "Well, maybe it means that—"

Suddenly a proud, majestic howl filled the thin Martian atmosphere. The other wolves raced forward, their furry white bodies standing out against the dark red sands. They disappeared over a small hill, then began howling with their leader.

"They found something," Herder said, an expression of pride on his square face.

Gameknight raced ahead, sprinting over the dark mound. When he reached the top, he saw the wolves standing around a large hole in the ground. The footsteps led straight to the shadowy abyss, then just disappeared.

"That must be the entrance to the dungeon," Crafter said.

"Great, another dungeon," Hunter said. "Just what I was hoping for."

"Hunter, sometimes you're so—" Stitcher began to say, but was interrupted.

"Come on, we need to get in there and catch up with Entity303," Gameknight said.

He ran to the edge of the hole and peered down. There seemed to be no movement down in the shadowy structure, but that could just be from the fact that it was so dark.

"You hear anything?" Stitcher asked.

Gameknight shook his head.

"That doesn't seem normal," Digger said. "Usually there are some noises."

The User-that-is-not-a-user leaned back away from the opening and gazed at his friends. They all had expressions of uncertainty and fear on their square faces, especially the pechs. Everything about this gaping hole terrified Gameknight999, but he knew they had to go in there, or else Entity303 would destroy everything he loved.

With a sigh, he stepped up to the edge of the hole, then turned and glanced once more at his friends.

"Are all of you ready?" the User-that-is-not-a-user asked.

They nodded, but said nothing. He didn't even get a sarcastic remark from Hunter, which he knew meant that they were all scared.

"Ok, here we go."

And then Gameknight jumped into the darkness, hoping that all of them would somehow survive this ordeal.

CHAPTER 13

INTO THE DARKNESS

Gameknight landed in a large room devoid of any noise. The silence was spooky, almost oppressive, making it seem as if a monster horde would jump out of the darkness at any instant. His breathing seemed amplified inside his helmet, the wheezing in and out synchronized with the drum beat of his quickening heart. His nerves tingled as he waited for claws to reach out at him or arrows to streak through the air . . . but the attack never came.

Forpech and Empech put glowstone torches on the walls, revealing a chamber lined with green bricks. Blocks of spider webs clung to the walls and ceiling, but no fuzzy black monsters, with their eight terrible green eyes, were visible.

"Where are all the monsters?" Gameknight asked softly. The silence made him want to be as quiet as possible.

"Are you complaining?" Hunter whispered.

"No, I just don't like surprises, and the fact that there are no monsters waiting for us is a surprise."

"The monster spawners have been removed, yes, yes," Empech said, his high pitch screechy voice echoing off the brick walls. The volume of it, even though he was really just speaking at a normal speaking level, was shocking as it sliced through the stillness.

Digger walked to the opposite corner from the pechs and knelt. "One's been removed over here as well."

"Why would Entity303 take away the spawners?" Weaver asked. "That makes no sense. He could have just destroyed the monsters that were here and then left before any more creatures appeared."

"Maybe he's worried for our safety," Hunter said with a chuckle.

"Yeah, I'm sure that's it," Weaver agreed with a wry smile.

"I think it's safe to say that Entity303 didn't destroy the spawners to make it easy for us." Crafter moved to Digger's side and stared down at the hole in the ground. "We all know, that's not his style. He'd rather we suffered as much as possible, so destroying the spawners would be the opposite of that."

"Hmmm . . . we must proceed with caution, yes, yes" Empech said. "Expect the unexpected and be ready—that is Empech's advice."

"Thanks for stating the obvious," Hunter said, her voice full of sarcasm.

Stitcher punched her in the arm.

"Ouch . . . you keep hitting me in the same spot!" Hunter complained.

"Well, that's because you keep saying dumb things," her younger sister replied, shrugging.

"We must continue on," Forpech grumbled, his deep voice making the walls of the dungeon vibrate just a bit. "Hmmm . . . we must find the Mars Boss and determine what he knows about our enemy, Entity303."

"Right." Gameknight drew his steeleaf shield and held it before him, enchanted diamond sword held at the ready. Waves of iridescent light flowed from the weapon, painting the walls with a faint purple glow. "Weaver, come up front with me. We need to place glowstone torches as we go." He glanced over his shoulder.

"Digger, you collect the torches as we move through the dungeon, so we won't run out."

The big NPC nodded, then scooped Tux up with his left hand, his big pickaxe in his right.

"Come on, everyone."

Gameknight moved through the dark passage, scanning the ground for pressure plates, trip wires, or holes. It would be just like Entity303 to leave behind some traps. They moved through the tunnel in almost complete silence, only the sounds of their footsteps echoing off the walls. The lack of any other noise made everything around them seem so much louder: the clank of iron armor, the scrape of a sword against the wall, the sound of a glowstone torch being broken. The silence in the dungeon was almost deafening, stretching their nerves to the limit.

The passage led to another chamber. And as before, it had been swept clean of monsters and spawners. The only evidence anything had ever been there were the two holes in the ground where the spawners had once sat.

Water dripped from overhead. The sound of the splashing droplet on the ground made Gameknight jump.

"What was that?" Digger asked.

Gameknight pointed to the ceiling with his diamond sword. "Water from the ceiling."

"Why is there water up there?" Stitcher asked. "I didn't see any lakes or rivers on the surface."

Gameknight shrugged. "It's just the way some of these dungeons are programmed. They've always been this way."

"Well, I don't like it," Hunter said.

"I'll tell Micdoodle8, the developer of Galacticraft, your complaint if I ever see him," Gameknight replied.

"Wait, that was sarcastic, but you didn't punch *him*," Hunter complained to her younger sister.

"His sarcastic comments are funny, at least," Stitcher replied with a smile.

"Funny . . . you call that funny?"

Stitcher punched her sibling lightly in the arm, then laughed.

"Come on," Gameknight said. "Let's get to the next chamber."

They moved quickly through the dungeon, the green bricks that lined the walls and floors looking eerie in the light of the glowstone torches. The occasional splatter of water from the ceiling continued, each drip sounding like a thunderous deluge in the empty silence. Gameknight's heart thumped in his chest, pounding faster and faster as they moved through the dungeon. When they reached the next chamber, Gameknight charged in, ready for a monstrous response. But like the first, this room was completely devoid of monsters, the spawners destroyed.

"This is gonna be easy," Hunter said.

"Shhh . . . you're gonna jinx us," Weaver said.

"Pffft, no big deal," Hunter added.

"Come on, let's keep moving." Gameknight dashed through the chamber and into the dark passage.

They ran through the passage, turning to the left and to the right, then entering another room that seemed larger than the rest, the walls shrouded in darkness. Again, there were no monsters visible. They moved through the chamber and headed into the next corridor. Gameknight and Weaver led, while Digger and Crafter brought up the rear.

Suddenly, the User-that-is-not-a-user skidded to a stop. A huge wall of cobblestone blocked off the tunnel, stretching from floor to ceiling.

"What is this?" Weaver asked.

"I don't think this is supposed to be here," Gameknight said. "It's likely Entity303 put it here."

Herder moved close to the wall and ran his hand across the cold surface. "But what is he trying to keep us from?".

"Perhaps the wall was not meant to keep us out," Forpech said. "Hmmm . . . but instead meant to just keep us *in*."

"But why would that annoying user want to just stop us here? He knows we could just dig through this obstacle," Gameknight said.

He glanced at Digger. The stocky NPC placed Tux on the ground and moved to the wall. With a gigantic swing, he smashed his pickaxe into the cobblestone. Cracks spread across the face as he tore into the cube until finally it broke. But behind it was another block. Digger carved into that block as well until it disappeared, revealing yet another block of cobblestone behind that.

"Hmmm . . . perhaps there is more to this wall than meets the eye," Forpech said.

Squawk, squawk! Tux screamed from the back of the passage.

"Tux, be quiet, we need to figure this out," Gameknight chided.

Squawk, squawk, squawk!

"What is wrong with that penguin?" Hunter said as she peered into the hole Digger had carved.

Suddenly, a moan filled the passage. It caused Gameknight to freeze as fingers of dread clawed into his soul, making him shiver. A clicking accompanied the sorrowful wails, followed by the clattering of bones.

"I don't think we're alone anymore," Crafter said in a soft voice.

"You think?" Hunter asked.

Stitcher punched her sister in the arm, then drew her bow and notched an arrow. Herder ran down the length of the passage and placed a glowstone torch on the ground, then retreated back. As they watched, zombies in glowing armor, complete with space helmets and oxygen tanks, moved into the light, followed by spiders and skeletons, their eyes all glaring at the intruders.

"We have no way out." Digger backed away from the sounds until his back bumped against the cobblestone obstacle. Turning, he hacked frantically at the cobblestone wall, but found only layer after layer of stone.

"It seems we have few choices, yes, yes," Empech said.

The little gray gnome moved away from the monsters and back up against the wall, his enchanted fishing pole held at the ready.

"I won't let a bunch of monsters slow us down." Gameknight turned to Digger. "Get to work on this wall. We need a way through as quickly as possible."

"What are you going to do?" Crafter asked.

"The only thing I'm good for," Gameknight replied.

He tossed his shield to Empech, then drew his iron sword. Turning, the User-that-is-not-a-user faced the approaching mob, then charged, yelling with all his might, "FOR MINECRAFT!"

CHAPTER 14

ENTITY303'S TRAP

Gameknight smashed into the lead zombie, striking it with both his swords before it had time to retreat. Pushing forward, he kicked a spider out of the way, then fell upon a skeleton wearing what appeared to be glowstone armor. The bony monster's arrow streaked over his shoulder as he dodged out of the way. Striking out quickly, he slashed at the creature, knocking the bow from knobby fingers, then smashing it with all his strength.

The User-that-is-not-a-user pushed the monster farther back until he entered a large, brick-lined room shrouded in darkness. A musty and dank smell permeated the chamber as water dripped from the ceiling. The stink of monsters was now almost overpowering. Creatures poured from the shadows as if there was a limitless supply of them; that had to mean there were spawners back there.

"Digger, I need you up here!" Gameknight shouted.

"Are you sure?" a deep voice came from behind.

Gameknight slashed at a spider, then pushed a creeper back with a booted kick.

"Yes, get up here!" The stocky NPC had still not found his courage after the loss of his daughter, but

Gameknight didn't care—he needed Digger's pickaxe right now or they were all in trouble.

The stocky villager pushed his way forward and stood next to Gameknight, swinging his pointy weapon at the approaching monsters.

"Digger, we're going spawner hunting," Gameknight said. "I'll take care of the monsters, you take care of the spawners."

The stocky NPC smashed a spider with his pick, destroying its HP, then sighed and nodded his head.

"Come on, to the right first." Gameknight sprinted into the chamber and followed the wall to the right.

There were monsters everywhere, but the hostile creatures didn't expect to see them in the darkness. The enchantments from Gameknight's sword and armor gave off enough of a glow to illuminate a two-block circle around him. Following the wall, Gameknight quickly found himself in what seemed like a side alcove, likely built by Entity303. It was dark and chock full of hostile mobs, but near the ground, a subtle yellow light flickered, giving off the faintest bit of illumination.

Monsters reached out at him from the darkness, zombie claws scratching at his armor while skeleton arrows whizzed past his head. Gameknight pushed them back with his iron sword as he jabbed at the creatures with his diamond blade, forcing the zombies and spiders to keep their distance.

"Creeper!" Digger shouted.

The stocky NPC leapt in front of Gameknight and smashed the mottled green creature with his dual pickaxes, halting the ignition process with his attack. In seconds, the creature disappeared, revealing a spawner under the monster's green, pig-like feet. It was a metallic cage with glowing embers sparkling within it. The shape of a tiny creeper spun within the cube, its body getting larger and larger. Digger brought his pickaxes down upon the cube again and again until the device shattered.

Digger smiled, then groaned as another zombie slashed at him with its dark claws. Turning, he stepped back, away from the attacking monster. The zombie moved closer, snarling. The big NPC stepped back again, but he bumped up against the wall of the chamber; he had nowhere to go.

Gameknight caught the movement of the monster out of the corner of his eye. He kicked a spider away, then turned and fell on the zombie. The monster, not expecting the attack, glanced around in confusion. Staying behind the creature, he kept attacking with his dual swords until the monster was destroyed.

"You okay?" Gameknight asked.

Digger nodded his head, his green eyes filled with fear.

"Let's find the rest of the spawners," the User-that-is-not-a-user said. "Come on, we're doing this together. You aren't alone, Digger . . . you're never alone."

Digger sighed, then headed into the darkness with Gameknight999 at his side. They moved through the small side-chamber as the rest of their friends battled near the passage entrance. The clash of swords and claws there seemed to draw most of the monsters away from the spawners, allowing Gameknight and Digger to move quickly along the perimeter of the chamber.

They smashed four more spawners before they had to face another monster. This time, it was a spider, its dark, fuzzy body blending into the darkness. The only thing visible was the creature's eyes. Instead of bright red, like they'd be on the Overworld, the evolved spiders of outer space had bright green eyes, the color of poison. Gameknight pushed the monster back, blocking its attacks with one sword and countering with the other. While he fought, Digger tore up the spawner. In seconds, they'd both completed their tasks.

"Come on, this way," Gameknight said.

They pair moved to the other side of the chamber, attacking monsters from behind when they could. On the opposite side of the chamber, Gameknight found another hidden room with more spawners, but had to urge Digger to break them. The big NPC's fear seemed almost overwhelming.

"Digger, we need to get these last spawners, then we're done," Gameknight said, trying to reassure his friend. "Come on, you can do it."

The villager hefted his pickaxe in the air and smashed one just as it spawned a zombie. Gameknight attacked the monster before it could turn its claws on Digger.

"Get the next one while I take care of this monster," the User-that-is-not-a-user said.

He shoved the zombie back against the wall, allowing Digger to pass. The stocky NPC moved past and shattered the last of the spawners while Gameknight finished off the zombie. They then headed through the darkness, moving toward the sound of iron clashing with claws.

With the flow of monster reinforcements eliminated, the sounds of battle changed from one of desperation for the NPCs to one of hopelessness for the monsters. Zombies shouted out for help, but none came. Spiders tapped claws on the ground, begging for assistance, but no more of their kin emerged from the darkness. The only things that approached were Digger and Gameknight999.

Charging forward, the User-that-is-not-a-user slashed at the monsters. Digger swung his pickaxes, hitting one monster with his left while defending with his right. When the villagers at the chamber entrance saw their two friends, they pushed forward, squeezing the monsters between two forces. Zombies stumbled over each other and fell while skeletons snagged their bow strings on the exposed ribs of their neighbors. Between the two groups, they slowly crushed the monsters between them, eliminating the last of them.

Digger glanced around the chamber, his green eyes filled with fear. "Are they all gone?"

Squawk! Tux added. The penguin was being held under one of Empech's arms; the other held his magical fishing pole firmly in a three-fingered hand.

"Yeah, I think so," Crafter said.

"Let's get back to that cobblestone wall," Gameknight said.

The friends ran through the passage until they reached the stone obstacle.

"Digger, you think you can dig through this?" Gameknight noticed the villager's face was a pale white color, square beads of sweat streaming down his forehead. He looked terrified by the battle they'd just fought. Gameknight had hoped being thrust into the conflict would have brought the big villager's courage back to the surface, but he could see that wasn't the case.

With a sigh, Digger moved to the wall.

"Just be ready when I break through," the villager said. "I've had enough monstrous surprises for today."

Holding his big pickaxe with both hands, Digger did what he did best . . . he dug.

CHAPTER 15

MARS BOSS

Digger labored with his pick, smashing the cobblestone blocks only to find more layers hidden behind each.

"Entity303 really didn't want us to get into this room, did he?" Hunter asked.

"I don't think it was that," Crafter said. "I suspect his goal was to keep us from escaping while all those monsters attacked."

"Hmmm . . . why would your enemy do this?" Forpech asked. "It serves no purpose."

"I know why he did this." Gameknight said as he pulled out his pickaxe and helped with the wall. "He must know, somehow, that we're pursuing him. This trap, with the wall and all the monster spawners, was put here for only one reason . . . to make us suffer. Entity303 is just like the evil Herobrine."

"When I was his captive in that weird forest, I remember Entity303 saying something once about how he created Herobrine," Weaver said. "He bragged that Herobrine was his greatest virus, and inserting that virus into Minecraft was all part of his plan for revenge."

"Our enemy feels good about himself only when other people suffer." Gameknight stopped digging for a moment. "He's like every bully I've ever known; they mask their own pain by making others feel worse. I'm sure everyone in the Minecraft programming team hated him; he probably did things to them, to cause suffering. I bet this was why he was fired from the programming group, because he wasn't a team player. He's alone in Minecraft, and probably in the physical world as well, and the only way he's able to make himself feel better is to cause anguish in others."

"But what do these bullies fear?" Stitcher asked.

"They fear they'll show some kind of weakness and become a target of the other bullies. They fear showing any vulnerability that can be exploited. They fear being alone instead of being surrounded by people that tell them they're awesome." Gameknight lowered his voice to just a whisper. "They fear being afraid."

"That's kinda pathetic," Weaver said.

Gameknight nodded. He turned back to the wall and continued to smash the cobblestone with his pickaxe, helping Digger with the laborious task. Weaver stepped forward and stood shoulder to shoulder with Gameknight and Digger, his iron pickaxe in his young hands. Swinging it with all his might, he tore into the gray, cobblestone blocks. In minutes, the wall was finally obliterated, revealing a dark passage opening into a large room, the walls and floor lined with the same green bricks. A smattering of glowstone blocks were set in the ground along the perimeter of the deathly quiet chamber, casting the smallest amount of light along the perimeter, but leaving the center of the room masked in darkness.

"You think the Mars Boss is in there?" Digger asked, taking a step back.

"Probably," Gameknight replied.

"It's pretty dark." Hunter notched an arrow to her bow and drew it back. "I don't like dark."

"I know," Gameknight replied. "But I have a plan."

He smiled.

"I already don't like it," Hunter said, eyeing him cautiously.

Quickly, he explained his plan, then stood next to the opening of the chamber.

"Everyone ready?" Gameknight asked. They all nodded their heads.

"NOW!"

Gameknight sprinted out into the room with Weaver at his side, a handful of glowstone torches in their hands. They followed the edge of the room, placed the glowing sticks on the ground as they ran along one wall, brightening the edges of the room.

Suddenly, the ground shook as a gigantic monster appeared at the center of the chamber, shrouded in darkness. Gameknight skidded to a stop as the floor quaked. The creature's feet pounded the ground as it drew loud, raspy breaths, its features masked in shadow.

"Come on, Weaver," Gameknight said.

They took off running, with Gameknight putting torches on the ground while Weaver placed them on the walls. Slowly, they painted the room with light.

"WHO DARES DISTURB THE MARS BOSS?" the creature boomed.

Gameknight said nothing. He just ran as fast as possible, not peeking up at the monster or the features of the chamber. Their goal was to illuminate the room before the fighting really started.

"We do not mean to intrude," Crafter called out from the entrance, trying to distract the monster. "We are just searching for the user that came before us."

Gameknight and Weaver moved faster, placing more torches on the ground.

"HE SAID YOU WOULD COME TO DESTROY ME," the Martian boomed. "THIS IS MY DOMAIN AND YOU WILL NOT BE ALLOWED TO PASS."

"We don't want to fight," Crafter continued, keeping the Mars Boss's attention away from the User-that-is-not-a-user. "We only want to find the user, Entity303."

"LEAVE AND YOU WILL NOT BE HARMED."

"We can't do that," Crafter said. "Entity303 means to destroy all of Minecraft. He must be stopped."

"SHOW YOURSELF," the monster demanded.

"Well . . . I'd rather stay in the darkness of this tunnel," Crafter replied.

"IF YOU ARE NOT IN THE CHAMBER, THEN WHO SUMMONED ME? . . . SOMEONE ELSE IS HERE!"

The monster moved out of the darkness and into the light of the glowstone torches. Gameknight was shocked at what he saw. Sparkling sheets of blue electricity sizzled through the gloom. The sparks danced across the creature like glowing spiders crawling all across the monster's skin. The electricity outlined the monster's body, making it glow with deadly energy. And just by the shape of the electrical blanket of energy, the User-that-is-not-a-user knew exactly what kind of creature they faced. It was a creeper, a gigantic creeper easily three times their height, if not more.

Gameknight skidded to a halt as the monster moved further into the light.

"Look at it," he said to Weaver. "It's massive."

"But did you see its heads?" the young boy replied.

"Heads? Multiple?" Gameknight asked.

And then he glanced up at the monster's face. Instead of having just one head, the Mars Boss had three, the left and right ones sticking out at an angle. The monster turned all of its creeper heads toward Gameknight and Weaver.

"THERE YOU ARE," the boss growled. "NOW LEARN THE PENALTY FOR DISTURBING THE MARS BOSS."

"Weaver . . . RUN!"

Suddenly, a flashing cube of TNT streaked down from the Martian Boss, heading straight for Gameknight999. He shoved Weaver to the right, then ducked and rolled to the left, allowing the explosive to pass over his head and detonate behind him.

"LET THE BATTLE BEGIN!" the monster roared, then pounded its four massive, pig-like feet on the ground, causing the entire chamber to shake. Its electrical coating grew bright, then the boss fired upon those in the tunnel, before turning to search for the two intruders who had entered its domain.

Gameknight and Weaver sprinted through the room, searching for some kind of safe place in the green, brick-lined chamber. But there was no safety to be had in the Martian Boss's chamber . . . there was only death and destruction.

CHAPTER 16
BATTING PRACTICE

With the room now lit, Crafter and the other villagers charged forward. Hunter and Stitcher fired arrows at the beast, but they simply bounced off the creature's electrical coating. Crafter and Herder moved up close and swung their swords against the creature's legs, but their blades just clanged harmlessly against the monster, as if they'd been fighting solid bedrock. They tried again and again, but just ended up damaging their own weapons.

"Nothing's working!" Hunter shouted.

She fired her bow, aiming for the creature's center head, but the arrow was deflected and clattered to the ground. The creature then fired a block of TNT at Hunter. She quickly dodged to the side as the explosive tore a massive hole in the side of the chamber.

Gameknight and Weaver ran to the creature, their swords flashing through the air. As with Crafter, their swords bounced harmlessly off the creature's legs. The Martian Boss glared down and kicked them with one of his four feet. They flew through the light gravity and landed with a thud, but before the monster could fire upon them, Gameknight and Weaver were both instantly up and moving.

Gameknight put away his diamond sword, and drew his glowing yellow blade. He hoped there wasn't some kind of limit to the power that pulsed within the deadly weapon.

"Weaver, stay back," the User-that-is-not-a-user said.

He ran to the monster again, swinging the infused-sword with all his might. Just as with the diamond blade, the glowing weapon bounced off the sheet of electricity as if it were just a stick; it had no effect.

"Everyone get out of the room," Gameknight shouted. "Go back into the tunnel!"

Gameknight stayed in the chamber while his friends ran for safety. The Martian Boss fired a block of TNT at the escaping villagers, but it flew wide and missed. The flying explosive cube reminded him of something in the Nether. And then the image of his ancient enemy, Malacoda, appeared into his head. That king of the ghasts had loved throwing fireballs at people while they retreated, not caring if those he fired upon were warriors, women, or children. All that creature had cared about was destruction, and fireballs were his weapon of choice. But Gameknight also remembered how to defeat a ghast. The User-that-is-not-a-user chuckled, drawing the gaze of the left creeper head.

"ANOTHER STILL DARES TO STAND IN MY CHAMBER?"

"Not for long," Gameknight replied, then sprinted to the entrance.

A stream of TNT followed him, but he ran a zig zag pattern, avoiding the explosive cubes. He made it to the entrance, and the instant he stepped out of the chamber, the three-headed Mars Boss disappeared.

"So, your plan about all of us attacking it at the same time?" Hunter said. "That was one of your worst plans ever."

"Yeah, it didn't really work like I thought."

"You have any other bright ideas?" she asked.

"I have one, but you won't like it."

"Let's hear it," Crafter said.

"I need all of you to stay near the entrance and out of the room. I know how to take care of the boss."

"I can't believe it's possible, but that plan is more idiotic than the last one," Hunter said.

"I know how to defeat it this time, but I need its attention focused on me," the User-that-is-not-a-user said. "Just stay out of the room and watch my back."

Gameknight put away the glowing yellow sword, hoping to conserve its energy, and drew his diamond blade. He then drew his iron sword with his left hand. Glancing at his friends, he gave them a smile, then stepped into the room.

Instantly, the Martian boss materialized at the center of the chamber. His three heads turned and stared down at the intruder.

"YOU'VE RETURNED?"

"I need what's in your locked chest," Gameknight said. "I'm sure you gave your key to Entity303. Now you're gonna give it to me."

All three heads smiled, changing the normally downturned mouth on each creeper head to a sort of jagged grimace. He then launched a block of TNT—which was exactly what Gameknight was expecting.

"Gameknight . . . RUN!" Hunter shouted from the doorway.

But the User-that-is-not-a-user stood his ground. The TNT moved closer and closer until . . . at the last instant, Gameknight batted the explosive back at the creeper with his sword. The TNT struck the creeper, then exploded, making the gigantic monster flash red as it took damage.

The boss roared in pain and frustration, then launched another attack, but this time, tiny charged creepers dropped from his body and approached Gameknight999. Running forward, Gameknight knocked the TNT back at the monster, then turned his sword on the little creepers.

The sound of digging filled the air . . . strange, he thought. He hit the first miniature creeper, driving it backward, then turned his attention to the next one. Before he could hit it, arrows streaked out from the doorway and struck the little monster. In the decreased gravity, the little creeper flew backward, but was hit in midair by more arrows, finally causing it to disappear.

"Incoming!" Herder shouted.

Gameknight looked up just in time to bat another explosive cube back at the Martian boss. It exploded against the monster's chest. Blocks behind him shattered as the digging sound became louder. Gameknight tried to glance over his shoulder at the noise, but the creeper boss fired another cube of TNT. The User-that-is-not-a-user waited until it was about to hit, then flicked his sword, batting it straight back.

Boom . . . the Martian boss flashed red again.

"Gameknight, let one hit the wall behind you," Crafter shouted.

He was about to ask why when the creeper launched another attack. Instead of hitting the TNT, Gameknight rolled across the floor and focused on a miniature creeper, letting the explosive cube detonate against the green brick wall behind him. The blast tore open the edge of the chamber, revealing an open space on the other side of the wall. Instantly, Digger, Herder, and Weaver moved in and fired their bows through the opening, targeting the little creepers that were continuing to fall from the Martian boss.

More TNT blocks streamed from the massive creeper, and each one was sent back to the source, blasting more and more of the creature's HP. With his friends concentrating on the little charged creepers, Gameknight could focus his attention on the boss and the flying blocks of destruction. Moving up close, he stood right in front of the monster.

The boss smiled and fired a stream of TNT down at Gameknight, but the User-that-is-not-a-user used both swords to swat the deadly blocks right back in its face. The creeper boss stepped back, trying to avoid the assault, but there was no place for the monster to flee. It continued to fire the explosive cubes as if it had no choice, but at the same time, the Mars Boss knew it meant its doom.

"NO . . . NOT AGAINNNNNN!" the Mars Boss screamed as he flashed red over and over.

Suddenly, the huge creature began to shake, then spin around. Gameknight backed up, scanning the ground for any of the miniature creepers, but none were present; his friends had taken care of them all.

Suddenly, the Mars Boss exploded, tearing a massive crater into the floor of the chamber. Glowing balls of XP showered the room, giving it an almost Christmas-y appearance.

Cautiously, Gameknight approached the rough-hewn hole. A couple of miniature creepers stared up at him from the bottom of the hole. He stepped into the recession. When the little monsters charged, he destroyed the first with his sword. Arrows rained down upon the remaining mini-creepers, eliminating them quickly. Gameknight glanced up and found the sisters standing on the crater's edge, bows in hand and arrows drawn.

Stepping further into the recession, he moved toward something shining at the very bottom, its shape hidden by the glowing balls of XP. The colorful spheres flowed into his inventory as he approached the golden thing. When he finally reached the bottom, Gameknight saw a bright key floating off the ground; it was the tier-four key. He allowed the key to flow into his inventory, then climbed out of the crater.

Along the rim, his friends stood, watching him. Crafter reached out and helped Gameknight up.

"That was fun," Hunter said. "Let's do that again."

Stitcher punched her, this time in the other arm.

"Ouch . . . now both my arms hurt."

Stitcher smiled.

"Come on, to the treasure room," Gameknight said.

He sprinted for the narrow passage that led out of the boss chamber. It turned to the left and right, then left again until it ended in a small room with columns of glowstone in each corner. At the center of the room sat a dark chest. Gameknight inserted the key and unlocked it, then slowly lifted the lid. It screeched with age as the rusted hinges strained against the ages of disuse. Dust fell from the lid, floating slowly to the ground.

Inside were more ingots of iron, some strange components from different mods that must be overlapping with Galacticraft, and some larger rocket components. Gameknight shuffled through the chest, looking for what he desperately needed.

"Well?" Hunter asked. "Is there anything useful there?"

The User-that-is-not-a-user shoved aside loaves of bread and potions of healing. There was so much stuff in the chest, it was difficult to find anything.

"You're not answering," Hunter said. "I don't like it when you don't answer."

"Umm . . ." Gameknight kept searching. Grabbing items, he started lifting them out of the chest and just dropping them on the ground. He threw a pile of coal, then a wooden sword, an iron chest plate . . . he littered the ground with items.

"It must be here," he moaned. "It must be."

Gameknight glanced up at Crafter, a worried expression on his square face.

Just keep looking, child, an ancient voice said in the back of his mind.

He pulled more items out of the chest, until . . . he found it.

Gameknight breathed a sigh of relief. "This is what Entity303 came for, and what we desperately need, so we can keep following him." He held a piece of paper in the air.

"What is it?" Crafter asked.

"It's the plans for a tier-four rocket," the User-that-is-not-a-user explained. "This will allow us to leave this solar system and go into deep space."

"Hmmm . . . Entity303 indeed seeks the edges of the Far Lands," Forpech said in a deep gravelly voice. "That is where the path will end."

"We gotta get to these Far Lands, wherever they are, fast," Herder said.

"It's not as easy as that," Gameknight replied. "We have to build the next ship to get to the tier-four planet, then build the next rocket to get to the farthest planets; those are tier-eight. This isn't easy, and we still don't really have a plan for when we finally catch up with Entity303."

"Well, I know one part of the plan." All eyes shifted to Hunter as she spoke. "We aren't gonna catch that terrible user if we stay here on Mars. Let's get going."

"Agreed," Stitcher said.

Pulling out his pickaxes, Digger carved into the wall, creating a tunnel that led to the surface, with Herder and Weaver at his side, a shower of ruddy Martian stone chips flying into the air from their pickaxes. As they dug, Gameknight thought about the danger he was putting his friends in. He had to stop Entity303, somehow, but he didn't want to see any of his friends—no, his *family*—get hurt in the process.

Maybe it's better if I do this alone, Gameknight thought. *I'm sure this is gonna get more dangerous as we move farther out into the universe. I couldn't bear the thought of being responsible for one of them getting hurt . . . or worse. But how do I tell them I need to do this alone? I feel like I'm betraying them, but what choice do I have if I want to keep them safe?*

He glanced at his friends, the pechs, the wolves . . . all of them were watching the three villagers digging upward through the Martian soil. None of them noticed the battle raging within Gameknight999 . . . one he felt he was losing.

CHAPTER 17

SIRIUS SOLAR SYSTEM

Entity303 peered out the window into the endless expanse of space. The stars twinkled as the ship slowly revolved, but the blackness was even darker than before. It seemed to suck the light out of his vessel, somehow even darkening the interior. He knew this was just his imagination, but the depth of outer space around him had an ominous and spooky feel to it, as if it were some kind of gigantic monster waiting to swallow him and his ship in a single gulp.

The reality of it was that Entity303 was very, very far from the Overworld and his native sun, Sol. With the Moon and Mars, the sun was always there in the distance, casting light on its orbiting children. But here, in deep space, there was nothing but distant stars shedding only the barest bit of light on the universe. The darkness felt cold and empty, amplifying his sense of being alone—not just on this journey, but in life. Programming Minecraft had meant everything to Entity303, and when they fired him for his overly violent sense of humor, it had stripped his sense of belonging and community away. They had no idea how much that had hurt him . . . or did they? Now, he was going to make them all pay.

Suddenly, a map surfaced in his mind. Entity303 closed his eyes and was able to see it all: it was a map of the Galacticraft universe. The Sol solar system, with the Overworld orbiting third from the sun, dominated the map. But off to the right were two other solar systems. The farthest, the Kepteyn solar system, had only a single planet orbiting its small red sun. Entity303 knew, from experience, there was nothing on that planet which would be of interest to him. What he needed was something teeming with life. When his final plan eventually took effect, it would drain the innocent lives from the planet while the tainted virus tore at the fabric of Minecraft.

It wasn't necessary for him to execute his plan on a planet filled with life; it was just a bonus, making the creations of those who had shunned him suffer a bit before they were swallowed by the void. Reaching out with his mind, the user imagined himself clicking on one of the planets. He first tried his target, but nothing happened; he'd need a larger ship to reach that planet, and for that, he'd need to battle another boss and take the tier-eight ship schematic from the treasure room. But for now, all he could do was reach a tier-four planet.

"Let's see, which tier-four planet is farthest from the sun?" Entity303 said, his voice echoing off the cold walls of his rocket ship. "Ahh . . . there it is, Diona. That's the one."

He thought about clicking on that planet with his wireless mouse. Suddenly, the map disappeared for a moment, then all the stars went out.

"What happened?"

There was a blackness around the ship that was darker than the void, darker than shadows at midnight, darker than . . . nothingness. Icy shivers of fear crept up his spine, making him shake for just an instant, then everything disappeared.

His ship was gone.

Entity303 found himself floating through space, unable to tell which way was up or down.

"Am I in the void?" he said.

There was no echo around him. His voice just seemed to disappeared into the endless darkness.

"Should I leave?"

Entity303 knew he could use the *EXIT* command, and the Digitizer that he had stolen would take him back to the physical world. But this was his best opportunity to destroy all of Minecraft, and take his revenge on all those programmers who had kicked him out. He had to see his plan through.

The darkness wrapped tightly against him, as if it were coiling around him like a snake getting ready to strike. Beads of sweat formed on his forehead and trickled down his face. They felt like tiny spiders crawling across his skin. Entity303 reached up and tried to wipe the sweat away, but his hand just bumped against his space helmet and left the tiny cubes of moisture clinging to his eyebrows and cheeks.

And then, just as quickly as the darkness came . . . it was gone. In what seemed like a burst of light, the stars suddenly appeared, their brilliance shocking him. He was surrounded by the sparkling universe, a harsh white sun hanging in the inky sky. It seemed as if he were completely motionless, the starry background remaining fixed, but then Entity303 felt the faintest tug on his body. There was a sensation of *down,* like something was pulling on his feet. This made it feel as if he were descending toward something, the gentle caress of gravity guiding him somewhere. Glancing at his feet, Entity303 saw a planet appear beneath him. It was pale, without any land features or vegetation; just a barren cube floating in space. Above him, a cratered blue moon suddenly appeared. It hovered over the planet, trapped in its gravitational embrace.

He'd never known of anyone going to the moon of Diona, but there it was. Turning his gaze back to the planet, he watched the pockmarked surface as he drew nearer. Off to the right, a wooden crate floated down, a large, billowing red parachute slowing its fall. Glancing up, Entity303 saw a similar parachute above him, controlling his descent.

Memories of the last time he'd been on this planet came to his mind. There had been a thriving ecosystem here, with tall, skinny trees that were able to reach up to the cloud level in the reduced gravity. Flying creatures soared from tree to tree on delicate wings, harvesting the brightly colored fruit that grew in the thick purple leaves. Fields of blue grass covered every inch of the planet, providing sustenance to the small herds of green and white striped six-legged creatures that were raised by the villagers on this planet. It had all been incredible . . . until Entity303 had arrived.

"I wonder if my tainted virus has finished destroying this planet?" he said aloud as he drew closer to the surface.

He had released a self-replicating virus that spread the Taint across the planet. It had first spread out, turning the ground and plants a dark, obsidian-like purple, making everything poison. When the tainted wave touched the animals and villagers, it had turned them into the evolved monsters that he now saw moving about on the surface.

"If only the Minecraft programmers could see my Taint working now."

This was one of the many reasons he'd been fired from the Minecraft development team. Entity303 liked focusing on destructive additions to the game, rather than things that could make the creative experience within the digital landscape more incredible.

Below him, he saw the end result of his creation. The Taint virus had worked exactly as he hoped. The planet was now stripped of the life that once covered the planet like a blanket of hope. Now, it was a hopeless place, with hopeless inhabitants . . . perfect.

Entity303 landed gracefully on the pale surface of the planet. The crate landed nearby, the parachute instantly disappearing as soon as the wooden box touched the ground. He ran to it and pulled it open. Inside were his tier-four rocket and launch pad. He gathered the two items and stuffed them into his bulging inventory.

A hissing sound filled the now poisonous Diona air. Entity303 spun around and drew his sword in a smooth, fluid movement. He slashed out at what he knew would be a creeper, without even looking. His glowing yellow blade struck the monster hard, making it flash red with damage. The monster stopped its ignition process and stepped back, but that would not save it. Entity303 moved forward and attacked again, hitting the creature two more times. With a confused and terrified expression on its mottled face, the creeper disappeared with a pop.

"Ha ha . . . that was fun," Entity303 said, then turned and scanned the landscape. "Anyone else want some?!" he shouted.

The monsters continued to shuffle about, ignoring his presence unless they happened to move nearby.

Entity303 laughed again.

"To think all of you were once villagers, and now you're mindless monsters."

Entity303 smiled, pleased with his cleverness. The lives he destroyed with his virus were of no real concern—after all, they were just computerized creatures, and of no importance to him.

"Now, let's see if the virus completed its work."

Reaching into his inventory, the user pulled out a lodestone. The dark, polished stone felt cold in his hands, but there was a pulse of magical power in the object that radiated into his fingers. Entity303 slowly turned in a circle, watching the stone. It remained dark and cold as he pointed it across the landscape. And then, suddenly, it grew warm and bright, a red glow emanating from within the enchanted device.

"So the transformation is not complete," he said just to hear his own voice. "There must be some tainted ground in that direction, still completing the poisoning of this land." He smiled, pleased with the level of destruction he'd caused on this planet. "That must be where the dungeon is located. They're always the last to change. And since the transformation isn't complete, that means there is no Diona Boss . . . at least, not yet. That'll make getting the supplies from the treasure room that much easier. "

He removed his furry white chest plate and replaced it with his jet pack. Activating the tiny rockets, he flew high into the air just as a group of zombies approached. The user was tempted to destroy the monsters, but there wasn't time to play . . . he still had work to do. The monsters glared up at him as he climbed in the air, then arced forward in the direction the lodestone had indicated.

"I'll quickly get the supplies in the dungeon treasure room. After I build the tier-eight rocket, and get to the next planet, then I can start the last phase of my plan. Soon I'll be in the Outer Lands of Thaumcraft. Let's see if Gameknight999 has the courage to follow me there."

He soared through the deadly air of Diona, toward the dungeon that lay hidden underground, his prize waiting for him. Soon, all of Minecraft would be as dead as this planet, and then even the pyramid of servers itself would be destroyed. And there was no one here to stop him, not even the meddling Gameknight999.

CHAPTER 18
IRREPARABLE DAMAGE

The rocket felt cold and empty, even though his friend Tux was with him. Gameknight glanced out the window at the vastness of space. Stars sparkled in the distance, but they seemed so far away; it made him feel even lonelier.

He knew he'd hurt his friends' feelings back on Mars when he suggested continuing after Entity303 on his own. It had actually made Crafter weep. The young NPC had said they were family and they should work together, no matter what.

Stitcher had just hung her head down . . . she'd probably been crying as well.

Hunter had refused to look at him, she was so angry. He'd tried to make her and the others understand that he was trying to protect them . . . but they didn't care. They'd felt abandoned and betrayed, just as he anticipated. Gameknight thought he could have handled that, but what he wasn't ready for was the expression on their faces, the disappointment and pain and tears.

Herder and Weaver had both been confused. They'd asked him why he was leaving them behind. Gameknight said they could stay there on Mars, in the oxygen bubble, until he finally caught Entity303. Weaver had pointed out that Gameknight wouldn't have any oxygen collectors or bubble distributors or anything; that was something the User-that-is-not-a-user had not considered.

That had ended up being the weakness in his argument. He knew he couldn't go on without his own oxygen generation equipment, and he couldn't leave his friends on Mars without any. He had no choice; they had to accompany him . . . to what might very well turn out to be the bitter end.

But the damage he'd done to the relationship with his friends might well be irreparable.

Suddenly, the stars went out. It was like a light switch for the universe had just been flicked off, leaving him in a darkness that seemed to seep into his very soul.

Squawk! Tux said.

"I know girl, it's okay. We're probably going from the Sol solar system to the Sirius solar system. This was why we needed the larger, tier-four rocket, so we could make this jump through the void to the next solar system."

Squawk, squawk! The penguin moved back and forth from one foot to the other.

Gameknight could tell she too was feeling the strange emptiness from the starless abyss.

"Just close your eyes, Tux. I'm sure it will pass soon."

The User-that-is-not-a-user closed his eyes. It seemed to make the blackness wrap even more tightly around him, digging its dark fingers into his sense of guilt. He'd unintentionally hurt those that meant the most to him . . . how could he be so foolish?

The darkness grew deeper, amplifying his feelings of guilt and sorrow. An overwhelming sadness spread through him like a deadly poison, devouring his courage. And just when he thought he couldn't stand it anymore, when he thought this might be the end of his hope and the end of his sanity . . . the darkness disappeared.

Gameknight opened his eyes. Through the window, he saw countless stars. They were very far away, too distant to reach with this ship, but it was something to drive away the sense of loneliness. The craft rotated slowly, allowing a pale-yellow sun to move into view.

"Tux . . . look, it's Sirius. We made it!"

Squawk, squawk! The little penguin jumped up, then started floating in the cabin of their ship, the lack of gravity giving the usually flightless bird wings on which she could soar.

Gameknight reached down and picked up his friend, holding her tight to his chest. Just then, the ship disappeared, and they were floating through outer space. The brilliant stars wrapped around them like a bejeweled blanket. It was beautiful in all directions, and filled his spirt with hope.

A force began to pull on him, slowly drawing him into the gravity well of Diona. Reaching out, he held her tight, then gazed down at his feet, where he saw the planet appear. It was a desolate place, with craters from countless meteors marking its surface. Off to the left, a blue moon hung in space, the cube possibly within reach if he were still in his ship. But he was committed; Gameknight999 was descending toward Diona.

As they drew closer, he saw countless monsters moving across the surface. There were evolved creepers, zombies, and spiders all moving aimlessly about. Each wore a glass space helmet and had oxygen gear to keep them breathing, but there was no plant life anywhere.

"I thought this planet had life on it other than monsters," Gameknight said to the little penguin under his arm. "In fact, I thought there weren't monsters at all on any of the planets in the Sirius solar system. The earliest videos of the More Planets mod, the add-on to Galacticraft, showed nothing but fantastic new biomes and interesting new creatures. But this planet seems dead."

Squawk, Tux agreed.

As they floated to the ground, a group of space wolves moved past, their white coats almost glowing in the light of the small, yellow sun. When he finally had his feet on solid ground, Gameknight set Tux down and drew his two swords. A pair of zombies approached, interested in the newcomers; that was their first mistake. They initially moved toward Gameknight999, but when they saw Tux, they decided to attack the little penguin; that was their second error.

"You stay away from Tux!" Gameknight shouted.

One of the monsters reached out with a clawed hand and swiped at Tux. She saw the attack coming and flopped down on her white belly, allowing the sparkling claws to pass overhead.

"No, you didn't!"

Gameknight fell on the monsters in a fury.

"No one tries to hurt my friends!" he growled.

He hit the first monster with his diamond sword, then followed with the iron blade. The monster flashed again, then let out a sad and sorrowful moan. It tried to back away, but Gameknight would not let it escape; he knew the creature would be back. With both swords, he hit the monster again, destroying the beast and leaving behind glowing balls of XP. Its companion growled and lunged at Gameknight, but he was ready. Knocking aside its attack, he slashed at the monster, hitting it over and over until it disappeared.

Turning to scan the landscape, Gameknight didn't see any other monsters nearby; he and Tux were safe . . . for now.

"Tux, come with me."

Gameknight moved to a large, flat area and started building their base. Their crate of supplies had landed nearby, but he didn't want to worry about those right now. Instead, he pulled out the blocks of leaves and oxygen collector and constructed their air bubble as he had on all the other planets. When he was finally finished, he used the teleportation ring and brought his friends to Diona. As before, they appeared in a flash of light, the slightest purple haze of teleportation particles left floating into the alien atmosphere.

"Glad you remembered to bring us here," Hunter said, pain still in her eyes.

"I got the base set up as quickly as I could," the User-that-is-not-a-user said.

"Look, wolves!" Herder shouted.

"They're space wolves," Gameknight said. "I remember hearing about them. For some reason, they aren't hostile to anything, even monsters."

"That's unfortunate," Hunter said.

Weaver sprinted to the wooden crate that had fallen with Gameknight and Tux. He yanked the lid off and pulled out the rocket and launch pad, then sprinted back to the air bubble before any monsters became curious. He placed the launch pad and rocket on the ground.

"Good work, Weaver," the User-that-is-not-a-user said.

The boy only grunted; he, too, was still angry at Gameknight.

"Well, I know you're all still angry at me, but you must realize . . ."

"A Third!" Forpech exclaimed.

"Yes, yes, a Third . . . Empech feels him as well."

"What are you talking about?" Crafter said.

Empech moved to stand in front of Gameknight999.

"There is another Third, yes, yes," Empech said. "They must be found and protected."

"Another Third?" Gameknight asked. "What are you talking about?"

"Hmmm . . . there is another Third . . . another pech, like Forpech and Empech," the pech said in a deep, gravelly voice. "They are in danger."

"Yes, yes, we can feel their fear," Empech said.

Gameknight glanced at Crafter. The young NPC's bright, blue eyes were filled with uncertainty.

"We need to catch Entity303," Hunter growled. "Getting distracted by a side quest will not help."

"Well, right now, we have no idea where to go on this planet," Gameknight said. "Heading toward another pech is just as good of a direction as any other." He turned to Crafter. "So far, the pechs have been critical to our success. I suspect this third pech will be the same."

"I agree," Crafter said. "Likely having three pechs with us will help our cause in the end."

"Then you agree with Empech and Forpech?" Gameknight asked.

He wasn't addressing Crafter, he was asking the whole party. They all nodded their heads, with the exception of Hunter. Instead, she glared at Gameknight, anger simmering behind those deep brown eyes.

"Well?" the User-that-is-not-a-user asked.

She finally nodded. "I agree, let's go get this pech. We don't leave anyone behind and we don't abandon our friends, no matter what."

Before Gameknight could respond, the pechs took off across the pale, desolate landscape. Forpech had his emerald-tipped wand out, the end glowing bright green when it pointed in the correct direction. Somehow, his magical weapon was guiding the party directly toward the new pech. The rest of the group followed the gray-skinned gnomes, leaving the safety of their oxygen bubble behind as they went out into the unknown of the planet Diona.

CHAPTER 19
THE TAINT

Entity303 hovered in the air, staring down at the monsters clustering together in the dungeon entrance. Spiders, zombies, skeletons, and creepers all stared up at him with hungry eyes.

Reaching into his inventory, the user drank a potion of night vision. Instantly, the details of the room below came in to clear focus. It was a large, square room with a circular hole in the ceiling, the opening stretching up all the way to the surface of Diona. In the corners of the chamber, he could make out the telltale signs of spawners: the faintly glowing embers dancing about their edges.

He lowered himself a bit and glared at the monsters below him.

"At one time, you were all villagers," the evil user said. "But thanks to my Taint virus, now look at you. If only you could remember your past lives a bit, then maybe this would be more terrible. Ha ha ha."

He slowly descended into the dungeon, but when he was just within the chamber, Entity303 activated his jet pack and flew through the room. Soaring along the ceiling, he shot into the next passage, staying out of reach of the mobs below.

"Sorry, but I don't have time to play with you," Entity303 said with a sneer. "I'm getting impatient and want the destruction of Minecraft to start. And to do that, I need to get farther into outer space."

He sped along the ceiling of the dungeon, the gray bricks that made up the walls, floor, and ceiling zooming by as he rocketed through the structure. Weaving around the occasional block of spider's web, he made it through the passages of the Diona dungeon in record time.

Slowly he settled to the ground as he approached the Boss chamber. Within the room were three creatures: one was one of those strange pechs, his gigantic backpack colored a deep blue. Nearby stood a female villager and her child. Likely, these were the sole survivors from the virus he used to infect this planet a while ago.

Most of the chamber was brightly lit, the floor and ceiling made of brilliant white quartz, but the walls were now a sickly purple color, like a bad bruise. In some places, the dark stain from his virus had already faded to the gray, lifeless brick he'd seen in the rest of the dungeon, while some of the pristine white quartz struggled against the relentless viral caress of the Taint.

"Ahh . . . I see my virus is finishing its job here," Entity303 said with a smile.

The pech turned and glanced at the evil user for just an instant, an enchanted pickaxe in his small, three-fingered hands, but then turned back to face the purple bruise that was slowly devouring more of the white blocks. The gray gnome was using his pick to break the tainted blocks and replace them with new blocks of quartz, but he couldn't keep up. The pech zoomed across the chamber, repairing damage here and there as the mother and her child stood in the center of the room, terrified.

"You seem like you're having fun, so I don't want to disturb you," Entity303 said with a smile.

"Wait, help us," the woman said. "Please, take my son and save him from this terrible thing. Please . . ."

"Now why would I want to do that, villager?" the user said. "I was the one who planted this virus here. This was my creation. I would hate to intervene; it is inevitable."

He then turned toward the little gnome.

"I see the developers put you here to try and stop my taint," Entity303 said to the pech. "Good luck with that. This virus, like the last one, is based on artificial intelligence. It will learn what you are doing, then take advantage of your weakness. You cannot win. You might as well just surrender to your fate."

"Never. I'll not give up," the pech said with a hurried voice, his staccato words short and fast. "I see the truth in your words. You overestimate your disease. I will not yield."

"Yeah . . . well, we'll see about that," Entity303 said with a smile. "Resistance is futile, but I'll leave you to your pointless attempts. It's only a matter of time until the virus destroys the last of this planet. Soon, all of the planets will be obliterated, but you won't be around to see that. My Taint will destroy this chamber and the last bit of Diona as the developers of Minecraft intended it, and then the virus will also destroy you. Don't worry, it won't be fast. I've been told when the Taint finally infects a living creature, the transformation is quite painful. But rest assured, you won't be gone—the last one of you will be changed into a three-headed creeper boss. Then, you will do my bidding."

"Never!" the pech said as he smashed a purple block and replaced it with quartz, then dashed to another spot in the room that was fading to purple.

"I leave you to your hopeless task," Entity303 said with a smirk. "But before I go, I will help myself to what's in the chest in the treasure room. You see, I left those items there long ago so I could finish the destruction of Minecraft."

He laughed again, then floated into the air and drifted across the chamber, careful not to touch any of the infected walls. When he reached the passage that led to the treasure room, he glanced one more time at the pech. The little creature was putting up a magnificent fight, but one creature was just not enough to hold off the virus from all sides. Eventually, his Taint would win and the last remnants of life on this planet would be erased and replaced with monsters.

Satisfied with himself, Entity303 streaked through the passage and entered the treasure room. Kneeling, he carefully opened the old wooden box, not needing a key since the locking mechanism would not engage until the transformation of the planet was complete. Reaching in, he pulled out some large rocket engines, pieces of hardened hull plating, and the plans for a tier-eight rocket. That single piece of paper would give him access to the outer planets of the Sirius solar system, where the destruction of Minecraft would begin.

Closing the lid, he drew his yellow-glowing pickaxe. With all his strength, he brought it down onto the chest, shattering it into a million pieces.

"Ha! Now the chest won't be spawned when the virus has finished with this planet." Entity303 looked at the flat side of the metallic tool, seeing his warped reflection in the pick. He smiled. "Let's see what you do, Gameknight999, without a tier-eight rocket schematic. You'll get here and you'll find nothing that can help you follow me deeper into outer space."

He smiled as he reached down and picked up a few ingots of iron.

"You'll be forced to watch the destruction of Minecraft from this lifeless planet, your failure complete. I hope you have just enough oxygen left to see the fabric of Minecraft tear itself to shreds."

He looked at the gray walls that had already been transformed. In a few places the purple stain of the taint was still fading from the walls and corners, the white quartz just finishing the transformation.

"I wish I could be here to see your face, Gameknight999, when you realize you're trapped, you've lost, and there is nothing you can do to save Minecraft."

With a smile, he soared to the ceiling and dug his way back to the surface, now one step closer to completing his mission.

CHAPTER 20
THE THIRD

They dropped into the shadowy dungeon, the light of their enchanted weapons the only thing to push back the darkness . . . as well as their fear. As before, Gameknight and Digger ran along the perimeter of the room, searching for spawners. Herder and Weaver darted between spider claws and skeleton arrows, placing glowstone torches on the ground, with Herder placing the glowing sticks while Weaver fought back the monsters, protecting his lanky, young friend. Hunter and Stitcher filled the air around the two youngsters with arrows, making the monsters think twice before attacking.

Digger and Gameknight shattered the two spawners in less than a minute while most of the mobs were focused on Herder and Weaver. The monsters, sensing they would not be joined by any more of their brothers and sisters, tried to flee the room, but Hunter and Stitcher stood in the passage, blocking their escape. A hail of arrows fell on the creatures while Gameknight and Digger—mostly Gameknight—attacked the creatures from behind. Unsure where to attack, the monsters clustered in a tight circle and fought for their lives.

Crafter, Weaver, and Herder added their blades to the attack, encircling the mobs. With no place to run, and escape seeming impossible, the monsters fought harder, pushing the NPCs back. A zombie claw found Hunter's arm, a skeleton arrow embedded itself in Herder's shoulder, and a spider's claw tore into Crafter's leg. The monsters battled with renewed strength; clearly, they knew there would be no surrender in this conflict.

Suddenly, Empech and Forpech were there. They threw splash potions of healing on their comrades, but also on the zombies. The decaying green monsters flashed red as the liquid poisoned them, sucking away at their HP until they disappeared with a pop. With the zombies gone, the balance of power had shifted.

"Close in, don't let any escape!" Gameknight shouted.

The villagers pushed forward, slashing at spiders and skeletons. With the monsters pressed in a tight group, their ability to fight was drastically reduced. They fell before the storm of swords and arrows until the last of the monsters finally disappeared.

Gameknight breathed a sigh of relief; no one had been seriously hurt.

"Must hurry, yes, yes," Empech said. "There is little time."

The wolves howled from within their space helmets, somehow sensing the urgency of the situation.

"Hmmm . . . Empech is correct, there is no time for battle," Forpech added. "Speed is more important than fighting."

"Yes, yes," Empech added.

"OK, we run through the chambers. Crafter, you lead with the pechs. Just run through the rooms and don't stop," Gameknight said. "I'll take the rear. Digger, I want you with me. We'll make sure none of the monsters think it's a good idea to follow us."

"Are you sure you want me?" the stocky NPC asked.

Gameknight nodded. "I need you by my side, old friend. For some reason, I feel as if there is something we must do together. I don't know what it is, a premonition, or maybe it's Minecraft telling me something . . .

I don't know. It's like when the Oracle used to plant thoughts in my head to give me hints about what to do."

"The Oracle?" Digger asked.

"That's right, you don't know about the Oracle, do you?" Gameknight said.

Digger shook his head, confused.

"You would have liked her," Gameknight continued. "She was . . ."

"Must hurry, yes, yes," Empech insisted.

"Sorry, let's go," the User-that-is-not-a-user said. "We run."

They sprinted through the tunnel, Crafter leading the way, Weaver placing glowstone torches on the walls, and Herder chopping at the cubes of spider web that blocked their way. The wolves howled and growled, sensing a battle, their space helmets muffling their voices a bit.

When they reached the next chamber, it was filled with spiders.

"To the left!" Crafter shouted.

The group darted through the room, not even slowing to strike at any of the monsters. By the time Gameknight and Digger had reached the room, the monsters were trying to block their way, denying the two friends an exit.

"Digger . . . JUMP!"

Both of them leapt up into the low Dionian gravity, soaring over the heads of the black, fuzzy monsters. Before the spiders knew what had happened, they were gone.

"Digger, slow down," Gameknight said.

With his two swords held before him, the User-that-is-not-a-user turned and walked backward, waiting for the spider attack; he didn't need to wait long. A wave of monsters charged at him. Fortunately, the passage had narrowed, and was only wide enough for two monsters to stand shoulder to shoulder.

"Digger, I need you!" Gameknight shouted.

He was battling two of the fuzzy monsters, his swords flashing through the air like lightning.

"Digger . . . now."

Pain exploded in his arm as one of the spiders landed a hit. Gameknight shouted out in agony.

"Digger . . ."

Gameknight dodged to the left, narrowly avoiding a wicked, curved claw, then slashed at the spider to the right. He blocked an attack with his iron sword, then struck with his diamond blade. The monster flashed red one last time, then expired. He turned to confront the last spider, but the creature chose the better part of valor and let the intruders continue down the passage, rather than continuing the fight.

Gameknight turned and found Digger standing frozen behind him, his face white as a ghast's.

"Where were you?" Gameknight asked. "I needed you."

"I'm so afraid . . . I'm always so afraid," Digger moaned. "I couldn't save my daughter, Topper, and you expect me to save you. I can't do it. I can't do anything." He lowered his gaze to the gray brick floor. "I should never have come with you. I'll just end up getting someone killed . . . like Topper."

"Digger, I have faith in you," Gameknight said. "You won't get anyone hurt. We're all here because we know Minecraft needs us. We need to work together so we can stop Entity303's plans."

"But you wanted to leave us all behind."

Gameknight sighed. "I know. I wrestle with the same fear: getting all of you hurt on this insane quest. But I know one thing for sure now . . . I need you at my side. All you need is faith in yourself."

"That's not likely to happen anytime soon."

"Digger, when I was younger, I—"

"HURRY UP, YOU TWO!" Hunter shouted.

"Come on," Gameknight said. "We have friends to protect."

He slapped the stocky NPC on the shoulder, then took off running, Digger following behind. They found the party waiting for them before the next chamber.

"GO!" Gameknight shouted.

The group shot through the next chamber, then the next and the next. A few monsters tried to slow them, but when they were running at full speed, the group was difficult to stop. The wolves learned they could use their helmets as battering rams, and collided into the monsters, taking them off their feet. This let them move even faster, with the white, furry animals and their sensitive eyes leading the charge.

In minutes, they made it through all the rooms and passages, and now approached the boss chamber. The pechs moved to the edge of the room and stopped.

"Oh no!" Empech shrieked.

"Nooo . . ." Forpech growled in a deep voice.

Crafter ran to their side and skidded to a stop.

"What's happening?" the young NPC cried.

"The pain . . . I can feel Minecraft's agony," Empech moaned.

"What is it?" Gameknight asked as he and Digger moved to the front of the column.

He was shocked at what he saw. Another pech stood at the center of the chamber, standing on a small circle of quartz. Next to him stood a villager woman and her son. The two NPCs clutched each other tightly, terror painted on their square faces. Surrounding the three of them was a sickly, diseased-looking dark stain moving closer and closer towards them. It was a dark purple, like the color of obsidian, but sickly and dirty somehow. The contaminated blocks were something Gameknight had seen before in Minecraft. It was the Taint. This was part of a mod called Thaumcraft, but this seemed much worse, and likely deadly to the touch.

The pech had dug up a number of the purple infected blocks and was replacing them with new pieces of quartz, his large blue backpack shifting about on his back. He dug as fast as he could, trying to keep the tainted blocks at bay, but he couldn't dig fast enough; he was losing the battle. In minutes, they'd be consumed by the taint, and Gameknight999 couldn't think of any way to help the doomed creature.

"Where's the Diona Boss?" Herder asked.

"The destruction of this world is not complete." Empech wiped away tears as he stared at the embattled peck. "When the Taint claims its last victims, it will create the boss, yes, yes."

"We have to get them out of there." Gameknight stepped into the chamber and stared at the villagers, struggling to come up with a solution.

"If we could somehow use a rope, maybe we could pull them out," Weaver said.

"But leads only work with animals," Herder said.

Suddenly, the puzzle pieces began to tumble around in Gameknight's head. Not a rope, but a fishing line, Gameknight thought. But who would be strong enough to lift it? His eyes then fell upon Digger.

"I know how to save them, but we must act quickly," the User-that-is-not-a-user explained. "Empech, can your fishing pole lift their weight?"

"Of course, my fishing pole is magically enhanced, yes, yes. It will hold their weight."

"Good," Gameknight replied. "Then all we need is someone strong enough to lift them once they are snagged by the hook."

"Whomever does this, will feel the pain the target feels," Empech said. "They must be more than just physically strong. It is emotionally draining as well. This person must not be afraid, or the magic in the fishing pole will consume them."

Gameknight glanced at Digger. "You're the only one strong enough to do this."

The stocky NPC stared at the embattled pech, then looked back at Gameknight999.

"I don't know if I can . . ."

"Digger, we have no choice," Gameknight said. "We must act now, before it's too late."

The big NPC turned back to the three besieged people within the ring of deadly purple Tainted blocks, then turned to Empech. The little, gray gnome had the fishing pole in his hands and extended it to the villager, an expression of fear in the pech's crystalline blue eyes.

Herder moved to the edge of the purple circle and quickly built a set of steps out of cobblestone that extended a few blocks into the air, then added a platform, allowing Digger to get up higher, making the lift easier. He extended the platform over the tainted blocks. Instantly, the cobblestone started to turn purple, somehow infected by the Taint spreading across the ground. Herder quickly shattered the block and stepped back.

Digger sighed then took the fishing pole from the magical creature's hands. He moved to the edge of the tainted circle, then stepped away as the sickly stain seemed to ooze toward him.

"It hungers for life," Forpech said. "Hmmm . . . must hurry, before it is too late."

Glaring at the purple stain, Digger climbed the stairs Herder had constructed and stood on the platform. He moved to the very edge, the tainted ground throbbing as if it had a pulse. Holding the fishing pole high over his head, he threw the line toward the trio. It missed them all and landed on the ground. Digger pulled the line back to him, then threw it again. This time it snagged on the oversized backpack of the pech. Instantly, sheets of magical power ran down the fishing line and enveloped the pech, causing the little creature to cry out in pain. Digger screamed as well, the same magical energy wrapping around his muscular body.

"Digger . . . PULL!" Gameknight shouted.

The stocky NPC yanked on the pole with all his strength, but the jagged bolts of magic that stabbed at him were sapping his strength. He was only able to lift the peck just a few inches off the ground.

The taint somehow sensed this, and began oozing upward, trying to snatch at the pech's foot. Digger pulled back on the fishing pole, but the pain was too great . . . his strength was failing. Suddenly, Gameknight was at his side, the User-that-is-not-a-user grabbing onto the big NPC's muscular arm and allowing the pain to wash over him. Gameknight yelled in agony as the magical energy flowed from Digger and into him.

"Pull!" the User-that-is-not-a-user moaned.

Digger pulled up on the fishing pole, raising the pech just before the Taint reached the creature's foot. Then, Hunter moved to Digger's other side. She tossed her bow aside and grabbed hold of Digger's hands. Shafts of magical energy moved away from Digger and stabbed at Hunter. She screamed out in anguish, but did not let go.

"You . . . can do . . . it," she moaned. "PULL!"

Digger leaned back, pulling the pech a little higher.

Stitcher ran up the steps and wrapped her arms around Digger's huge barrel chest. She screamed in pain, but held on, drawing some of the pain away from Digger and into her small body.

"You can do it, Digger," Crafter whispered into his friend's ear, then put a hand on his shoulder, allowing the magical energy to flow into his own body.

Herder and Weaver ran up the steps and added their strength to the painful hug, their screams of agony combining with the others, creating a symphony of torment.

Digger suddenly pulled with all his strength, and yanked the pole backward. It sent the pech flying through the air, passing over their heads, to land with a thud on the gray stone near Forpech and Empech. Digger fell backward, bringing all his friends with him. He released the fishing pole and the pain finally stopped.

A strange rushing sound filled Gameknight's ears, as if a strong breeze were blowing past him.

"Quick, the others," Crafter said.

Digger dislodged himself from the tangle of arms and legs, then stood and readied the fishing pole for another cast. But the tainted stone had finished its work. The last of the pristine white quartz was gone, replaced with the lifeless gray brick. Where the mother and boy had last been, now stood an evolved zombie villager and zombie child, space helmet and oxygen gear covering their scarred faces.

They were too late.

"Noooooo . . . not again!" Digger moaned, and then collapsed to the ground, unconscious.

CHAPTER 21

GAMEKNIGHT'S FAILURE

"Digger, are you alright?" Crafter rushed to his side and cradled his head in his hands. "Come on, Digger, wake up . . . please wake up."

He gently shook his head, trying to draw his big friend back to consciousness. Gameknight knelt at his side and checked his oxygen tanks; he still had lots of air.

"What's wrong with him?" Hunter asked.

Crafter pointed at the two zombies that stood on the ground, staring up at them. There was a pained expression in their beady red eyes, as if they could somehow remember the horror that had befallen them, but then the expressions changed from sadness to overwhelming hatred as the newly-transformed monsters glared up at the intruders.

Gameknight sighed.

"Those poor villagers," the User-that-is-not-a-user said.

"They'd be better off dead," Hunter said grimly.

She notched an arrow and aimed it down at the zombie mother.

"No," a hoarse voice croaked. Digger reached out and grabbed Hunter's ankle. "Leave them be. This is my fault. Just like with Topper. I was too late and my failure has doomed more innocent lives."

"Digger, you can do only so much," Gameknight said. "We do our best and then we deal with the consequences. It's all any of us can do."

"That's easy for you to say," Digger bit back, trying to sit up. "You didn't just condemn a mother and child to a life of misery."

"Digger, it wasn't your—"

"The other pech," Crafter suddenly shouted.

Gameknight glanced down at Forpech and Empech. They had put a space helmet and oxygen gear on the newly rescued pech, as the transformed air in the chamber was now completely poisonous. Empech shook the tiny gray creature, trying to get him to wake up. The new pech had been knocked out by the fall, and maybe even gravely injured.

"I think it best we get out of here," Hunter said. "We need to stay on Entity303's trail."

Gameknight nodded, then cast Digger a worried glance. The stocky villager was struggling to his feet, an expression of despair on his square face as he stared down at the zombie child glaring up hungrily at him. The wolves growled at the zombie and formed a line between the pechs and the monsters' razor-sharp claws, but the two zombies made no attempt to attack . . . at least not yet.

Gameknight leapt off the raised platform and landed on the cold brick floor. Not slowing a bit, he sprinted for the passageway that led out of the boss chamber. Following the corridor, he ended up in the treasure room. Columns of glowstone lined each corner, as they always did in the treasure rooms, stretching from floor to ceiling. Scattered across the floor were small pieces of wood, a single metallic hinge mixed in with the sprinters.

"There should have been a chest here . . . a tier-eight chest," Gameknight said, his voice getting softer and softer, until it was but a whisper. "What are we gonna do?"

He sank to his knees just as the others came into the room, the pechs carrying their unconscious brother.

It was here, Gameknight thought. *The chest was here, but we were too late . . .* I *was too late.*

Waves of despair crashed down upon him as the reality of the situation hit him.

"It's gone . . . it's gone," the User-that-is-not-a-user moaned.

"What's gone?" Crafter asked.

"The chest," Gameknight said. "The tier-eight chest is gone. Entity303 destroyed it and now it's gone."

"We have lots of chests, can't we just use another one?" Crafter suggested.

"You don't understand," Gameknight said, his voice barely a whisper. "The mod will only put the items in the original chest if it's already here. Entity303 destroyed the tier-eight chest before the Boss was created. So when the Dionian Boss is destroyed, nothing will spawn here. I've failed all of you . . . as I knew I would."

Waves of despair crashed down upon Gameknight, the overwhelming sense of failure making it hard to breathe. His heart pounded in his chest like a jackhammer as his eyes burned. Emotions surged within him; grief mixed with guilt and despair. He gazed across the faces of the friends he'd doomed to a long and drawn out death on this planet. It was all his fault, just like the deaths of Fletcher and Woodcutter.

How many people must suffer because of me? Gameknight thought .

"It'll be OK, we can just—" Stitcher started to say, but was interrupted.

"You don't get it," the User-that-is-not-a-user snapped, frustrated and upset. "We need to keep following Entity303. You can be sure he is heading farther into this solar system. But we have no rocket that can follow him."

"Hmmm . . . yes, the enemy seeks the edges of the Far Lands," Forpech said.

"So let's use the one we have and get moving," Hunter said.

"You don't understand. We can't follow him with our rocket. It will only take us to tier-four planets. I'm sure Entity303 is heading for the tier-eight planets, and without the plans that were stored in the chest he destroyed, we can't go any further."

"What do you mean?" Hunter asked. "You saying he's won?"

Gameknight sighed. Tears of frustration and helplessness began to trickle down his cheeks. He hoped his helmet would hide them from all his friends. One of the tears became dislodged from his face and floated in the lower Dionian gravity for a moment, then stuck to his faceplate, creating a long smear on the glass.

Glancing up at Hunter, he nodded his head. "We can go no further," the User-that-is-not-a-user said. "All we can do is go back to the Overworld and wait for . . ."

He grew silent, not wanting to say the words.

"For what?" Stitcher asked. She moved to Gameknight's side and put an arm around his shoulder. "Wait for what?"

"For the end," Gameknight moaned.

Suddenly, an explosion shook the planet. Pieces of debris fell or were dropped through a hole in the corner of the room. A laugh echoed through that vertical shaft.

"Ha ha ha . . . enjoy your time down there, losers!" Entity303's voice shouted down from above.

Gameknight stood and stared up through the narrow opening. The hole stretched all the way to the surface. At the other end, Gameknight's nemesis glared down at him.

"You messed with the wrong user, Gameknight999, and now you must pay the price. Either stay there and wait for the destruction of Minecraft, or betray your friends and abandon them by going back to the physical world . . . your choice." Entity303 laughed again, his maniacal voice echoing through the chamber. "I've enjoyed our little game, but now it is time for me to go. Sorry about blowing up your rocket, but maybe you shouldn't have just left it lying around; accidents happen all the time."

He laughed again, then disappeared from view. Minutes later, the sound of a rocket blasting off trickled down through the shaft, filling the dungeon with thunder, then everything became deathly silent. They were stuck here, on Diona, and there was nothing Gameknight or any of his friends could do but wait for the destruction of Minecraft.

CHAPTER 22
CONSEQUENCES

Digger sat down next to Gameknight999 and leaned against him, their helmets touching. They just sat there for a moment, the room completely still. One of the zombies out in the boss chamber gave a sorrowful moan, then moved through the room, its growls and wails of despair getting softer and softer. Digger turned and gazed into Gameknight's eyes, their helmets slightly fogged up from their breathing.

Gameknight glanced around at his friends. A myriad of emotions stared back at him, with everything from anger, to hate, to a thirst for revenge, to sorrow, to sadness; all of them being displayed on their square faces. But the one constant amongst them all was sympathy for the User-that-is-not-a-user.

"This is why I wanted to continue alone," Gameknight said. He lowered his gaze and stared at the ground, ashamed to look any of them in the eyes. "I didn't want to do something that would get any of you hurt, and now you're all sentenced to death on this desolate planet because of my failure."

"This wasn't your fault," Crafter said. "Entity303 was just too far ahead for us to catch him."

"I agree with Crafter," Stitcher said. "This isn't your failure . . . it's *our* failure."

"You don't get it either," the User-that-is-not-a-user said. "I could have done this whole thing on my own. I could have gone through the Twilight Forest, then gone through Mystcraft and eventually come to Galacticraft all by myself, but I was afraid. I didn't know if I was strong enough to save Weaver on my own, so I selfishly took you all along for the ride. And now see what I've done. You're all stuck here on Diona, and you'll never leave this place alive."

"Gameknight, that might all be true," Hunter said.

"Hunter, be nice just for once," Stitcher chided, but her older sister raised a hand, silencing the younger girl.

"You might be right," Hunter continued. "This might all be your fault. Maybe you could have left us behind. Maybe you could have done all this on your own. And maybe you could have stopped Entity303 without our help, but the fact is . . . it wasn't your call to make!"

Gameknight saw her eyes sparkle with anger.

"Sometimes, you think you have to do everything on your own. You want to do all the suffering for all of us, and you want to take all the blame . . . every time, and I'm getting pretty sick of it!"

"Hunter . . ."

She ignored Stitcher and continued. "Let me tell you the way it is, Gameknight999. When I first met you, my family and village had been destroyed and my sister Stitcher had been taken as a slave. I was alone and had nothing but hatred in my heart, yet you still took me in. You made me part of your family, as you did with Crafter. And then you adopted all these other people around you, gathering people with different strengths and weaknesses. You formed us into an unbreakable family, and now, because things are bad, you think you can break us apart and say you should have gone on alone? Well . . . you don't get to make that decision.

"This is a family. We take care of our own, and that includes knuckleheads like you." She pointed a finger at him. "You don't get to decide if you need to be a martyr or not. We do things together, regardless of the risk, because that's what families do. What one of us does . . . *all of us* do." She moved a step closer. "What you don't understand is the incredible gift you've given to all of us."

"A gift?" Gameknight pulled his gaze up to her chocolate-brown eyes, confused.

"Yeah . . . a gift." She knelt so that they were face to face. "All of us know what it means to be alone in this world, and you made it so that none of us would ever be alone again. That's what made your attempt to continue on without us hurt so much. We weren't mad at you, we were mad because we wouldn't be able to help you, and that's our job . . . to help each other. And none of us will allow anyone to ever take that away. We're a family, we're together, and that's the way it's always gonna be . . . forever." She then stared at him with an intensity that almost made him look away. "In a family, you are never alone."

The words resonated in him, bouncing off the walls of his mind like an endless echo. She was right . . . they were a family, and nothing could ever change that. He thought they hated him because he wanted to go on alone, but they just wanted to keep their family together.

At least they don't hate me, Gameknight thought. *That's something, but I still led them here, and now we're trapped. I failed them all.*

"I know what you're feeling," Digger said softly. "You think this is all your fault."

The User-that-is-not-a-user didn't reply.

"I get it. I feel the same. I should have been able to save that mother and child, but I didn't. I have no idea what I could have done different, but I still feel guilty, maybe because of my past, or maybe it's my own insecurities at being a bad father."

"You aren't a bad father," Gameknight snapped. "Your kids love you!" Then he grimaced when he realized what he said. "I mean Filler loves you, and . . . uhhh . . . Topper loved you and . . . um . . ."

"I know what you're saying," Digger said. "Maybe in your timeline, where Topper is still alive, things are different, but here, in this timeline, I must own my guilt. But like you told me earlier, we do our best and then we deal with the consequences. We can't just stay down here and feel sorry for ourselves. You and me . . . we have things to do. You have to get us off this planet, and I have to save Topper by helping you, and neither of those things are gonna happen if we stay down here and feel sorry for ourselves. So now it's time to deal with the consequences."

Digger stood up, then reached down and lifted Gameknight to his feet, whether he liked it or not.

"I'm digging my way to the surface, because that's something I actually know how to do without getting anyone killed. By the time we get to the surface, you're gonna have some ideas for us to try, or you and me are gonna have a serious discussion, and that's gonna hurt you a lot more than it hurts me . . . you got that?"

Gameknight stared up at Digger and saw that, for the first time, his seafoam green eyes had something in them nobody had seen for a long time: courage.

"But how do we go on?" the User-that-is-not-a-user asked.

"I think you told me a long time ago, 'If you quit, then you guarantee the outcome.' Well, this outcome is not acceptable. So instead of giving up, we're gonna keep fighting and get it done." He pulled out his pickaxe and gave him a wry grin. "You better step back if you want to keep all your fingers."

The stocky NPC started to dig. His pickaxe rang out as it smashed through the Dionian soil, the metallic tool vibrating like a struck bell. The wolves picked up on the sound and started to howl, their voices cutting through their helmets and filling the chamber with pride and strength.

Gameknight glanced around at all his friends and saw the same thing he saw in Digger's eyes: courage and hope. Crafter stepped up to him with his bright blue eyes.

"I think it's time we got Weaver back where he belongs," the young NPC said.

Hunter moved to his side. "Yeah, and after we catch that Entity303, I was thinking of doing some target practice, with that evil user as the target."

Stitcher laughed and put a hand on her older sister's shoulder.

Weaver moved next to Crafter, his blue eyes matching his distant nephew's in brightness and clarity.

"I think maybe it's time to stop following Entity303, and start attacking him, like Smithy of the Two-swords did with Herobrine." Weaver took a step closer, the wails of the zombie barely audible. "It's payback time for what that evil user has done to Minecraft."

Gameknight nodded, then closed his eyes and listened to the puzzle pieces in his head, but all he heard was silence. He had no ideas, no great plans, nothing. His mind seemed devoid of thought or images or sound, like the dark emptiness of outer space. But as he searched for an idea—any idea—a distant voice came to him from out of the darkness. It was a scratchy voice that seemed ancient and powerful, yet soothing and understanding at the same time. There was a grandmotherly kindness to it that seemed to ease his fears.

There is help around you, child. You need only open your eyes and see it.

It was the Oracle, he was sure of it. Her scratchy voice filled him with courage and strength, even though he still had no idea how to solve this problem and get them off Diona. But right now, that didn't matter. The only important thing right now was to keep fighting and not give in to despair. Maybe there was a solution here . . . maybe the

Oracle was right. But how could that have been her? The Oracle didn't exist in this timeline.

Is that what you think? I've been with you all along, child. You just need to open your eyes and do the math.

And then the voice was gone.

"Do the math?" Gameknight said in a soft voice, confused.

"What?" Crafter asked.

"Ahh . . . nothing," the User-that-is-not-a-user replied. "Let's just get to the surface."

"Are you OK?" Hunter asked.

"No, I'm still terrified. I might have stranded all of us on this lifeless planet, but staying down here, hiding from myself, isn't gonna help anyone." He pulled out his own pickaxe and looked at his friends. "I'm helping Digger, because at least that's one thing I can do that won't get anyone killed."

Gameknight999 smiled, then moved into the freshly carved passage that ascended upward. He moved to Digger's side and started to dig.

CHAPTER 23
TRUPECH

The soil of Diona was soft, much softer than stone, but not so light that a shovel could be used. They dug quickly with their picks through the planet, filling their inventory with the pale blocks. When Digger grew tired, Herder took his place. When Gameknight's arms felt heavy, Weaver stepped forward and took his turn. Each of them helped out, with the exception of the pechs and, of course, Tux. They were a family, and each helped the others whenever they could.

In a family, you are never alone. The words resonated in his head like a sacred chant. It filled him with hope and strength as he thought about those around him.

I must find a way off this planet, the User-that-is-not-a-user thought. *I won't believe this is the end.*

When they reached the surface, Gameknight could see the remains of their camp in the distance. A wall of leaves still stood in a large square where he'd placed his oxygen collector. Who knew if it was still there; he wouldn't put it past Entity303 to destroy it out of spite.

The wolves dashed across the red sands and inspected their base, howling loudly to let them know all was well. Digger lifted the still-unconscious new pech in his strong arms and ran across the surface of the planet, the rest of the party following. When they reached the camp, they found the oxygen-generation equipment still functioning, a stable bubble of air enveloping a large part of the landscape. Off to the side, a large crater marked the position where the launch pad and rocket had once stood. Pieces of the ship lay all around them.

Hunter and Weaver collected all the pieces while Digger placed the pech on the ground, leaning him up against a block of leaves. For the first time, Gameknight noticed this pech was different from the other two. He seemed ancient, with skin that was wrinkled and marked with age. His jaw stuck out just like with the other pechs, but this new one had only one tooth, the other likely lost to time.

Slowly, the gray-skinned gnome opened his eyes. Gameknight was shocked at their familiar color; they were a steely gray, like metal forged in the hottest of furnaces. They seemed old beyond the pech's years, as if they had seen many lifetimes and held an ancient wisdom.

"Are you OK?" Crafter asked.

He reached out and pulled the glass helmet off the tiny creature's head and set it aside. Sitting up, the pech glanced around at his new companions. When his eyes fell upon Empech and Forpech, the gnome smiled, his single tooth shining in the light of the Sirius sun.

"Brothers, we are well met," the pech said, his words flowing from his mouth like a rapid stream of bullets. "I am Trupech. Diona has been my home for a long time. Now it is a wasteland." A tiny square tear tumbled from his eye. "The enemy spent much time planning this attack. It seems he has been successful."

No one said anything, they just looked to the ground, all except Gameknight999.

"I should have been able to stop him, but I couldn't," the User-that-is-not-a-user said. "Now we're stuck here."

"What is your name, child?" Trupech asked.

"I'm Gameknight999, and this is Crafter, Digger, Hunter, Stitcher, Weaver, and Herder."

The wolves howled.

"And of course, those are Herder's wolves out there, keeping us safe."

"The two pechs are Empech and Forpech," Gameknight said, pointing to the gnomes.

Squawk! Squawk!

"Oh, and last but not least, this is Tux."

The penguin came forward and stared up at the pech. Trupech reached down and patted the little penguin on her soft head.

"Good to meet all of you," the gnome said. "Why are we stuck here?"

"Entity303 destroyed our ship and took the plans to the tier-eight rocket," Gameknight explained. "We have nothing."

"Well, that's not entirely correct," the old pech replied.

"What do you mean?" Crafter asked.

"Your enemy, who is mine as well, has been preparing this for a long time," Trupech explained, his words coming out staccato and fast. "I have been watching. I have been investigating." Trupech stood up and peered into Gameknight's eyes. "And I have been stealing."

He reached into his inventory and began taking items out, dropping them on the Dionian sand: hull plating, nosecone, fins, canisters of fuel, and the critical piece: a huge rocket engine.

"I took all this from our enemy," Trupech said. "It was one piece at a time. He tried to trap me, but never could. We should have all we need, right?"

"Not everything," Gameknight said. He picked up the NASA workbench and placed it on the ground, its spindly arms sticking up into the air like the crooked legs of an overturned bug. "We still need the tier-eight rocket plans, so we can put all this together. I'm afraid that, without that piece of paper, we're lost."

The User-that-is-not-a-user sat on a block of leaves and looked down at all the components as they hovered just off the ground, rising and falling ever so slightly. The pech moved to his side and glared down at Gameknight.

"So quick to give up?" Trupech said. "Disappointing, I thought you'd be different."

"What?" the User-that-is-not-a-user growled, his anger rising.

But before he could speak another word, Trupech pulled out a piece of paper and held it before Gameknight's eyes. Intricate drawings of rocket components were scrawled on both sides, and an "8" was printed on one corner. Trupech's single tooth slowly emerged from behind his lips as the gnome gave him a strange, satisfied smile.

Gameknight reached out, grabbed the plans, and held them up over his head, jumping up and down. Tux waddled next to him and jumped up and down as well, squawking. The wolves, hearing the ruckus, started to howl, filling the alien landscape with their proud song.

"It's time we got to work!" the User-that-is-not-a-user exclaimed as the puzzle pieces tumbled about in his head.

"But Gameknight, I thought there were more planets out there in the farther reaches of space," Crafter said. "We have to pick the right one, or miss Entity303 completely. How will you choose?"

The User-that-is-not-a-user glanced at his friend, the turned and faced the pechs. They sat huddled together, the three of them talking quietly.

"Forpech, you and Empech both agreed that Entity303 wanted to get to the furthest reaches of the Minecraft, to the edge of the Far Lands."

"Hmmm . . . yes, that is where the fabric of Minecraft is the thinnest."

"But wouldn't the fabric of the universe be the most fragile where all the life is congregated?" Gameknight asked.

"Yes, yes," Empech said, "Life and creativity draw heavily on Minecraft. Where there are many living things, and a rich, creative world, the fabric of Minecraft will be quite fragile."

"Entity303 has gone out of his way to destroy all the life in this solar system, except for one planet," Gameknight said.

"What do you mean?" Crafter asked. "There is still life here on this planet."

"No, not here, but I remember one planet in the Sirius solar system that was teeming with life. It's not the farthest planet, but it's close to the edge. I bet Entity303 is gonna attack that planet and start the tear in the fabric of Minecraft there."

"If that planet has all the remaining life in this solar system, then . . . hmmm . . . the rip will go from there straight to . . ." Forpech paused to consider his words.

"What is it you aren't saying?" Hunter asked.

"Well," the little gnome continued, his deep voice sounding scratched and aged. "If the rip starts on a planet with life, it will go to the next planet with life still on it."

"And there's only one planet left with living creatures other than monsters," Gameknight said.

"The Overworld," Crafter said slowly as he realized what that might mean.

"Exactly." Gameknight started to pace back and forth. "But now we have an advantage."

"How do you figure?" Hunter asked.

"Entity303 thinks we're stranded here, but we aren't, thanks to Trupech." Gameknight stopped and turned toward Hunter. "He won't be expecting us on the next planet. That will give us the element of surprise."

"That might be true, but it will only work if we do one thing," Hunter added.

"And what's that?" Digger asked.

"We need to get off this rock!"

Squawk! Tux added.

"OK, I'll get started on the new ship," the User-that-is-not-a-user said.

"But first," Digger said, "tell us where we're going. What's the name of the planet that will be the home of the Last Battle for Minecraft?"

Gameknight looked at each of them. He could see the hope and courage burning bright in their eyes. They were a family and none of them were ever going to be alone, even him. That knowledge brought a sense of peace and determination to the User-that-is-not-a-user. There was no way he was going to let Entity303 hurt anyone in his family.

"The planet," Gameknight999 said in a loud, clear voice, "is called Fronos. Now hand me those rocket designs. I have a space ship to build."

CHAPTER 24

FRONOS

Entity303 removed his space helmet and oxygen and put them into his inventory; the air on Fronos was breathable, though it always smelled of strawberries and candy. That was likely because of the small pinkish clouds scattered across the sky. He knew they were strawberry clouds, though he never could figure out their purpose.

Off to the left, his supply crate settled to the ground next to a fluorescent yellow bush. He walked to the crate and took out the rocket and launch pad, then stuffed them into his bulging inventory. He didn't really plan on leaving this planet via rocket, but he felt it best to have the supplies with him anyway.

When he eventually started the chain reaction, it would be unstoppable and would decimate this planet. A rocket into space would not save anyone from the tear through the universe he was going to cause; it would destroy everything. So his escape from the destruction would not be to another part of Minecraft, but out of the doomed servers forever and back to the physical world. He'd just give the *EXIT* command to the Digitizer, and the miraculous invention would transport him back into his body.

At the thought of all the destruction he was going to cause, Entity303 smiled evilly.

"We'll see what those Minecraft programmers have to say after I destroy their prized creation."

Glancing around at his surroundings, he was disgusted by all the colors. He was standing in a bright yellow field, with golden blades of grass swaying in the usual east-to-west breeze. Clumps of colorful flowers dotted the landscape, their flamboyant petals like candies on scoops of lemon sherbet.

Yet stranger still were the creatures: a large, square thing that resembled a blueberry approached on two short legs, the berry's stem acting as the nose, and its pair of small, white eyes stared up at Entity303, a complete absence of fear on the being's innocent face.

Foolish creature.

Entity303 gave it a kick, sending it tumbling across the ground. A group of slimes approached. Entity303 drew his sword and moved slowly away from them. They were not normal-looking monsters; instead of a green, translucent outer shell and a darker green face at the center, these slimes were solid purple and blue and red. Moving closer, Entity303 detected an aroma that reminded him of . . . jelly.

"Jelly slimes?" he said to no one. "Those are slimes . . . made of jelly? This place is ridiculous."

He moved closer to the purple one, then struck it with his glowing, infused-sword. The monster screeched but made no attempt to fight back. It wasn't hostile like a normal slime; the creature was just a huge bouncing cube of jelly. Entity303 hit it again and again, causing the monster to flash red as it took damage. It divided into smaller cubes, each of which he attacked, causing them to divide again. Finally, he destroyed the last of the slimes, making them vanish, leaving behind three glowing balls of XP and some clumps of grape jam.

"This is the strangest place I've ever seen, but it will serve my plans perfectly. All of this life and these interesting creations will amplify the tear in Minecraft's fabric . . . it will be unstoppable."

Fronos was not the most distant planet in the Sirius solar system, but it was the center of creativity in the Minecraft universe. The developers must have thought themselves to be pretty clever, hiding this world as a tier-seven planet. Most users chose to head for the tier-eight planet, overlooking Fronos, but not Entity303. He checked everything to find just the right spot for his virus to do the most damage. On Fronos, with all these new biomes, creative animals, glowing plants, and sparkling clouds, the fabric of Minecraft was stretched the tightest . . . which meant it would rip apart the easiest here.

Moving away from the remaining jelly slimes, the user sprinted to the top of a hill and surveyed his surroundings. To the left was a forest of purple oak trees, bright green grass covering the ground. Next to the oak forest, there stood what seemed like a jungle of some kind. But instead of your typical jungle wood trees, this biome boasted tall coconut trees, with large green fronds sprouting out of the tops of the trees like leafy fireworks. Large brown coconuts sat nestled amidst the large leaves.

Next to that sat another grassland biome, but the grass there, instead of being golden yellow, was a fluorescent green. A village was just barely visible in the distance, the peaked roofs sticking up from behind rolling hills. More of the strange-looking animals, walking strawberries, and short, waddling things that resembled flattened rabbits moved through the verdant grass, all of them ignorant of the danger nearby. Large green creatures that resembled half of a watermelon bounced near the village, their red faces standing out against their green outer skin.

All of this seemed bizarre, but none of these biomes were his target. What he needed was the true center of creativity at the edge of the Far Lands: the Candy Land biome. That was where he'd left something critical to his plans . . . the Eldritch shrine. Likely, that evil structure had already brought some dangerous creatures into these lands. The thought made Entity303 smile.

Good, let some of the Guardians feast on these harmless creatures, Entity303 thought.

Once he awakened the Eye, that portal would bring forth more monsters of destruction. They would devour these creatures, but not before his Tainted virus started to tear through Minecraft.

The evil user smiled.

"I hope you have a good seat to watch all this destruction, Gameknight999," Entity303 said to the colorful landscape. "The end of Minecraft is coming fast, and with you being stuck on Diona, there's no one to stop me."

He laughed a maniacal laugh, then picked a random direction and shot into the air, his jetpack lifting him high into the strawberry cloud-filled sky, in search of Candy Land.

CHAPTER 25

LANDING

As Gameknight descended through the clouds, he was shocked at the landscape below him. It was as if a colorful quilt had been pulled across the world, leaving huge swatches of yellow and green and pink and blue and purple interlocking with each other in the most complicated jigsaw puzzle ever seen. Tux, held tightly in his arms, squawked excitedly as she looked down at the planet's surface. As the ground neared, trees of every color became visible in many of the biomes, with vibrant grasslands of bright green and golden yellow lining the edges of the forests.

Slowly, they settled to the ground, landing in the most amazing forest he'd ever seen. The grass covering the ground was a bright pink, with tall stalks of the fluorescent grass sparkling with some kind of magical enchantment contained within. The trees themselves appeared to be oaks, but the leaves were a deep red, the same color as the cherry candies Gameknight's mom liked so much. None of the trees showed any of the normal, forest-green leaves that would be expected in the leafy canopy; only the rich crimson topping was visible.

In the distance, the pink grass gave way to rich chocolate brown, then eventually faded to a sharp cerulean blue, the red caps to the trees stretching throughout; it was so spectacular, Gameknight thought he might not be able to turn away.

Just then, a strange creature approached. It resembled a half of a watermelon, with a dark green outside, and a red central core. The creature had two small, widely spaced, beady eyes. A row of shining white teeth that almost seemed to glow in the sunlight marked the creature's mouth. Atop the green and red cube sat what looked like a slice of a watermelon with a huge bite taken out of the center, making a large "U" shape on the creature's head and reminding Gameknight of green horns. But even with all those teeth and curved watermelon horns, for some reason, the creature did not seem threatening at all.

The creature approached Gameknight, bouncing across the pink grass. He wasn't sure if it was a hostile mob, or just an aimless creature moving about the surface of Fronos. Though he felt no fear, Gameknight took a few steps back, getting out of the strange creature's path. His legs felt the reassuring presence of gravity; it felt the same as the gravity on the Overworld.

Good, we're used to this gravity, he thought. *No floating up into the air.*

He stood perfectly still and waited for the melon to approach, his hand ready to reach into his inventory and draw his weapon. The bouncing fruit turned its eyes up to him for just a moment, then continued to hop past, apparently uninterested.

With a sigh of relief, Gameknight walked to the edge of the forest, heading for the supply crate that had fallen nearby. The crate sat on a bright green plain of grass. Strange creatures moved about, all of them either unaware of or uncaring about his presence. Moving to the box, he knelt and opened the top. Inside, he saw the tier-eight rocket and landing pad. Gameknight gathered them and put them in his inventory.

Squawk! Tux said, but for the first time in a long time, her tiny voice did not seem muffled.

"Tux . . . your helmet!"

The penguin was glancing about, her space helmet lying on the fluorescent grass. Gameknight dashed to her side and picked up the glass cube.

"Quick, put it on, Tux."

But the penguin just waddled away, unconcerned. Staring across the grassy plains, he noticed none of the other creatures were wearing space helmets either.

Maybe the atmosphere hasn't been destroyed . . . yet, Gameknight thought.

Carefully, he lifted his helmet off his head and took a tentative sniff. The air smelled clean and dry and had a faint taste of fresh fruit, especially strawberries. A creature shaped like a large blueberry waddled nearby on two tiny black feet. The stem of the berry formed the creature's nose while two bright white eyes on either side of the woody stem gazed up at him. The aroma of fresh berries wafted through the air as the creature neared; it smelled fantastic.

Tux squawked, then stepped up to the berry and rubbed her beak on the creature's side. The berry smiled, then ran in a wide circle, Tux chasing it playfully. Gameknight glanced around, taking in the fantastic landscape; this was truly the creative center of the Minecraft universe.

With a smile, he removed his space suit entirely and shoved it into his inventory with the rocket and other assorted items. Pulling out the teleportation ring, he pressed the ruby red gemstone.

Instantly, a cloud of purple mist formed to his right. A whooshing sound filled his ears, then went away as the lavender cloud evaporated. Standing before him were his friends. They took in the surroundings, each of them shocked at what they were seeing.

"Gameknight, your helmet," Hunter exclaimed. "Put it on, quick, before you—"

"It's OK, you can take off your suits," the User-that-is-not-a-user explained. "There's air here."

Herder was the first to take the advice. He drew in a huge breath of air and smiled.

"That smells much better than my own bad breath and sweat," the lanky boy admitted with a grin.

Running from wolf to wolf, he removed each of their oxygen gear and put the equipment in his inventory. By now, everyone had their gear off and was basking in the clean, scented air of Fronos.

"This world is incredible." Crafter tucked his space helmet into his inventory. "Look at all the colors. There's pink grass over there and blue shrubs to the left. And look at those tall trees—what are they?"

"I think they're coconut trees." Gameknight pointed to their tops. "See how the huge green leaves sort of explode out of the top? And the square things with three dots are coconuts. I bet we can use them for baking, somehow."

Stitcher instinctively pulled out her bow, but left the arrow in her inventory. "This is beautiful. The creativity here is unbelievable."

"Hmmm . . . that is why Entity303 brought us here," Forpech said. "All of these fantastic biomes, new creatures, explosive colors . . . they all strain the fabric of Minecraft."

"Yes, yes, Entity303 is here to start the destruction of Minecraft," Empech added, his crystalline blue eyes taking in the surroundings with wonder.

"A tear in the Minecraft universe would be a disaster," Trupech said, his words short and clipped. "He must be stopped."

"First, he must be found," Crafter pointed out.

"But how do we find him?" Digger asked.

"I see a village out on the plains," a voice said from atop a deep-red oak.

Gameknight glanced upward and found Weaver standing on top of the largest tree. He was pointing to the north.

"How much time do we have until night?" Hunter asked.

The sun was a small white square with a delicate, blue halo glowing around its edge. Clumps of translucent blocks floated everywhere across the sky, each colored a very faint pink. Gameknight suspected those clouds were the source of the ever-present strawberry aroma, though he had no idea what their purpose could be. Above them floated huge, fluffy white clouds that drifted forever to the west, as with all worlds in Minecraft, and yet the strawberry clouds stayed fixed overhead, in one place.

"I don't know how long a day is on this planet," Gameknight said. "But I'd say let's head to that village and see what we can learn."

"Great idea," Hunter said. "At least it doesn't involve any terrifying battles with huge monster armies, like most of your grand plans."

Gameknight stuck his tongue out at her, then started walking. Herder whistled and moved a finger around in a circle over his head. The wolves formed a protective ring around the party, warily eyeing the strange creatures of Fronos.

As they moved across the bright green plains, Gameknight thought he heard something in the deepest recesses of his mind. At first, he thought it was Crafter humming some strange song, as he'd been known to do, but the young villager was silent. Closing his eyes, Gameknight walked along, not really focused on where he was going as much as just walking in a straight line. He turned his thoughts inward, listening for the faint thing he'd heard.

There it was again. It sounded as if it were some sort of melody, but the tones were so soft, they were difficult to identify. For some reason, it seemed as if the music was coming to him from very far away. It was a soothing sound, but sad at the same time . . . too distant to really hear.

Gameknight opened his eyes and glanced at his friends. He found the newest pech, Trupech, staring at him with a strange smile on his face. His solitary tooth stuck up from the jaw that jutted out, giving his oversized head a comical appearance. But his eyes, those steely-gray eyes, seemed ancient and wise, the skin around them wrinkled with age. It was like gazing into the eyes of an old friend . . . Gameknight didn't understand.

Was the music coming from Trupech? he wondered.

But just as the User-that-is-not-a-user was about to ask, the music disappeared.

Was that the Music of Minecraft? Oracle, are you there?

No response came, just empty silence.

"Did any of you hear anything?" Gameknight asked.

His friends looked at him, confused.

"Are you finally going crazy?" Hunter asked. "I knew this day would eventually come. Gameknight999 has lost it . . . ouch!"

Stitcher readied another punch to her sister's arm, but suddenly Weaver shouted out from the top of the next grassy knoll.

"There it is . . . the village!" the young boy shouted.

The comrades sprinted to the top of the hill. By now, the pale sun and its blue halo had sunk much closer to the horizon; it would be night soon. But did nighttime mean monster time on Fronos? They would soon find out.

CHAPTER 26

NIGHTTIME ON FRONOS

They ran across the bright green grass, weaving around blue and green and orange and pink slimes, each with a different fruity aroma. Trupech seemed to possess a bit of knowledge about the creatures of Fronos; he explained that these creatures were called jelly slimes, and each was a different flavor: lime, blueberry, grape, orange, and pink bubble gum. Most of the bouncing, flavored cubes watched the party from afar, but a large red one was more curious. The huge gelatinous cube charged toward the party.

"What is that slime doing?" Hunter asked.

They stopped and watched it charge, though charging for a slime meant still moving slower than a casual jog for an NPC.

"It seems to be attacking," Crafter said. "Why would it do that?"

"I can take care of it," Hunter said.

"No," Gameknight said. "Let the wolves chase it away. I don't want to destroy it if it's not necessary."

He glanced at Herder. The young boy nodded, long, dark tangles of hair falling across his face. He pushed the rebellious strands aside, then whistled three times and pointed at the slime. The wolves moved toward the threat and nipped at the corners of the monster, not sinking in their teeth, but making it clear it would not be allowed to come any closer. The monster refused to halt its attack.

Gameknight drew his swords and moved out to face it, but before he could reach the creature, Herder whistled again, this time a long, piercing tone that hurt their ears. Instantly, the wolves attacked, causing the gelatinous monster to divide into smaller cubes. The wolves fell on the smaller slimes, making them divide and divide again, then destroyed the smallest monsters. Gameknight moved to where the creature had perished. Instead of finding slime balls, like he would have expected in the Overworld, he found globs of cherry jam, as if the monster were actually made out of jelly.

"This is the strangest place I've ever seen," the User-that-is-not-a-user. He turned away from the piles of jam and continued toward the village.

"I'm not sure we're gonna make it to our destination before dark," Digger said, his voice shaking a little.

The halo that ringed the sun was dipping below the horizon; it would be night very soon.

"You're right," he replied. "We'd better hurry."

They shifted to a sprint, moving quickly across the colorful rolling hills. As they neared the village, Gameknight saw torches being lit within the buildings. For some reason, the windows on all the homes were orange-stained glass instead of just clear . . . strange.

Suddenly, the sorrowful moans of zombies drifted across the grasslands. Monsters began moving out of the nearby forest, heading straight for the cluster of wooden homes. Spiders, with strange green eyes instead of their usual red, emerged from holes in the ground and joined their decaying comrades as they converged on the cluster of buildings.

"We have to protect this village," Crafter said.

"Get the zombies first, yes, yes," Empech suggested. "They can break through the doors."

"Hmmm . . . that is correct," Forpech added. "The pechs will calm the villagers . . . hmmm . . . while the rest of you protect them against the monsters."

"Thanks for taking the easy job," Hunter said, then shouted as her sister punched her in the arm. "Ouch . . . why'd you do that?"

Stitcher just scowled at her sister.

"Yeah . . . okay, I guess I deserved that."

"You always do," the younger sister added.

"Hunter, Stitcher, I need you two up on top of the blacksmith's house," Gameknight said. "Watch for skeletons and take them out. The rest of you, with me."

When they neared the village, the sisters peeled off and headed for the largest of the buildings while the User-that-is-not-a-user and the others charged. The wolves shot out into the now darkening plain, sharp teeth quickly finding decaying zombie legs. As the wolves kept the zombies busy, Gameknight attacked the spiders. With Herder on one side and Weaver on the other, the monsters lasted only seconds.

A clattering of bones sounded off to the left. Gameknight glanced in that direction only to see a flaming arrow already streaking toward the bony monsters. Instantly, it was aflame; Hunter's and Stitcher's enchanted arrows had found their first target.

More zombies approached. Gameknight charged at them, swinging his enchanted diamond sword with all his might. One creature reached out with sharp claws, but they were blocked by Digger's big pickaxe. Gameknight readied his counterattack, but Crafter appeared suddenly behind the monster, silencing its moans forever. In another minute, the last of the zombies were destroyed and the remaining skeletons all burned with the sisters' magical flames. A small group of creepers emerged from the edge of the bordering forest, but chose to stay clear of the conflict.

"That wasn't so bad," Weaver said. "These monsters aren't really all that strong."

"Maybe Herobrine's shadow-crafters didn't have an effect all the way out here," Gameknight replied. "I wonder if . . ."

Suddenly a cold sensation spread throughout his body as his vision narrowed, the periphery slightly blurry. A gray, smoky fog drifted across the landscape, making it hard to see.

"What's going on?" Digger asked, his deep voice cracking with fear.

"I don't know," Gameknight replied.

Suddenly, his ability to sense his health seemed to vanish, making the User-that-is-not-a-user's body feel slightly numb, replacing any feeling he had with a sense of dread.

"Oh no . . . is this the wither effect?" Gameknight said. "Everyone look around, watch for a wither. If it fires flaming skulls at you, scatter."

Before anyone could reply, an eerie whispering drifted out of the gray smoke. The voices sounded desperate and terrified, like lost souls caught in the terrifying fog.

"I don't like this." Weaver's voice sounded as if it were far away, even though Gameknight could see him standing nearby.

"Everyone get to the village." The User-that-is-not-a-user put away his iron sword. "We need to stay near Hunter and Stitcher's bows."

"Which way is it?" Crafter asked. "I'm lost. I can't see anything in this dark haze."

"Everyone, just come to my voice!" Gameknight banged the hilt of his diamond sword against his chest plate so the others could find him. "Follow the sound."

They moved toward him, Gameknight continuing to shout and bang his armor, hoping the sounds could cut through the terrible, whispering mist. As his friends emerged from the fog, each had terrified expressions on their square faces.

"Come closer," Gameknight said. "Stay within arm's reach."

Herder and Weaver moved to either side of him, then Digger and Crafter approached. The wolves yelped and whined as if the mysterious fog was somehow hurting them—or perhaps it was just their first taste of fear.

They backed up as the strange mist became darker, blotting out the stars overhead and encasing them in a gray pall that sapped their courage and turned their blood to ice.

"What's going on?" Hunter yelled from overhead.

Gameknight glanced over his shoulder. They had backed up to the village and could now see Hunter on the roof, an arrow notched, but the User-that-is-not-a-user could barely hear her voice. His heart pounded in his chest as cold beads of sweat tumbled down his face. Taking shallow breaths, as if he were afraid to inhale the nightmarish mist, he peered into the darkness. Slowly, a dark figure emerged from the haze. It was stocky, like Digger, but much bigger, and wore ornate armor that he'd expect to see on some ancient ninja or knight from a history book. Long, shadowy robes were draped across the creature's broad shoulders, the seam in the front flying open, revealing the shadowy armor underneath. The creature was somehow transparent, as if made of smoke.

"Oh no," Gameknight moaned.

"What is it?" Crafter asked.

"I can't believe Entity303 would load this mod into Minecraft." Gameknight shook his head. "It's incredibly violent, and dangerous for everyone. He's a madman."

Crafter moved closer and lowered his voice. "What is it?"

"That creature isn't a wither. It's something far worse. I've only battled one of them once . . . it didn't end well."

"Gameknight, you're scaring us," Crafter said. "What is that thing?"

"It's an . . . Eldritch Guardian." Gameknight's voice cracked with fear. "They're from a mod called Thaumcraft. This is not good."

"Why?" Weaver asked. "What do they do?"

Suddenly, the ethereal knight made a terrible, screeching sound that cut through the mist and smashed into them like an iron fist. As the sound faded, the Eldritch Guardian fired a ball of dark magic straight at Gameknight999.

CHAPTER 27

ELDRITCH GUARDIAN

Gameknight dodged to the left, but he wasn't fast enough. The black sphere of magic slammed into his shoulder, causing pain to blast down his arm and making him feel suddenly weak. Gray spirals floated around his head as the weakness enchantment slowly spread to the rest of his body.

The Eldritch Guardian then sprinted forward, closing the distance between himself and Gameknight999. Dropping his iron sword, the User-that-is-not-a-user pulled out his shield and held it firmly in his hand. The armored nightmare drifted closer, riding on puffs of smoke instead of feet, its raspy breathing like some demonic robot panting through a rusted, metallic pipe. The Guardian crashed into Gameknight's shield, striking it with all its strength, and the wooden rectangle shuddered as it took the force of the blow, cracks slowly spider-webbing outward across the back.

Gameknight swung his sword as hard as he could, but the diamond blade just clanked against the creature's armor, doing little damage.

"Gameknight, get back," Hunter growled.

Rolling to the left, the User-that-is-not-a-user moved back just as a pair of flaming arrows struck the terrifying monster. The arrows hit but had no visible effect. The Eldritch's armor failed to catch on fire, for its transparent body was insubstantial, made of smoke and shadow.

"Watch out, it's gonna shoot!" Herder said.

Just then, two dark balls of magic flew up at the two girls, one of them hitting Stitcher, the other narrowly missing Hunter.

Squawk, squawk, Tux shouted just as the Guardian fired another volley at the sisters, who were now pressed low against the roof.

The dark creature turned toward the sound. The penguin was standing before the monster, squawking in anger. The Eldritch started to reach out, its ghostly hands like clawed, skeletal things that held no mercy. But then, a shout that sounded like a hundred warriors echoed across the landscape.

"NO!" Digger screamed as he charged forward.

With a pickaxe in each hand, the stocky villager threw himself at the monster.

"You aren't hurting our friends anymore!" the villager shouted.

His picks were a blur as he swung them with all his strength. They rang out like hammers hitting an anvil when they landed squarely on the creature's armor. Trupech tossed Gameknight a golden apple, which he gobbled down, then stood and attacked, his diamond sword flashing through the air like blue lightning.

The Eldritch Guardian backed up, trying to get away, likely to use its dark magic again, but suddenly Herder was behind the monster, placing blocks of cobblestone on the ground. Herder joined, building a short wall to keep the monster in place. The Guardian struck back, smashing Digger in the chest and causing him to stagger for a moment, but Crafter was there to catch his friend, and then moved next to him and added his sword to the attack. Flaming arrows streaked between the comrades, striking the Eldritch repeatedly, adding more damage to the assault.

The monster flung an armored fist at Crafter, knocking him to the ground, then shoved Digger hard until the villager fell backward. Turning his nightmarish attention on Gameknight999, the monster attacked with a flurry of punches and kicks, the User-that-is-not-a-user barely able to block them all.

Suddenly, a wave of white surged around the monster. The wolves had thrown themselves at the creature, drawing its attention to the ground. At the same time, Herder and Weaver leapt up on top of the wall they'd built, and attacked the Eldritch from above. Gameknight dropped his shield and held his diamond sword with both hands. Using every bit of strength, he hacked at the shadowy Guardian. Digger and Crafter reengaged, adding their weapons to the attack. The creature turned from one attacker to the next, not sure which to strike, and all the while its HP dropped lower and lower.

Trupech moved forward and pulled out some kind of magical staff. It appeared to be a straight, waist-high stick, the ends capped with bright, silver metal. The gray gnome pointed it at the creature. After a tiny flash from the tip, the staff began to draw something out of the Guardian. The creature shook violently, then fell to the ground and writhed in terrible agony.

Trupech moved a step closer. The Eldritch Guardian tried to crawl away, but the cobblestone wall kept the creature from escaping.

"Attack it now," Trupech said, his short words spat out quickly.

The friends resumed their attacks, smashing the monster with their weapons. The smoky nightmare flashed red as their blades tore into its HP. It tried to strike out at them, but the Eldritch Guardian was getting weaker and weaker. Suddenly, it shuddered and moaned a hollow sort of wail that echoed, artificially, as if it were in some long stone tunnel. Gameknight swung his blade with all his strength, as did the others. The creature moaned again, then shook violently; its last act.

The Eldritch Guardian fell to the side and crumpled to the ground, finally disappearing in a puff of dark smoke.

The gray mist around them cleared as the whispering sounds slowly dissipated. Gameknight turned and faced Trupech, then glanced at the staff in the creature's three-fingered grasp.

"Is that from Thaumcraft?" the User-that-is-not-a-user asked.

The gnome nodded his head.

"What are you talking about?" Crafter asked.

"That staff . . . it comes from the same mod that brought the Eldritch Guardian into existence," Gameknight999 explained.

Hunter jumped down from the roof and approached. She turned to Trupech. "What's the deal with that cane of yours?"

"This is the Staff of Truth," the aged pech replied. "It has been in my possession for all my life."

"What does it do?" Crafter asked.

"This magical tool forces the target and the wielder to confront their true self," Trupech explained, his words coming out short and fast. "They're shown all the truths they've been hiding from. For creatures of evil, this is not easy. Good and evil are universal truths. We all know which side we are on. The Eldritch was forced to realize that it was an instrument of evil and destruction. It has no purpose in Minecraft other than harming others. The Guardian refused to accept this and resisted the images of its true self.

"A person can never win a battle with themselves. We must all accept who we are, with our strengths and weaknesses. No one can deceive themselves fully; we all know the truth. For the Eldritch, the truth about all the harm it had caused to others was too much to bear. It refused to accept the reality of its existence, and thus, the Staff slowly drained its life force. The Eldritch Guardian could never accept the truth, and that cost it its life."

"That's a nice little toy," Hunter said.

"It is not a toy, it is a weapon—a dangerous weapon," Trupech snapped, the words sharp and pointed, as if the gnome had suffered as well. "It asks a price of the target and the wielder. It forced me to accept the truth about myself. It showed me my failure on Diona. I should have been able to stop Entity303, but I wasn't strong enough. Because of my weakness, the villagers of that planet are now nothing but evolved monsters. The Staff of Truth forced me to accept both my successes and failures. If I hadn't, it would have destroyed me as well."

"That doesn't sound so nice after all." Hunter put a comforting hand on the gnome's small shoulder.

Everyone was silent for a moment as Trupech contemplated what he had confronted in the battle while the rest of them scanned the terrain for any more threats.

"You know, Entity303 isn't making this very easy for us," Crafter said. "Warriors made of smoke was not something I thought we'd need to fight."

"Me neither." Gameknight lowered his voice. "It's making me think that there are lots of other things Entity303 can bring into this land with that mod if he wanted. Some of them are pretty mean . . . and tough."

Empech stepped forward and gazed up at Gameknight999. "He uses Thaumcraft to weaken the fabric, yes, yes. Empech can feel the strain."

"I can feel it too," Trupech said, his words short and clipped. "Soon, he will start the tear in Minecraft. He'll use the dark magic held within Thaumcraft to start the destruction."

"Hmmmm . . . we must hurry," Forpech grumbled in a deep voice.

Squawk, Tux agreed.

"I know, I know," Gameknight said. "But first we must heal and rest. Everyone find a bed in the village. All of us need food and sleep. In the morning, we'll find our enemy, Entity303."

Digger looked at the User-that-is-not-a-user with fear in his green eyes. "What if he and his dark magic finds us first?"

No one answered. They glanced at each other as they considered the question, but none wanted to put a voice to their fear . . . no, their nightmare.

CHAPTER 28

OPENING THE EYE

Entity303 soared high over the tops of the trees, using his jetpack to fly quickly across the landscape. Below him scrolled biomes of pink and purple and yellow and blue, all of it making him sick.

"If I'd been on the development team for this planet, I would have never agreed to these colors," he said to himself, the jetpack almost drowning out his voice. "It's like I'm trapped inside some kind of cartoon . . . it's ridiculous."

He banked to the left when he spotted a pool of lava nestled in the center of a strange forest. The trees were tall, with leaves that reflected the light from the stars overhead. It was as if each leaf were crafted from the finest silver, the individual blades shining like tiny little mirrors. One of the trees looked ablaze, but as Entity303 drew near, he realized the leaves were just reflecting the bright glow from the pool of molten stone below.

He banked away from the lava and headed to the south. The landscape was dark, but with the clear sky, the stars added a faint silver hue to the surroundings. The sun had sunk below the horizon and the world was now plunged into a mystical twilight, but Entity303 had no problem seeing; he'd used a potion of night-vision to give himself an extra edge.

A large green plain of fluorescent grass stretched off to the right. There was a village out there, with the flickering light from torches spilling through the colored windows. It was barely visible in the distance, but he was sure there would be villagers there to torture.

"Maybe I should go destroy those NPCs, just for fun." The idea amused him, but he knew he had to stay focused. "No, I need to find the Altar and get this party started."

He angled down, zooming just above the shining leaves of the forest, the pink grass below making the leafy canopy stand out in stark contrast. Far off to the left, he saw a bright something that stretched out for dozens of blocks. He angled toward it, heading south-east. As he neared, Entity303 realized it was just another grassy plains biome, but this one had an annoying golden yellow grass that glowed, lighting up the landscape even on the darkest of nights. The sparkling blades of grass made him sick.

"What a waste of programming," he mumbled.

He turned away from the glowing fields and headed to the southwest. Ahead were some steep mountains with multi-colored trees decorating their slopes. Curving around the peaks, Entity303 passed through the mountain range only to find another forest.

"This place is sick with forests," the user growled. "Couldn't those developers think of anything original?"

And then he saw what he was searching for. Off to the right there was a biome that at first glance looked covered with snow, but Entity303 knew there wasn't any snow on Fronos. The trees in the white biome were completely devoid of branches, just multicolored pillars sticking up into the air. As he neared, the user smelled what he thought was cake . . . how could that be? He accelerated toward the bright land and descended closer to the ground. The jet pack sputtered and coughed, the last of the rocket fuel getting sucked into the engines. Slowly gliding to the ground, he landed gracefully in the strange biome. He loosened the straps and removed the jetpack, then replaced it with his Alpha Yeti chest plate.

Around him, the ground reminded him of an endless frosted cake, with tiny little candies embedded in the frosting. Colorful shrubs that resembled clumps of cotton candy dotted the surroundings. The trees were actually spiral-striped candy sticks, each a different flavor and color. Entity303 reached out and touched the sugary stalk, then brought his finger to his mouth.

"Strawberry and banana?" he said aloud, astonished. "It's really all candy. I found Candy Land!"

That was the name of this biome. They were extremely rare on Fronos, and the evil user knew this would be where the Altar would be located; he had put the bug in this software himself before being fired from the Minecraft team.

Surveying his surroundings, he saw creatures of all kinds moving about. There were large strawberries with little feet. They had yellow eyes and the strawberry's stems made their noses. Tiny kiwi fruit with eyes and mouths on their fuzzy green bodies walked about as if all this were normal. Blueberry creatures and small jelly slimes moved about, with large watermelons, complete with half-eaten slices on their heads, followed nearby. It was the strangest area he'd ever seen in Minecraft.

"I must find the Altar, fast," he said to himself.

A curious blueberry walked up to him. He viciously kicked the curious berry, then stormed toward a bouncing candy. The tiny green creature curled up into a ball and rolled quickly away.

Entity303 growled in frustration, then stormed across the landscape, searching for his prize. He climbed a small hill covered with the candy pillars. When he reached the top, an eerie chill filled the air. The faint sound of ritual chanting seemed to float softly across the landscape, causing tiny little square goose bumps to form on his arms; it was really spooky.

"It's near," Entity303 said.

He glanced around, expecting to see monsters nearby, but fortunately, the only creatures nearby were the ridiculous fruits and candies. Frustration was beginning to blossom within him, making the user angry. He wanted to punch something or do some damage to something substantial, but all there was around him were these ridiculous candies. Drawing his infused-sword, he swung it at one of the candy canes, cleaving it in two. The top half tumbled to the ground. Entity303 looked down at the candy, but the act did nothing to relieve his frustration.

Putting his sword away, he ran up the next pink-frosted hill of cake. The chanting grew louder as he swerved around cotton candy bushes and sugary pillars. The spooky voices made him glance over his shoulder to see if anyone was there. Chills ran down his spine. Tiny beads of sweat trickled down his forehead, even though he felt as if he were wrapped in an icy blanket. Entity303 knew he was getting closer. At the peak, the evil user skidded to a stop and smiled; he'd found what he sought.

Near the bottom of the sweet mound, a shadowy altar sat between a group of candy cane trees. Dark blocks that seemed alien and completely out of place sat on the frosted cake, their presence like a festering wound in an otherwise completely healthy landscape. The blocks were laid out in the shape of an octagon, and were even darker than the void. Small, ornately-carved pedestals dotted each side of the altar, a larger pedestal at the center. Floating above the structure was a tall column of stone, the ends sharpened to points. It was the Eldritch obelisk, dark as midnight, with a shadowy aura about it caused by the dark magic radiating from within.

The sun crested the eastern horizon and cast rays of light upon the altar. But that did nothing to illuminate the stones or obelisk. The enchanted thing seemed to emanate pure darkness, and, in fact, the surrounding Candy Land forest seemed dimmer than the rest of the forest as a result; the altar was sucking light *out* of the landscape.

Standing on the edges of the dark thing were four NPCs. Each one was wearing a long, blood-red cloak that covered them from head to foot, with a thick, billowing hood over each of their heads. The shadows within the cowls completely hid their faces as they stood and faced the center of the altar. These creatures, Crimson Clerics, as they were known in Thaumcraft, were the source of the chanting.

Entity303 drew his sword and moved closer. He knew the Clerics were harmless, but the very dangerous Crimson Knights could spawn at any time, as well as the dreaded Eldritch Guardian. Moving behind one of the Clerics, the user noticed a stream of dark smoke that flowed between the obelisk and the NPCs. It wasn't clear if the Clerics were breathing in the dark magic from the shadowy column of floating stone, or whether they were providing the mystical smoke to the structure. In any case, this was what he'd been searching for on Fronos.

"Now it's time to open the Eye," he said to himself.

Reaching into his inventory, Entity303 pulled out four round plates, each one identical. They all had a drawing of an eye on them, with a gold rim around the edge and a purple pupil at the center. The user stepped up to the obelisk, the Crimson Clerics ignoring his presence. Kneeling, he placed one of the disks on the pedestal that sat under the floating obelisk. It instantly stuck to the dark stone. Moving around the pedestal, he placed the rest of the eyes on the structure.

Suddenly, a hissing sound filled the air. It sounded like a gigantic snake getting ready to strike, but then it faded away as a dark stain formed in the air between the pedestal and the obelisk. The stain grew darker and larger, stretching outward until it encompassed the pedestal and part of the floating stone. It was roughly shaped like an eye, with an inky black pupil and a dark blue halo surrounding the edge.

The Eye was now open.

The clerics looked up for just a moment, then lowered their cloaked heads and continued to chant.

Entity303 laughed as he approached the dark and menacing portal. He had the urge to destroy the clerics, just because he could, but he liked the sound of their frightening chants.

"I will let you live, for now," he said to the NPCs.

They ignored them and just continued their spooky incantations.

Turning, he glanced around the Candy Land terrain. All of the strange candy and fruit-like creatures were now slowly moving toward the rift, as if in a trance . . . it was strange.

"Well, if you foolish creatures want to come to the Outer Lands and be destroyed by things more frightening than your worst nightmares, then please come on."

He reached down and picked up a blueberry creature. Its tiny feet squirmed as he held it high in the air, then he threw it into the portal. The innocent creature vanished when it entered the eye-shaped rift, transported to another dimension, a dangerous dimension: the creature was transported to the Outer Lands.

The user turned around, hoping someone would be there to see the terrible act, but the only creatures nearby were more of the jelly slimes, berry creatures, and hopping melons, all of them approaching the Eye, their faces emotionless, as if they were each in a trance.

He sighed, then pulled out some special armor. It was dark blue with a hint of magical enchantments. Removing the Alpha Yeti armor and throwing it to the ground, he replaced it with the Voidmetal armor. Entity303 knew the kind of monsters that lurked on the other side of the portal; the furry white Yeti armor would not have been enough protection in the Outer Lands. But with Voidmetal wrapped around his body, he stood a very good chance of being able to withstand just about anything.

The magical enchantments on the armor cast an iridescent blue glow on his surroundings. But as soon as the cerulean light touched the ground, it was extinguished, as the black magic of the Eldritch Altar overpowered it with its dark hue.

With his powerful infused sword in his hand, he stepped up to the portal and stared into the dark abyss.

"So begins the end of Minecraft," Entity303 said in a loud voice, his self-inflated ego growing even bigger. With a malicious grin on his square face, he stepped into the Eye and headed for the Outer Lands, where he would light the fuse of the destruction of Minecraft. And not even the great Gameknight999 would be able to stop what he was about to start.

CHAPTER 29

TO CANDY LAND

"Gameknight, get up, get up," someone said in his ear.

He was still tired and sore from the battle with the Eldritch Guardian. Throughout the evening, he'd had terrible dreams: armies of Eldritch guardians, strange red knights, gigantic armored robots . . . it had been impossible to get any peaceful rest. Now, he was paying the price for his restlessness: he was exhausted.

Suddenly, a cold nose rubbed against his cheek, followed by a rough, wet tongue. Gameknight shook his head and sat up, wiping his cheek with a sleeve.

"What is it?" he said, annoyed.

Herder was standing before him with one of his wolves, the alpha male and pack leader.

"Herder, what are you doing? I was sleeping."

"I know, ahhh . . . sorry, but I think you should come see this."

Without waiting, Herder darted out of the house, leaving the door wide open. Gameknight glanced at the other end of the room. Crafter and Digger were still fast asleep and Tux was curled up on the floor.

He stood up and stretched, trying to get a knot out of his back, then put on his armor and followed Herder outside. The NPCs in this Fronos village were already awake and doing their chores. After the battle with the monsters and the Eldritch Guardian, the villagers had welcomed them into their homes, but just like on the moon, these NPCs were unable to communicate with them; they likely only spoke Fronosian and weren't able to understand the User-that-is-not-a-user or his friends. But the villagers could tell their defenders were hungry, and had given them food and places to sleep in exchange for their help chasing away the monsters.

"Come on, Gameknight, come on." Herder's voice sounded far away.

Woof! the wolf added.

Turning, the User-that-is-not-a-user found the lanky boy atop a nearby hill behind the blacksmith's shop. Gameknight ran to his side.

"Now tell me, Herder, what was so important that you had to wake me?"

"Look." Herder pointed out onto the grassy plain.

Gameknight stared out at the green, rolling hills. Instantly, he noticed something was wrong. All of the animals were moving in the same direction, heading southward. It was like watching a parade.

"Why are they all heading to the south?" Gameknight asked.

Herder just shrugged.

"They feel it," a voice said from behind.

The words were fast and short, like three quick shots from a gun. Trupech stepped up from behind, the tiny little gnome gazing out upon the plain, his wrinkled face creased with worry. His steely-gray eyes took it all in as if he were recording every detail in his mind.

"Feel what?" Gameknight asked.

"The power," the gnome replied. "Some kind of portal opened near dawn. It is bleeding power into Fronos, but also sucking life out of this world. The animals feel its presence."

"Can you feel it?" Herder asked.

Trupech nodded his head. "I can hear its song through the fabric of Minecraft. I know what it is." He stared up at Gameknight999. "And you know as well. It is related to last night."

"The Eldritch Guardian, you mean?"

The gray-skinned gnome nodded his head, his oversized backpack jingling as items inside the dark blue pack banged against each other.

"You think it's a portal?" All the features of the Thaumcraft mod cycled through Gameknight's mind; all the creatures, all the magic, and . . . "You think Entity303 opened the Eye?"

Trupech nodded his head, causing more jingling from his pack.

"But why would he want to make one of those portals?" the User-that-is-not-a-user said. "All it would do is give him access to the Outer Lands."

"Wait, what are the Outer Lands?" Herder asked.

"They're another dimension within Minecraft," Gameknight said. "Some say the Outer Lands exist on a separate server plane within our pyramid of servers, some say it's on a totally different pyramid . . . no one is sure. But what everyone agrees is that the Outer Lands materialize far, far away from the portal that sends you there."

"You mean the Eye?" Herder asked.

Gameknight nodded. "The Outer Lands are so far away that the sky and land no longer exist; it's just a series of tunnels built from ancient stone bricks that are floating in nothingness. The endless void wraps around the structure, and in some places even leaks into the passages. Touching the void will kill you."

"If our enemy opened the Eye out here, in the Far Lands, far away from the central core of Minecraft, then the Outer Lands that was created by this Eye portal will be the farthest point ever loaded into this universe." A worried look came across Trupech's oversized face. "If a tear in the fabric of Minecraft starts out there in that evil and unforgiving land, nothing will be able to stop it."

"We have to stop him." Gameknight turned to Herder. "Go wake up the others. We're leaving in five minutes."

Herder whistled. All of the wolves converged on him. The skinny boy pulled his long hair from his face, then held a finger up in the air and moved it in a circle. Instantly, the wolves fanned out, forming a protective circle around the village. Herder then took off running for the wooden buildings, yelling at the top of his lungs.

Gameknight shuddered as icy chills ran down his spine. He knew the terrors that lurked in the Outer Lands. They would be tested to the limits of their strength and courage in those twisting and confusing passages. But on top of that, they'd need to stop Entity303 as well. Gameknight never imagined that the evil user would try to do this. No sane person went into the Outer Lands on purpose, yet now they had no choice but to follow their enemy there. It was likely that many of their party would not survive. But he knew they had no choice.

How can I protect my friends in those shadowy passages? the User-that-is-not-a-user moaned to himself. *How many lives will this cost because of my decisions? This is too hard, it's too dangerous . . . it can't be done.*

Gameknight glanced down at the pech and was terrified.

"Fear not, child . . . it *can* be done. We have not given up yet," Forpech said.

The pech looked up at him with those ancient gray eyes. There was something hauntingly familiar about them, as if he'd seen them a hundred times before. But how was that possible? He'd only just met this creature.

Just then, the rest of their companions came running up the hill, their armor polished, their weapons sharp and ready, courtesy of the Fronos villagers.

"What's up?" Hunter said. "What's the deal with the animals—they're all heading the same way?"

"They're leading us to Entity303," Gameknight said. "He's built a portal to a dimension called the Outer

Lands, and it's likely he'll try to destroy Minecraft from there. We have to go stop him."

"Let me guess, there are tons of monsters there?" Hunter asked.

Gameknight nodded.

"And you have no idea how to defeat them?"

He nodded again.

"This does sound like fun. Another great plan by Gameknight999."

Stitcher aimed a punch for her arm, but this time Hunter was quicker and dodged her sibling's attack. She flashed her younger sister a smile, then turned to the User-that-is-not-a-user.

"If that's the plan, let's get going," she said. "None of us are getting any younger, and quitting isn't an option, regardless of the odds."

She took a step closer and stared straight into Gameknight's eyes.

"You lead and we follow, that's the deal. So let's get it done."

"I like her," Trupech said.

"You just haven't gotten to know her yet," Stitcher added with a rueful smile.

This time, Hunter was the one doing the punching. Stitcher rubbed her arm, then smiled at her sister.

"Hunter's right," Crafter added. "It's time to go."

"You all need to know something. There are terrible monsters in the Outer Lands," Gameknight explained. "I don't know if we have the armor and weapons to defeat them. This may be a hopeless cause."

Just then, Trupech took off his huge backpack and set it on the ground. He reached into its dark interior and began pulling pieces of orange armor from the sack and tossing them on the ground. He then pulled out swords, each made from the same orange material.

"Now we're talkin'," Hunter said as she removed her iron armor and replaced it with the shining, ornate new armor. She banged her hand on the orange chest plate. It rang like a gong.

"What is this stuff?"

"It is Ichorium armor. This metal is the strongest and hardest in Minecraft . . . the best Thaumcraft has to offer," Trupech said. "It will give us an edge."

The others removed their iron coating and replaced it with the glowing orange armor.

"Wait, there is more," the tiny gnome said.

Trupech reached into his pack and pulled out something made of the same glowing orange metal at the end of a long handle. He extended it to Digger. The stocky NPC dropped his pickaxe, then reached out and took it into his muscular hands.

"It is an Ichorium pickaxe," Trupech said as he pulled another out of his backpack and extended the handle to the villager.

Digger took the second pick, then held them both out in front of him. A wry smile crept across the big NPC's face as he swung them through the air.

"I like!" he exclaimed.

"Great, now let's get . . ." Gameknight said but was interrupted.

"There is one last thing," Trupech added.

He pulled two Ichorium longswords from his pack and extended both, handles first. The User-that-is-not-a-user's eyes lit up as he took the swords. There was power in these blades, power put there not just from enchantments, but also from the dark magic of Thaumcraft.

Gameknight smiled.

"We're gonna use Entity303's mod, Thaumcraft, to ruin his plans. He won't know what hit him," the User-that-is-not-a-user said.

With his new Ichorium swords held at the ready, Gameknight999 headed off across the landscape of Fronos, following the spellbound animals toward the portal that would take them to the deadly Outer Lands.

CHAPTER 30

THE OUTER LANDS

They followed the animals through the morning. It seemed as if every creature on Fronos was answering the call of the Eldritch Portal. Nothing seemed to stop the strange animals; the candy and fruit creatures waded through lakes and forded rivers, regardless of how difficult the crossing.

At one point, the companions entered a forest with silver, mirror-like leaves, a large pool of lava near its center. As they approached, Gameknight saw a group of strawberry-like creatures walk right into the lava, the boiling stone directly in their path. In their trancelike state, they never even saw the pool of death. When he closed his eyes, the User-that-is-not-a-user could still hear their screams, though they were mercifully cut short.

Approaching the lava carefully, Gameknight placed blocks of cobblestone along its edge, making a covering over the lava to protect other creatures from meeting the same fate. Herder came to his side and helped by adding blocks of dirt to the structure. The two companions covered the pool just as a group of kiwi-looking animals approached. The green creatures crossed the newly-made lid without harm, though some of the heat from the lava underneath still bled through the stone.

Satisfied the animals would be safe, the party continued running to the south, following the direction dictated by the beasts of this planet.

When the sun had just passed its zenith, a snowy-looking biome appeared in the distance.

"We draw near," Trupech said.

Empech nodded his gray head. "Yes, yes, we are close."

"Hmmm . . . it is in that white land ahead," Forpech growled, his voice deep and gravely. "I can feel it pulsing like a dying heart."

"Come on, let's speed it up," Gameknight said.

He sprinted across the landscape, the rest of the party following close behind. They moved through a forest, then past a fluorescent swamp and around a group of small mountains.

Finally, they reached the snowy landscape, only to realize that it wasn't snow that covered the biome . . . it was frosting! Incredibly, the ground was made of cake, and spread on top was frosting decorated with candies of every color. Tall, multi-colored trees stood like sentinels over the landscape. As Gameknight neared one of the striped trees, he caught the aroma of sweet candy. Stepping to the tree, the User-that-is-not-a-user touched his tongue to the bark to taste.

"It's not a tree . . . it's candy . . . really good candy!" Gameknight reached down and pulled off a clump of a pink bush and put it in his mouth. It tasted like the best cotton candy he'd ever had. "This biome is probably called Candy Land. I wouldn't be surprised to find Princess Bubblegum here surrounded by her Banana Guards."

"What are you talking about?" Hunter moved to a nearby candy pillar and ran her hand down its sticky length. "Sometimes, you are so weird."

"It's from a show I used to watch, called—"

"Look, this one's been cut down." Herder was staring down at a fallen candy tree.

Gameknight moved to the boy's side and gazed at the ground. One of the candy trees was cut in half, the severed end melted a bit as if it had been cloven in two by a hot knife.

"Entity303," Weaver hissed softly. "He used his glowing blade on this."

The User-that-is-not-a-user nodded. "Come on, let's keep going."

They ran over the next hill, the constant stream of Fronosian creatures still marching toward the distant portal. After cresting the frosted knoll, they came across another hill of cake, this one topped with pink frosting. When Gameknight was almost at the top, he thought he heard something; a chanting of voices drifted to his ears. It sounded as if they were right behind him. The User-that-is-not-a-user glanced over his shoulder and found Digger behind him, his green eyes filled with fear; he heard it too.

Suddenly, a chill cut through his new armor, making him shiver. Gameknight moved to the top of the pink-frosted hill and gazed down the other side. At the foot of the cake-mound sat that which they sought: the Eldritch Portal.

The dark stones that made up the structure were similar to obsidian, but somehow darker. Small, carved stones, known as capstones, marked the perimeter of the altar, with a similar stone at the very center. The tiny pedestals had ornate carvings on them, giving the dark little blocks a magical appearance. Above this central stone floated a tall column; it was the Eldritch Obelisk. Below the obelisk floated what looked like a hole in space; it was a dark portal with a sinister blue halo marking its edge; it was the Eye. It pulsed as if it had some kind of undead heartbeat. Though it looked the same from any direction, Gameknight felt that the Eye was staring straight at him. Surrounding the shadowy gateway were four NPCs, each cloaked in bright red robes.

"Who are they?" Stitcher asked.

"They're Crimson Clerics," Gameknight replied. "They aren't hostile, but they'll summon Crimson Knights through the portal if we're not fast enough."

Just then, a bouncing green jelly-slime approached the altar. Without stopping, it jumped through the dark portal and disappeared. It was followed by a blueberry creature, then a strawberry one.

"They're walking right into the thing," Digger reached down and turned the blueberry creature around. It quickly turned and headed back toward the Eye. "We need to stop them."

"The only way to stop them is to defeat the enemy," Trupech said.

"Come on, we can't wait," Gameknight said.

They ran down the hill, then drew their new Ichorium weapons and slowly approached the portal. Suddenly, the Crimson Clerics began chanting louder, their incantations no longer just a whisper. Hunter notched an arrow and aimed it at one of the cloaked NPCs.

"Don't worry," the User-that-is-not-a-user said. "They do that. All we need to do is . . ."

Suddenly, a gray fog floated across the landscape. A sad, mournful whispering came from the fog, as if a thousand souls were trapped within the smoky cloud, struggling to get out—or maybe draw new souls in. Gameknight suddenly felt numb, unable to feel his health.

"It's another Eldritch Guardian," Gameknight shouted. "Quick, everyone through the portal."

He stood by the ominous eye as his friends dove through. In the gray fog, he saw the Guardian approaching, its smoky body like a formless apparition. The monster threw a ball of dark magic at him. Gameknight rolled to the other side of the portal, allowing the shadowy sphere to pass by overhead. He then dove into the Eye, just after the last of the wolves.

When he materialized in the Outer Lands, the User-that-is-not-a-user found himself in a stone-lined chamber, the walls, floor and ceiling all a dark, lifeless gray. Stepping away from the dark portal that existed on this side as well, he glanced at his friends. They all had terrified expressions on their square faces. This place had an ancient feel to it, as if it were the oldest thing in existence, but there was also an inherently malevolent feel to it as well. It had been made with dark magic, and everything in this place was dangerous . . . and evil.

"This is a really nice place you have here, Gameknight," Hunter said with a strained smile. "What's with the windows in the corners?"

Gameknight looked at the corners of the portal room. The bricks were missing, and through the holes he could see the Void on the other side. The Void was the space that filled the End, and was the barrier that surrounded Minecraft. Nothing survived the Void; it was instant death.

"It's safe to say we aren't tunneling out of here like we did the dungeons," Hunter added.

Gameknight nodded his head in agreement.

"So when we destroy Entity303 and want to leave this horrible place, we need to use this portal?" she asked.

Gameknight nodded again.

"But there's one of those Guardian things waiting for us on the other side."

The User-that-is-not-a-user sighed and nodded.

"This is great!" Hunter exclaimed sarcastically.

Stitcher didn't even try to punch her sister in the arm; she was too afraid to move.

Gameknight walked to the doorway in front of them. Before him stretched a long gray passage whose end was not visible. In multiple places, it branched off, the side corridors going who knew where. Each passage appeared the same, with the occasional pale-yellow block glowing on the wall or ceiling, casting just enough light to see. Cobwebs hung from the ceiling, which meant that there were spiders in the tunnels.

Hunter moved to his side, then notched an arrow and pointed it down the passage.

"There aren't any monsters here . . . yet," Gameknight said, his voice almost a whisper.

She nodded then glanced at her sister. They took up defensive positions near the wall.

"Herder, see if your wolves can pick up Entity303's scent," Gameknight said.

The pack leader seemed to understand and lowered his nose to the ancient stone floor. He sniffed around, careful to stay away from the portal. Moving to the tunnel entrance, the animal sniffed some more, then began to whimper, his tail falling between his legs. Herder reached out and patted the animal on the side, then whispered something in their ear. The wolf stood tall, wagging his tail, looking affectionately at the boy.

Herder turned to Gameknight999 and shook his head. "They can't find a scent."

"Doesn't matter," Hunter said. "We'll just search the passages until we find him."

"You don't understand," Gameknight said. "The Outer Lands is like a maze. We could get lost in here and lose track of the portal, and be stuck in here for the rest of our lives."

"Hmmm . . . if the enemy is not found soon, then the length of our lives will not be important," Forpech said.

"Agreed, yes, yes," Empech added.

"Then if we are going to . . ." Gameknight began to speak, but stopped when a strange little creature emerged from the portal. It was similar to a rabbit, but was flatter and smaller.

Forpech reached down and patted its soft head, but the creature did not respond. "It's a grappy, from Fronos."

The creature hopped away from the portal and into the passage. It moved to the nearest intersection and turned right. Then a purple berry creature with short stick-like legs and large white eyes shuffled out of the portal and followed the grappy, as if drawn by some external force.

"They can sense the power Entity303 brings to this place," Trupech said in a rapid fire string of staccato words. A light green kiwi jumped out of the portal and followed the other creatures.

"I guess this makes the maze a little easier to solve," Hunter said. "I say we follow them."

"Okay," Gameknight adjusted his Ichorium chest plate. "Everyone stay close and watch out for—"

"Look out!" Stitcher shouted.

A dark, crab-like creature suddenly scuttled across the ground toward them, its single eyeball staring at them hungrily. The monster snapped its two huge claws together, the razor-sharp edges making a clanking sound like a blacksmith's hammer striking an anvil.

Stitcher fired an arrow at the creature, causing the crab to squeal with a strange sort of ghostly voice. She fired again, as did her sister, their arrows lighting the monster on fire. It flashed red multiple times, then flopped over on its side and disappeared.

"What was that?!" Hunter exclaimed.

"Eldritch crab," Gameknight raised a finger to his lips. "Shhh, keep your voice down."

She was shaking. "Keep your voice down . . . are you kidding? That was a one-eyed crab with massive claws. It wanted to eat us."

Gameknight put a calming hand on her shoulder. "Welcome to the Outer Lands."

He glanced around the room at all his friends. Terror was visible on all their faces, except for the pechs. For some reason, they seemed calm, as if they knew some secret and their faith in the User-that-is-not-a-user was unshakable.

"The portal leads back to Fronos and can be used at any time. Eldritch Guardians are weaker when they aren't in the Outer Lands, so you'll have a better chance of survival if you go back." He sighed and took a tentative step into the passage. "I'm going after Entity303, by myself if necessary. I have to get Weaver back into the past so that this timeline can be repaired and all of this madness can be stopped. I'm not gonna rest until everything is fixed."

Gameknight adjusted his armor, making the orange plates hang a little more comfortably on his blocky frame, then moved off down the corridor. At the intersection, he peeked quickly around the corner, then turned to the right and followed the strange fruit creatures from Fronos. The walls of the passage were cold and lifeless and ancient. Their colorless appearance made the User-that-is-not-a-user feel empty and alone. But as he walked, the sound of boots clicking on the stone floor echoed off the walls. Glancing over his shoulders, Gameknight saw his friends following, all of them. Breathing a sigh of relief, he continued, moving deeper into the Outer Lands, a smile on his face.

I only hope I'm worthy of the sacrifice many of them are about to make, Gameknight999 thought.

Just then, faint musical tones echoed in the back of his mind. They were just whispers at first, but they slowly grew in volume. Like an ocean wave, they grew stronger and stronger until the lyrical notes crashed down upon him, washing away his fear and uncertainty. But, like all waves, it then receded again, leaving his mind in silence.

Have faith in your friends, child, a scratchy old voice said in his head.

Gameknight turned to see if anyone else had heard it, but all of his friends looked at him as if he were a little crazy.

"Any of you hear that?" he asked.

They shook their heads, confused.

Gameknight shrugged, then smiled.

I know it's you, he thought. *I've missed you.*

There was no reply, but somehow, Gameknight could imagine her smiling. With a strong grip on his two

Ichorium swords, he moved down the dull, gray passage, heading deeper into the Outer Lands, and closer to his enemy, Entity303.

CHAPTER 31

RUNED TABLET

They ran through the gray passages, the occasional glowing tile spilling light onto the walls and floors and providing just enough illumination to see. There were clusters of white crystals hanging from the ceilings, and strange rune-covered blocks occasionally dotting the walls. These features seemed distributed randomly throughout the Outer Lands, but could be found in every passage, making every tunnel appear identical. That was what made this maze was so dangerous; people often entered but never found the exit.

"What's that?" Weaver asked.

Ahead was something like an ant hill in the middle of the floor, a puff of steam floating up from the dark opening at its peak.

"I don't remember," Gameknight said. "But I don't think it's good."

Suddenly, an Eldritch Crab spawned on the mound. The dark creature's purple shell blended in with the shadows, but its single, oversized eyeball glowed bright. It scanned the passage, glancing to the left and right, then focused its hateful orb onto Weaver. It charged, snapping its gigantic claws together like deadly castanets. The terrifying monster jumped up into the air and landed on the young boy's head, wrapping its spindly legs around his helmet. An eerie screeching sound came from the dark creature as its claws bit into his Ichorium helmet.

"Get it off . . . get it off!" Weaver screamed.

The sharp claws scratched and scraped against the metallic coating as the crab tried to reach the soft flesh that hid beneath the boy's helmet. Weaver dropped his sword and reached up, frantically scratching at it with his fingers, but it had no effect.

Gameknight pulled a shovel out of his inventory. He moved close and struck at the creature, not trying to hurt it. Instead, Gameknight was just hoping to knock it off his friend's head. A solid hit landed right on the creature's eye. The crab staggered for a moment, then slackened its grip with its eight pointed legs for just an instant. Striking it again, the User-that-is-not-a-user knocked the crab to the ground. Before Gameknight could drop the shovel and use his sword, Digger was there with his glowing pickaxe. He hit the creature hard. The tip of his orange Ichorium pick tore through the shell and stuck into the gray stone floor, pinning the crab in place. Crafter then struck it over and over again until it disappeared with a pop.

Leaving the pickaxe embedded in the ground, Digger moved to the crusted mound and smashed it with his second pick until it shattered, leaving behind a hole that opened to the void. The stocky NPC used a block of cobblestone to seal the hole, then retrieved his pickaxe.

"I guess we know what those do now," Hunter said.

A squeaking sound from behind made everyone turn with weapons ready. Shuffling across the floor was a kiwi-fruit creature. It scurried past the group of companions, then turned left at the next intersection.

"You see its eyes?" Stitcher said. "It seemed as if that fruit-thing was dazed and in some kind of trance."

"It is the power Entity303 brings to this place," Trupech said, his words coming in short, quick bursts. "It blinds the weaker creatures."

"The enemy is planting something in this dimension, yes, yes, to start the tear in the fabric of Minecraft," Empech said. "Its power grows, Empech can feel it. Soon, it will begin to affect us all. We must hurry."

"Agreed," Crafter added. "I can start to hear a faint whispering sound in the back of my head. It makes me kind of . . . sleepy."

"Yeah . . . I hear it too," Herder added.

"Empech's right," Gameknight said. "We need to hurry. Let's follow that kiwi and see where it leads us."

They ran through the passages, dodging lightning traps and invisible spiders. Crimson knights in red armor and flowing robes attacked, but were vastly outnumbered by the group . . . for now. Continuing to follow the kiwi, they turned this way and that until the fruit finally led them to a narrow passage. This corridor headed straight into a room filled with ancient pedestals positioned around the chamber, clay vases lining the walls. In the center of the room, a column of ancient stone stood higher than the rest. On it sat a stone tablet covered with runes. It was shaped like a rectangle, with sharp corners along the bottom but the top corners shaved off, creating a smooth curve. The magical piece of stone gave off a pale glow, as if lit by enchantments held within.

Gameknight stopped at the edge of the room and peered inside. He could see the kiwi-creature leaving the chamber through a tunnel at the back of the room. It seemed unharmed after passing through the room, but Gameknight999 had heard of many traps in the Outer Lands; he wanted to be careful.

"What is that?" Digger asked, pointing to the glowing sheet of stone.

Gameknight pulled out the steeleaf shield and held it in his left hand, a glowing Ichorium blade in his right. "That's a Runed Tablet. We'll need that to unlock the boss chamber. That's probably where Entity303 is setting up his . . . whatever he's doing."

"Then let's just get it," Hunter said as she stepped into the room.

"NO!" Gameknight yelled, but it was too late.

Instantly, an Eldritch Guardian appeared. Black smoke billowed out from beneath the creature's robes, obscuring the floor. The monster's body was no longer transparent, but was now solid and dark as coal. A gray haze crept across the passage and chamber, the wither effect again making Gameknight999 feel numb all over, narrowing his vision. He shivered as needles of fear jabbed at him from all over.

The monster fired a ball of black magic at Hunter, striking her in the shoulder and knocking her to her knees. She tried to stand, but the weakness enchantment tore into her strength.

"Come on," Gameknight shouted and charged forward. "FOR MINECRAFT!"

The Eldritch turned and fired a ball of smoky magic at the User-that-is-not-a-user's chest. From pure instinct, he batted at the smoking sphere, knocking it away, then sprinted forward, closing in on the terrifying creature. His blade struck the dark monster's chest plate, making a loud clanking sound. But this time, with the new weapons, he felt the creature's protective coating give a bit. Gameknight moved to the side and noticed a pronounced dent in the monster's armor.

Just then, a group of helmeted guards, called Shambling Husks, entered the room from the opposite side. Each wore a heavy gray cloak with a wide leather belt over enchanted chain mail. Atop their heads, the Husks wore a square helmet with a narrow opening across the front for their eyes. They jingled as they charged into the chamber, their chain mail sounding like deadly wind chimes. It didn't seem that the monsters had any weapons, but Gameknight knew these creatures were dangerous.

Gameknight slowly advanced on the monster, his shield held high. "I'll take care of the Eldritch Guardian. The rest of you, take care of the other monsters."

A wave of white dashed through the room as Herder sent his wolves into battle, the rest of the companions following close behind. Crafter and Weaver ran forward and attacked one of the Shambling Husks together while the wolves were confusing the others. Hunter and Stitcher stood on either side of the entrance and fired their arrows at the creatures, quickly lighting the helmeted monsters on fire. They flashed red and took damage, but the flames quickly faded; it was as if the fire was afraid to touch the terrifying monsters.

Gameknight glanced at the entrance. He found the pechs set up in a defensive formation across the tunnel in case any creatures attacked from behind. But Digger seemed lost. The stocky NPC stood near the entrance with his pickaxes in his hands, but was unable to join the fray. He shook with fright, his normally bright, green eyes dulled with fear.

"Okay, Eldritch, it's just you and me," Gameknight said as he turned to face his adversary.

The monster hissed, a cloud of dark steam coming from the creature's helmet. The black mist smelled of rotten meat and decaying flesh, making the User-that-is-not-a-user momentarily gag. The Guardian gave off a loud screech that made Gameknight's ears ring, then fired a shaft of dark magic. It was like dark water from an evil fire hose. It shot straight out from the center of the monster's chest and hit Gameknight with the force of a giant's hammer, pushing him back a step or two. Bringing his shield forward, he deflected the beam as best he could, then advanced and swung his glowing Ichorium sword. It landed squarely on the monster's shoulder, tearing into the shadowy armor and cutting deep. The Eldritch Guardian groaned, then threw a fist at Gameknight's head. He ducked and slashed at the monster's mid-section. A satisfying *clank* resounded as his blade crashed into the monster.

On the other side of the room, Hunter and Stitcher were firing on crabs that had appeared, while the others battled the remaining Husks.

Duck, a scratchy, grandmotherly voice said in the back of his mind.

Gameknight crouched and rolled to the left just as a ball of dark magic streaked overhead. He stood and brought his sword down upon the monster, then dropped his shield and pulled out his second Ichorium blade.

The Eldritch Guardian saw the second weapon and tried to back up, but suddenly a group of wolves fell on it from behind, biting at its smoky form. It flashed red as the monster turned and tried to attack the animals. Gameknight leapt high into the air and brought both blades down on the creature. It screeched again, then tried to turn and face him, but arrows from Hunter and Stitcher rained down upon the dark monster. Gameknight swung both swords, hitting the monster hard in the side, his blades slicing through the enchanted armor. The Guardian wailed in pain, then fell to the side, and shook violently. Finally, with one last, hollow wail, the monster disappeared.

Gameknight readied himself for attacks from the other monsters, but they were all gone. Before any more creatures could appear, Trupech moved to the ancient stone pedestal. Reaching up, he grabbed the glowing slate and stuffed it into his backpack.

"Come on, we need to finish this!" Gameknight shouted. "Follow me."

He ran through the chamber, taking the passage he'd seen the kiwi go down. It led through more tunnels, many of them booby-trapped with crab spawners that Digger quickly destroyed. Ahead, they could see the kiwi scurrying along until it turned right at another intersection, and then it just stopped. Gameknight reached the passage and was shocked at what he saw.

Before him were hundreds of the fruit and candy creatures from Fronos. They stood crowded together in a narrow passage, the end blocked by what looked like a door with a set of stout braces crossing its entrance.

Gameknight carefully pushed through the crowd, trying to get up to the barricade. When he drew near, he had a better view of the barrier. It was a huge door preventing access to some sort of chamber, two strong bars of metal extending across it in the shape of a "+". Behind the bars, the strange emptiness of the Void sparkled, the shimmering points of light shifting as Gameknight moved his head. If anyone tried to climb past those braces, they'd be instantly destroyed by the Void.

At the center of the crossed bars, a small recession shaped like a rectangle with a curved top was visible. Gameknight was sure the braces were some kind of a lock, and that the recession was a keyhole.

"What's this?" Crafter asked.

The NPC reached out to touch the surface, but Gameknight grabbed his hand and pulled it back.

"Let's just smash open this door," Hunter said. "This waiting around is getting annoying."

The User-that-is-not-a-user didn't answer her. Instead, he turned and pointed at Trupech.

"You still have the Runed Tablet?"

The gray, wrinkled gnome nodded his head, then pushed through the congregation of colorful animals to reach his side. Pulling the stone tablet from his pack, Trupech reached up and carefully placed the Tablet into the recession, then backed up. Instantly, the ancient runes on the surface of the tablet began to glow bright red, the letters clearly part of the Standard Galactic Alphabet, which was the mystical writing used all throughout Minecraft. Gameknight felt a chill pass through the corridor as the braces slowly dissolved, allowing the star field of the Void to completely cover the opening. Each of the stars twinkled, then faded to darkness. Slowly, the shadowy depths of the Void parted, revealing the Outer Lands Boss chamber.

Gameknight stepped forward and peered into the room. Standing at the side of the chamber was his enemy, Entity303, leaning over a crafting bench. But more shocking was the unthinkable horror that writhed at the center of the room.

Waves of fear and hopelessness crashed down on Gameknight999. "Oh, no . . . Entity303, what have you done?"

The dark magic of Thaumcraft bled across the room like a lethal bruise on the skin of the chamber, causing ripples in the fabric of the universe. Filling the center of the room was the most lethal of bosses ever brought into existence in Minecraft, but there was not just one, but five of them. It was horrific and impossible.

"How are we going to defeat them?" the User-that-is-not-a-user whispered to his allies.

Entity303 glanced up from the crafting bench and saw Gameknight999, then started to laugh a maniacal laugh.

"Welcome to the destruction of Minecraft," the vile user said. "It's unfortunate that you're too late to stop it."

And then Entity303 laughed again as icicles of fear stabbed at Gameknight's soul, chilling him to the bone.

CHAPTER 32

TAINTACLES

Inside the chamber writhed five dark tentacles of differing sizes. They looked like they were growing right out of the floor, sticking straight up into the air and squirming about. The nightmarish things bent this way and that, squirming like a tortured squid. One of them appeared to be armored with shining, metallic plates along the side, while another had sharp thorns running down its length. The tallest of them splashed a green liquid on the surroundings that sizzled when it landed on untainted blocks. Gameknight guessed it was one of the venomous types; the poison would be lethal if left untreated.

A diseased-looking purple stain spread out from the flailing things, slowly seeping into the dusty gray blocks that made up the floor and walls and ceiling. When it spread to the ancient slabs, they instantly took on a sickly and brittle appearance. Cracks spread across the stone blocks, a moldy texture covering the surface as they faded to the bruised-purple. Gameknight instantly recognized the dark bruise as the Taint. And that meant these twisting and bending monsters were Taintacles.

One of the Taintacles flailed to the left and right, then reached out and grabbed one of the creatures of

Fronos that was among those streaming into the chamber. The little blueberry screeched in agony as it flashed red, taking damage from the dark monster's crushing strength.

"What are those?" Hunter asked.

"Taintacles. They grow from the taint our enemy has planted here." Trupech's words were fast and clipped. "When they grow large enough, they will break through the ceiling and floor. That will be the beginning of the tear. It will rip apart the fabric of Minecraft."

"Then we need to destroy those things," Stitcher replied.

"It will take all of us to destroy just one," Trupech said, his words growing tense.

"And while we battle the Taintacles, we can't defend ourselves from Entity303," Weaver pointed out.

"You leave him to me," Gameknight said. "I've had just about enough of him."

"Then let's do it!" Crafter shouted. "FOR MINECRAFT!"

They stormed into the room, pushing aside the Fronosian fruit-people. Choosing the smallest of the Taintacles, the comrades surrounded it, chopping at it with their Ichorium blades. The dark monster slashed at Herder like a whip, smashing into his chest plate. It sent him sprawling backward, landing hard on the floor. The wolves tried to defend their master, but as soon as the animals touched the tainted purple ground with their paws, they yelped in pain.

"Herder, keep the wolves back," Crafter commanded. "Our boots will protect us for a while, but the wolves are defenseless."

Suddenly, a large strawberry creature howled in pain as it was picked up by the armored Taintacle, then slowly crushed, its HP diminishing until it disappeared.

"Keep the creatures from Fronos out of the room," Herder commanded to his animals. "Don't let them enter."

The wolves barked, then turned and herded up the creatures of Fronos like sheepdogs, their sharp teeth nipping to back the creatures out of the chamber.

Herder stood and stared down at his boots. He could see tiny cracks forming across the Ichorium shoes; the taint was slowly degrading their armor. Rushing forward, the boy moved next to Weaver, his sword poking at the writhing creature.

The comrades battled the monster, taking turns between defending when it was slashing at them to attacking when it was trying to hit someone else. Each time the Taintacles struck one of the defenders, it left a dark stain across their armor, the diseased taint slowly corroding the Ichorium metal. The pechs ran back and forth, splashing the NPCs with some kind of potion. The magical liquid seemed to erase some of the taint, but not all. It kept the dark bruise from spreading across their armor and eventually enveloping the wearer. But how many potions did the little gnomes have?

Gameknight glanced at his friends as he walked straight toward Entity303, tiny little daggers of fear poking at him from all sides. He gave the deranged user an angry glare.

"Well, well, well, what have we here?" the evil user boomed.

"We're here to stop you, Entity303," Gameknight999 said in a loud voice. He squared his shoulders and tried to appear confident, but he was still shocked by the presence of the squirming mass of tentacles sticking up out of the floor, and that uncertainty was plastered all over his face.

The evil user sneered, then slowly drew his glowing infused-sword from his inventory. The razor-sharp edge of the blade burned white hot, casting a harsh illumination across the terrifying scene, but did nothing to illuminate his armor. The Void Metal coating he wore was as black as night and reminded Gameknight of Herobrine's ender-armor from so long ago. The shadowy metal sparkled with magical enchantments and seemed to drink up all light and hope. Entity303 growled, then swung his shining blade in a flourish of complicated moves, as if he were in a cheap martial arts movie.

Gameknight held his hand up and shaded his eyes for a moment as they adjusted to the glare.

"Well?" Entity303 said with a raised eyebrow. "You gonna come stop me, or just stand there and look like a fool?"

He laughed a mocking, malicious laugh that made Gameknight's skin crawl.

Can I do this? the User-that-is-not-a-user thought. *Can I really defeat him?*

Have faith, child and do what you do best, an ancient, scratchy voice said in the back of his head. It sounded as if it were coming to him from a thousand miles away, yet at the same time, it filled every part of his soul, the grandmotherly tone calming his doubt and fears.

What I do best? What's that?

And then the answer burst into his mind like an explosion of hope: *Refuse to give up!*

Gameknight stood a little taller as confidence began to flow through him. He drew his Ichorium blade with his right hand, then drew his second sword with his left.

"It's time you were stopped," Gameknight said. "You have caused harm to Minecraft and the electronic lives that rely on it for their existence. You have destroyed creatures for no reason and caused the death of many dear friends."

Entity300 smiled, as if satisfied.

"You lack the compassion to be a real developer of Minecraft and create something meant to be shared and enjoyed by others," Gameknight said, taking a step closer. "All you can do is destroy and focus on yourself. The programmers of Minecraft were right to fire you. Now, I'm gonna make your termination complete."

The User-that-is-not-a-user charged at his enemy, slashing at the dark armor with his orange-glowing Ichorium blade, but Entity303 was fast . . . really fast. Gameknight could see spirals floating around the user's head; he must have taken a potion of swiftness. It didn't matter, the User-that-is-not-a-user would not give up.

Entity303 swung at him with his glowing sword. Gameknight brought up one blade, blocking the attack, then swung with the other, slashing at his enemy's side. The blade landed with a *THUNK*, making the user grunt with pain. Entity303 quickly stepped back, moving away from him. It gave Gameknight a chance to glance at his friends battling the Taintacles.

Instantly, he noticed how much larger the squirming things were getting; the terrible monsters were growing, even as they fought.

"It's almost touching the ceiling," Forpech shouted, his deep rumbling voice making the tainted ground shake. "We must hurry!"

Just then, the smallest of the squirming Taintacles disappeared with a pop. The group of warriors moved quickly to the next most vulnerable. After destroying the first purple creature, it looked as if they had a plan. With Herder and Weaver on one side, Crafter and Hunter on the other, they took turns attacking it, one side moving in and stabbing at the thrashing tentacle while the others distracted it with noise. Stitcher stayed back and fired her flaming arrows into the base of the creature, where the segments separated the most, one in three slipping past the hard exoskeleton and finding soft flesh. The monster flashed red again and again until it finally flopped to the ground and disappeared, leaving the three largest.

The next Taintacle's thick base and long reach made it a more dangerous adversary; they had no choice but to fight. Instead of waiting to think about it, the companions charged forward, attacking the monstrosity.

"You know, they'll never defeat the last one in time," Entity303 mocked. "Say goodbye to Minecraft."

"Perhaps, but you'll be stuck here when it happens," Gameknight said. "As soon as you try to use the Digitizer to escape, I'll destroy you with my Ichorium swords."

"Ha . . . your *Ichorium* swords. Those are pathetic." The evil user took a step closer. "You know, those blades of yours are no match for mine. Here, let me show you."

Entity303 charged at Gameknight999, swinging his glowing sword with all his strength. Gameknight swung one of his swords up to block the attack, and the blades crashed together, making a sound like a clap of thunder. Gameknight's arm buzzed with pain as the force of the blow vibrated through the weapon and into his shoulder. Stepping back, Gameknight glanced at his blade. Cracks spread across the weapon, the point of impact glowing slightly.

"You see, what you don't understand, fool, is that the energy in these weapons can be increased." Entity303 laughed, then did something to the handle of the weapon that made the blade glow brighter. "But if you really knew anything about Minecraft, then you'd know this, wouldn't you?"

"Well . . ."

Before Gameknight could finish his reply, Entity303 attacked again, his infused-sword leaving a trail of sparks in the air as it sped toward its target. Instead of blocking the weapon, the User-that-is-not-a-user rolled to the right, then attacked the evil user's dark legs. The tip of his blade sliced deep into Entity303's thigh, causing cracks to spread across the shadowy armor. Not waiting, he rolled back to the left and attacked the legs again, causing more cracks to appear on the Voidmetal.

Entity303 grunted and stepped back. Gameknight thought his opponent was considering retreat, but then the evil user suddenly charged at him, his blazing sword streaking down at him in a vicious overhead strike. Gameknight's only choice was to bring up his blade and block the attack. Sparks flew out in all directions as more cracks spread along the length of the weapon. Feigning an attack with the damaged blade,

Gameknight slashed at his enemy with his left, scoring a glancing hit that did little more than annoy Entity303.

The evil user smiled.

"You see, fool, it's impossible to defeat me," Entity303 said. "I have more knowledge and skill than you'll ever have."

Suddenly, a strange squeal filled the air, followed by a cheer.

"We got one more," Crafter yelled, "only two left."

"The big one's getting closer to the ceiling," Hunter yelled. "When it punches through, it's all over."

Entity303 said with a smile. "You can't stop my plan . . . it's too late. You might as well give up and just watch the show."

Gameknight growled and swung his blade at the user's head. Entity303 brought up his blade just in time. The weapons smashed together in a mighty crash. More cracks spread across Gameknight's blade until it finally splintered in a shower of white-hot metal. Stinging shards of Ichorium nipped at his face and arms as the shattered pieces of his sword flew all around them, only the handle of the orange weapon remaining.

Gameknight threw the handle aside, then transferred his remaining Ichorium blade from his left hand to his right. He stepped back and sighed as he glanced at the remaining Taintacles dominating the room. Looking at Entity303 with a defeated expression on his face, he threw his sword to the ground.

"Oh, are you giving up?" Entity300 asked. "Are you expecting mercy?"

"Gameknight, what are you doing?" Hunter yelled, her blade slashing at the base of the Taintacle. "Pick up your sword and defend yourself."

"It won't do any good," the User-that-is-not-a-user said. "It will only shatter after a few impacts with Entity303's sword."

"A wise decision, giving up," the evil user said.

"Who said anything about giving up?" Gameknight replied. "This isn't over, not while I still draw breath."

"As you wish," Entity303 growled.

Raising his glowing infused-sword high in the air, he swung it directly at Gameknight999.

CHAPTER 33

ENTITY303'S REVENGE

It was like watching a disaster happen in slow motion. Entity303's blade was moving toward his head and Gameknight's hands were empty. The User-that-is-not-a-user thought he could hear the glowing sword hiss as the superheated weapon burned through the air. It came closer and closer, but Gameknight felt no fear. This was his moment—it was why he was here, why he was the User-that-is-not-a-user. It was the culmination of everything he'd learned and experienced in Minecraft, and now, all he had to do was let his instincts take over and he would either live . . . or die.

Just before the shining blade reached him, Gameknight dropped to the ground and rolled to the side. He could feel the white-hot, razor-sharp edge zip past his ear as he rolled, the heat from the weapon singeing his hair. While he rolled, Gameknight reached into his inventory and pulled out the sword King Iago had given him on that floating island in Mystcraft so long ago.

Pressing the blood-red ruby in the pommel as he'd seen Entity303 do, Gameknight arose with his own blazing-hot infused-sword.

Entity303 growled at having missed his target. He tried a counter attack, swinging his blade at

Gameknight's midsection, but the User-that-is-not-a-user was ready. Their identical infused-swords clashed together in a shower of sparks that was brighter than the biggest firework.

"We destroyed one more," Crafter shouted. "Only the large one is left."

Gameknight didn't look; instead, with their blades locked, he stared into the surprised eyes of his enemy. Entity303 glanced at the blade in his hands, and growled.

"Iago," the user hissed.

Gameknight smiled.

"Now it ends," the User-that-is-not-a-user said. "Come on, Entity303 . . . let's dance."

The evil user snarled and pushed away, trying to kick the User-that-is-not-a-user hard in the leg. But growing up with a mischievous younger sister, Gameknight had learned to avoid kicks, and he dodged the attack.

Then, with his sword a blur, Gameknight999 slashed at his enemy, first hitting the tip of his sword, then sliding his blade down the keen edge until he was able to strike at his enemy's hand. The evil user snarled, then charged in a fury. Gameknight stepped aside and slashed at him as he moved past, tearing a chunk out of his Voidmetal armor. Entity303 threw a flurry of fast attacks aimed at Gameknight's head, then stomach, then shoulder, then neck . . . but the User-that-is-not-a-user blocked them all, then countered. He thrust his blade through Entity303's defenses, scoring hit after hit.

The evil user yelled in frustration, swinging his blade wildly. This was his chance. Gameknight stepped to the side, then sliced his blade against his enemy's wrist. He knocked the weapon out of his hand. The glowing sword skidded across the floor, stopping next to the giant single remaining Taintacle. Entity303 stepped back as Gameknight advanced, his hands in the air.

"Hunter, Stitcher, get over here," Gameknight shouted.

He heard the thud of boots pounding against the ancient stone floor.

"Well, what do we have here?" Hunter said, an arrow drawn back and aimed at Entity303.

"If he tries to flee, shoot him," Gameknight said. "If the Gateway of Light forms and he tries to escape to the physical world, shoot him. He doesn't leave this place until we all do . . . got it?"

"We understand," Stitcher said.

"This is gonna be fun," Hunter added with a snarl.

Gameknight turned and moved to Crafter's side. The last and largest of the Taintacles was almost touching the ceiling. It oozed some kind of green poison that had destroyed the many Fronosian creatures that had fallen within its grasp. Suddenly, the thing expanded and grew taller. The tip of the scaly, purple Taintacle was now just scraping the ceiling, leaving charred scratches on the gray stones overhead.

"Gameknight, we don't know how to attack this," Crafter said. "Anytime one of us get close enough, it stabs them, infecting them with its poison."

A strawberry with two tiny little feet and large black eyes walked in a daze across the floor of the chamber. It had somehow gotten past the line of wolves and was now moving right up to the monster. Without hesitation or mercy, the Taintacle slammed its thick body down upon the red creature. When it arose, the creature was shaded a sickly green, flashing as it took damage, then disappearing with a pop.

"Hey, that wasn't nice!" Herder shouted.

The wolves moved away from the chamber entrance and growled at the monster, Tux squawking loudly, her piercing voice rising above the others. The little penguin looked infuriated. She waddled right up to the Taintacle as if it were going to peck it with her little yellow beak. The thing writhed and shook.

"Digger, do something," Crafter shouted. "You're closest."

Squawk, squawk!

The Taintacle tried to slam its bulk down on top of the penguin, but she was able to step aside at just the last instant.

"Tux . . . get back," Digger shouted, his voice cracking with fear.

Squawk, squawk! she shouted—maybe it was her battle cry.

The Taintacle raised itself high in the air, then started its attack again, aiming right for Tux.

"No," Digger said, then sprinted for the penguin. "NOOOOO!"

Instead of picking up the penguin, Digger leapt high in the air and grabbed hold of the squirming Taintacle. He wrapped his arms and legs around it, his weight pulling the tip of the monster to the ground. Digger moaned as he flashed red, his armor taking most of the damage—his protection would completely fail soon if he didn't let go.

"Digger . . . NO!" Gameknight screamed.

He ran to his friend, but as he came close to the purple monster, he saw some of the hard, segmented plates that covered the monster's purple flesh were now spreading open, revealing the dark flesh that hid beneath.

"Everyone, attack the gaps!"

Gameknight swung his infused-sword at the soft tissue. It hit deep, making the creature flash red. Now Crafter and Weaver were adding their Ichorium blades to the fight, attacking different gaps. The User-that-is-not-a-user's sword was a bright yellow blur as he chopped at the Taintacle with all his strength.

He glanced at Digger. The three pechs were standing side by side, throwing healing potions on the stocky villager, giving him a few more minutes of life as the others attacked the monster. Each of the gnomes had their magical weapons in their hands in case they were needed, but that much magic unleashed on the monster might tear the fabric of Minecraft just as much as Entity303's creation. They didn't dare try to use them.

The monster flailed and tried to escape Digger's grasp, but the big villager refused to let go. The writhing creature flashed red as the villagers' blades bit deep into the creature's flesh. Flashing two more times, the terrible monster gave off a strange tearing sound, then finally disappeared. Digger fell to the ground, unconscious.

The pechs threw rejuvenation potions on him as Gameknight and his companions rushed to his side.

"Is he gonna be okay?" Herder asked.

The wolf pack leader licked Digger's face with his rough pink tongue.

"What do we do?" Weaver moaned.

Suddenly Hunter and Stitcher went skidding across the floor; Entity303 had used the distraction to knock the sisters aside. The evil user picked up Gameknight's discarded Ichorium sword and struck at the three pechs. He hit them again and again before anyone could move, causing them to fall to the ground, dropping their wands.

Reaching down, Entity303 quickly scooped up the magical weapons and held them in his right hand, the Ichorium sword in his left. He pointed the cluster of enchanted weapons at the sisters when they tried to stand up and retrieve their dropped bows. They stopped in their tracks.

"All of you back up and stand next to your hero, Gameknight999, or I let the two little girls have it with these wands," Entity303 growled.

They all stepped back, wary of the power the user held in his hand.

"Entity303, you need to be careful with those," Gameknight said. "We don't know what they'll do if you use them all at the same time. They could destroy everything."

"You're right, we don't know what they'll do," Entity303 said with a sneer. "Let's find out."

He glared at the three pechs, who were struggling to stand, then flicked his wrist and fired the three magical weapons at the helpless gnomes. Gameknight gasped, knowing nothing could survive all that magic, and all he could do was watch as the horrific scene unfolded before his eyes.

CHAPTER 34

THE THIRDS

Gameknight watched in utter horror as Entity303 used Empech's magical fishing pole, Forpech's gem-capped wand, and Trupech's metal-tipped staff on the three gnomes. Waves of magical power flowed from each of the three enchanted talismans. The sparkling energy washed over the three pechs, making them writhe and convulse in pain. They flashed red with damage; Gameknight didn't think they could last much longer. Each one shouted out in agony, as did Entity303. The evil user's face grimaced as the pain flowed through his own body as well as the pechs', but the vile, hateful expression on his square face never changed. He would likely never relent; he didn't care what pain he felt, as long as he could destroy these three creatures, as well as the whole of Minecraft at the same time.

The pechs continued to flash red, the bursts of crimson light from their little bodies getting brighter with each pulse. The flashing increased, the time between each throb of damaging red light getting shorter and shorter until the space between pulsations was no longer visible. In fact, the bodies of the pechs gave off such bright red light that Gameknight had to turn away.

He glanced at Entity303 and saw an expression of pain and surprise as the vile user howled in agony, his eyes wide with shock. He shook his hand, as if he were now trying to drop the enchanted weapons, but they refused to fall from his grasp, the magical power continuing to flow unabated.

Hunter and Stitcher ran toward the user, arrows drawn and ready to fire. Entity303 quickly turned the weapons on the sisters, his visage still one of anguish. Instantly, the girls fell to the floor, bathed in magical light. The sisters writhed and convulsed as they screamed in agony. Gameknight and Weaver ran forward to go to their aid, but Entity303 turned the wands on them. Instantly, the User-that-is-not-a-user was enveloped with an explosion of pain. Every nerve was aflame as the magical energy seemed to burn away at his very soul as if it were consuming him from the inside.

But, at the same time, the power of the pechs' magical tools linked Gameknight999 to his attacker. Empech's enchanted fishing pole allowed the User-that-is-not-a-user to feel the emotions of his attacker, and he felt so sad for his enemy. Deep inside, Entity303 was consumed by loneliness . . . such terrible loneliness. The evil user's feelings were dominated by such a profound sense of isolation that it hurt. Entity303 felt rejected by the entire world after being fired from the Minecraft development team, and rather than come to terms with his emotions and look inward at his own shortcomings so that he could correct them, he instead had chosen a path of revenge and destruction. Without any family or friends or his job helping program Minecraft, Entity303 felt as if he had nothing; he was completely alone.

Gameknight understood that feeling—he'd felt it himself many times at school: *I'm invisible . . . I'm useless . . . I'm alone.* And for some reason, whenever he was drowning in self-induced sorrow, that was when the bullies would strike, making him feel even more isolated. These feelings of loneliness and being a victim flowed back up through the stream of energy to his adversary; Entity303 was now feeling what Gameknight was feeling as well. Their eyes locked and they realized how similar they really were.

Their feelings then shifted from focusing on each other to focusing on themselves. Forpech's wand made Entity303 and Gameknight face their choices, acknowledging their successes, and, more importantly, accepting their failures. They were confronted by the feelings they'd caused others and forced to experience them all. Gameknight smiled as he experienced the emotions of his friends, how they felt comforted by his presence and accepted into their community. And there was something even deeper from one of them that the User-that-is-not-a-user did not fully understand. Through the connection of the magical energy, Entity303 felt that Gameknight999 was feeling wanted, feeling friendship . . . feeling love.

But then Entity303 groaned as he began to face the emotions he had caused in others. The evil user fell to his knees as he felt all the pain and sorrow he'd caused others, both in the physical world and in Minecraft. All of the people he'd wronged on the Minecraft development team materialized in his mind. Their emotions smashed into Entity303 with enormous impact, and, through Forpech's magic wand, into Gameknight999 as well. Then, the suffering of the innocent creatures Entity303 had tortured and destroyed in the digital lands of the game crashed down upon the two users. Gameknight arched his back as he felt imaginary swords and claws tear into him, just as the evil user's victims had felt. Entity303 fell to his side and moaned as the same thing happened to him.

The awareness that he'd caused these emotions surfaced in the evil user's mind. He'd done these things because of his own feelings of insecurity and loneliness, and, rather than deal with his own failures, he'd lashed out at others, hurting them. He had tried to make others suffer so his pain would somehow be more tolerable . . . but it hadn't worked, and he realized that now. Entity303 knew, instead of punishing others for his failures, that he would need to take ownership for his actions, and forgive himself as he tried to right the wrongs he caused. Maybe those he'd hurt would give him the smallest bit of forgiveness.

Then, the full power of Trupech's Staff of Truth smashed into the two users. The images of their true selves came crashing down upon them. Gameknight saw himself as a leader who was afraid and sometimes uncertain. He had known there were terrible monsters on the planets of Galacticraft, but he hadn't told his friends, for fear of being abandoned.

That's ridiculous, a voice said in his head. It was Hunter's voice; she was still in the stream of magic from the three wands. *We'd follow you anywhere.* Her thoughts were calm and peaceful. *I'd follow you anywhere.*

And me too, Stitcher's thoughts said in his mind.

Suddenly, Crafter reached out and grabbed Gameknight's hand, trying to take some of the damage onto himself to help his friend. Then Herder did the same, as did all his wolves. They piled on one another, hoping to share the damage, to keep their friends alive for just a moment longer.

Gameknight could feel the love they all had for each other, but especially for him. He was their glue, the thing that kept their family together, and they would do anything for him.

You think we wouldn't follow you because it was dangerous? Hunter thought. *Sometimes, you truly are an idiot.*

Stitcher laughed even though she was raked with pain, and then Hunter laughed as well. Soon, all of them were laughing and crying at the same time, the strength of their family holding back the damage.

But for Entity303, this was the harshest possible lesson. His true self was a selfish, bitter, childish person who needed his pride and ego constantly reinforced so that he could feel good about himself, even if it meant hurting others. He lacked any self-esteem because of how others avoided him, adding to his sense of isolation. But he also realized that his coworkers had stayed away, not because they wanted to exclude him, but because they felt their companionship was unwanted by him. As a result, Entity303 realized, he had always been the cause of his own isolation. And his loneliness had made him angrier and more bitter, which led to him pushing people even farther away. If he had only accepted himself, and come to terms with his strengths and weaknesses, and stopped driving others away, then he might have felt that which Gameknight999 did within Minecraft . . . a sense of belonging . . . a sense of community. He was a member of a family.

And, now that Entity303 had realized the source of his hostile actions, he was able to allow the feelings of being part of a group to flood through him.

Gameknight felt what Entity303 was experiencing and wanted to help. He reached out with his mind and drew the user closer.

What you have with your friends . . . that's what I want, Entity303 thought. *I never knew it before, because I was so focused on hurting others to hide my own pain, but that's not what I want anymore. Not revenge, but acceptance.*

Gameknight struggled to stand and face his adversary. *You get acceptance by letting people into your life*, he mentally told the user, *instead of shutting everyone out.*

But what if they won't accept me? asked Entity 303.

Try helping others first, Gameknight thought. *What you do for yourself dies when you die, but what you do for others creates ripples throughout their lives, even long after you're gone. What you do for others can live forever. Help people and they will accept you.*

As the magical power from the pechs' weapons slowly faded, Entity303 groaned in realization. "I'm the source of my own problems," he said. "I can change. I can become better. It's not necessary for me to hurt others."

And then, the flow of energy from the wands ceased, but the harsh light did not go away. The pechs were still glowing, the illumination so bright that they all had to turn away. It grew steadily more intense, as if the three gnomes were about to explode.

And then, suddenly, a bright flash of light filled the room. It didn't come from the wands or the pechs or the ground; it seemed to come from within each of them.

When the light had faded, and Gameknight's eyes had adjusted, he found the pechs were gone, and standing in their place was an old woman with wrinkled skin, and bright, steely gray eyes. In her hand, she held a crooked wooden cane, its end capped with metal.

It was the Oracle. *IT WAS THE ORACLE!*

Gameknight's head felt as if it were spinning, he was so confused.

"Oracle . . . you're here?!" Gameknight said, still struggling to stand. "YOU'RE HERE!"

"You don't need to yell, child, I'm right here," she said, her voice scratchy and aged.

"What are you doing here?" Gameknight asked. "What's happening? Where are the pechs?"

"Each of the pechs was a part of me all along. Empech was my empathy, Forpech was my forgiveness, and Trupech was my sense of truth and justice," the Oracle explained, smiling. "The mods that were loaded into Minecraft by Entity303 had fractured my artificial intelligence software code, splitting me into the Thirds. But now that the wands brought me together, I can continue the battle to protect Minecraft as a whole."

"I'm . . . sorry I did those things," Entity303 said. "I didn't understand. I thought my pain and loneliness came from others, that it was someone else's fault. But now I realize that I'm in control of myself, and I need to be responsible for myself. And it's time I helped fix the damage I caused."

"Well said, child." The old woman turned to the User-that-is-not-a-user. "I can't believe you didn't expect this," She pointed at Gameknight999 with her cane.

"How could I have known?" he asked.

"'*When the three became one*' . . . didn't you hear the prophecy?" the Oracle asked.

"Well . . . yeah, but I didn't think it meant you would—" Gameknight started to reply, but she cut him off.

"Really, child?" she replied, sarcastically. "'*The Music of Minecraft will return*' . . . you couldn't connect the dots?"

"Well . . . um . . ."

"'*Do the math?*' Didn't you hear that?" The Oracle shook her head, just like his favorite teacher, Ms. Shorey, always did whenever he forgot his homework.

Gameknight lowered his gaze, embarrassed and frustrated. But, just then, a beautiful melody floated through the air, filling the chamber and every occupant with soothing notes. Gameknight just stood there and smiled as the harmonious tones passed over him like a gentle spring breeze, carrying with them peace and contentment, and taking away any fear or uncertainty.

"No more time for questions," she replied. "We have much to do. The tear in the fabric of Minecraft has begun, and it's ripping through the pyramid of server planes as we speak."

She pointed to the ground near her feet. Thin cracks spread outward, bright white light shining from within. One of the cracks extended to the wall and just seemed to keep going, stretching out into the void that surrounded the Outer Lands.

"What can we do to stop it?" Gameknight asked.

"Yeah, what can we do to save Minecraft?" Entity303 added, wiping tears from his eyes.

Gameknight could see that the normal, hateful scowl that had seemed perpetually carved on the user's face was now gone, replaced by a softened and empathetic expression.

The Oracle glanced at the formerly evil user and smiled, then turned and pointed her cane at Weaver.

"We must get young Weaver back where he belongs," the old woman said. "And we don't have long before it's too late."

"So what do we do?" Gameknight asked.

"We go back to the Overworld," she replied.

"But how?" Hunter asked.

The old woman smiled, then turned her gaze to Digger. "We dig."

CHAPTER 35
THE OVERWORLD

"Digger, what happened back there with that Taintacle?" Gameknight asked. "You went from meek and afraid to a raging maniac."

"I couldn't just stand by and let Tux get hurt," Digger said. "She was bravely standing up to that monster, and I knew that if I didn't do something, Tux would be destroyed. Something sorta bubbled up from inside me. It was like a raging fire, or a pot boiling over, or . . ."

"Or maybe it was courage?" Hunter said quietly.

Digger nodded his head, his green eyes finally bright with bravery. "I'd let Topper down when I wasn't there for her. That wasn't gonna happen with Tux."

Squawk! the penguin added.

Digger reached down and patted the little animal on her fluffy head.

"But what good is digging gonna do? How will that get us back to the Overworld?" Gameknight said to the Oracle. "If we go back the way we came, we'd have to refuel the rocket, then fly back to where we started, which was on the sky islands of King Iago. And then we'd still need to use our Mystcraft linking book to get back to . . ."

"You forget, child, that we are still in the Twilight Forest."

"What are you saying?" Crafter said as he stood and helped the sisters to their feet.

"I am so disappointed in all of you," the old woman said. "You really should pay attention. You followed the first of the thirds into the Twilight Forest, remember?"

"Empech," Stitcher chimed in.

"Exactly." The Oracle's scratchy voice sounded like sandpaper scraping against a piece of hard wood. "Then you went into the Ages of Mystcraft."

"We used the books in that dungeon under the White Castle to follow him." Weaver said, pointing at Entity303.

"That's right," the Oracle said. "You used the books to go to the different worlds in Mystcraft. Then you used the rocket ships to get out here in space."

"So?" Hunter asked.

"So you're still in the Twilight Forest. Everything has happened from *inside* that mod." A huge grin spread across the Oracle's wrinkled, square face.

Entity303 nodded. "Yep, she's right. We're still in the Twilight Forest mod. There are just other mods running inside that one."

The old woman turned and faced Digger.

"Use your new pickaxes and dig up a four-by-four hole in the ground. Be careful not to fall in, as the void is on the other side."

Digger pulled out his Ichorium picks and tossed one to Weaver. The purple taint had mostly disappeared, since the source of the disease, the Taintacles, was gone, but a small bit still lingered. Digger found an area far from the bruised ground and, with Weaver at his side, started to dig. Chips of gray stone flew into the air as the duo tore into the ground, the sparkling void slowly showing its terrifying face beneath the slabs. The two villagers carved out a square of sixteen blocks in total, then turned and looked expectantly at the Oracle.

"Now put a line of dirt blocks around the edge," she said.

Crafter stepped forward. He pulled blocks of dirt from his inventory and walked to the hole. Moving carefully along the edge of the opening, he placed the brown blocks around the perimeter, leaving a two-by-two hole in the center. When he finished, he cast the Oracle a confused glance.

"Please fill the center with water, children," the old woman said.

"I have water," Herder said.

The lanky boy walked to the edge of the dirt with a bucket in his hands. He poured water onto the side of the dirt blocks and it spread partway across the opening. Then he pulled out more buckets and filled the remainder of the opening with the liquid so that there was a calm pool of water in the middle of the dirt.

"I see what you're doing," Gameknight said. "You're making a portal."

"Exactly," the Oracle replied. "Now, my favorite part."

She reached into her own inventory and pulled out a handful of tall sunflowers. She planted them in the cubes of dirt, the twelve tall plants all facing the same direction.

"We need one more thing," she said.

"A diamond," Gameknight said.

The Oracle nodded, her long gray hair waving back and forth.

"Does anyone have a diamond?" the User-that-is-not-a-user asked.

The companions glanced at one another, each holding out their hands, empty.

"I have one," Entity303 said. "I was saving it for . . . I don't know."

"Perhaps you were saving it for this moment," the Oracle said, her gray eyes shining bright.

Entity303 nodded, but looked uncertain. Gameknight could see the humbled expression on the user's face, as if he were still seeking forgiveness. The user stepped forward and looked at his former enemies, clearly uncertain how to behave now. But with the shared experience they'd all had through the magic of the pechs' magical weapons, these villagers were no longer his adversaries, but his comrades. It is impossible to be enemies when you understand another person's hopes and fears and desires, the user had come to understand. Communication has a way of bringing people together, even when they are as different as NPCs and users.

Gameknight nodded to Entity303.

Crafter flashed the user a smile.

Digger's bright green eyes approved.

They all understood what Entity303 had struggled with, for there were no more secrets amongst them.

Reaching into his inventory, the user pulled out a sparkling blue gem. It resembled a piece of ice and almost seemed to glow from within. He threw the diamond into the pool of water. Instantly, bright light filled the chamber as bolts of lightning stabbed down at the water, making it boil and froth. When the lightning faded, the water was now a sparkling purple instead of the translucent blue.

"How do we know when we jump in that we won't just pass through the portal and end up in the void?" Entity303 asked.

Hunter leaned over and stared down into the pool. "He makes a good point."

"I suppose you just need to have faith," said the Oracle.

Gameknight moved to the edge of the portal and gazed down at the sparkling surface. Small purple particles floated about near the edge of the magical surface, floating away for a brief moment, only to be drawn back into its lavender pool again.

"I'll go first," Entity303 said. "If I hit the void, you'll know because of my screams."

Before anyone could stop him, he jumped into the portal and disappeared.

They heard no screams of anguish.

"You think he's okay?" Hunter asked.

"I don't know," Gameknight said. "Let's find out."

With a determined expression on his square face, the User-that-is-not-a-user jumped into the portal and was instantly wrapped in chilling darkness.

CHAPTER 36

OMINOUS FOREST

The swirling blackness was icy cold, chilling Gameknight's skin and almost numbing his body.

Is this the void? he thought.

Jolts of fear ignited his nerves, making him start to panic. But before he could utter a sound, he materialized in a gray forest, a pale, featureless sky stretched out overhead. Instantly, a sour, biting taste filled his mouth. He inhaled and tasted it again; it was as if he were breathing something putrid and rotten. Around him, colorless grass, dead trees, and crumbling plants covered the landscape. Even the air in this desolate place seemed to be decaying. Then he realized he was back in the Ominous Forest.

At his feet sat the portal that had taken them into the Twilight Forest, the sparkling purple membrane pulsing as if it were alive.

"It's nighttime, we need to be cautious," a voice said from behind him.

Gameknight turned and found Entity303 standing with the Ichorium sword in his hand. The dull orange glow of the sword pushed the monotone gray pall back a bit and added a warm hue to the poisoned, dying biome. More of his friends materialized around the portal, each relieved to be out of the inky-black darkness. The Oracle was the last to emerge from the portal, her aged frame seeming frail and tired. She looked as if she was in pain.

"Are you OK?" Gameknight asked.

She nodded. "The tear in the fabric of Minecraft is moving faster . . . it . . . hurts."

"We need to hurry," the User-that-is-not-a-user said. "We must get Weaver back into the past before this server fails. Entity303, which way?"

Gameknight999 glanced at the user and found him on one knee. Reaching out, he was running his hand through the gray grass. It crumbled under his touch, turning to ash.

Entity303 glanced around at the deteriorating landscape. "Did I do this to the land? What was I thinking?"

No one answered.

"Let's deal with regrets later," Hunter said. "Right now, we need to deal with Weaver."

"Right." Entity303 stood. "It's to the east, come on."

He took off running, the rest of the party following. Gameknight moved next to the Oracle, ready to reach out and help if needed. Crafter moved to her other side, then cast Gameknight a worried glance. The old woman's skin was slowly losing its color, the wrinkles across her checks and neck becoming more pronounced. It was as if the tear in the fabric of Minecraft was somehow drawing on her life force. Even the wolves sensed her pain. They formed a circle of fur and fangs around the companions, the alpha male gently pushing Crafter aside so he could lope along at the Oracle's side.

The growls of a direwolf floated across the landscape, followed by the clicking of spiders, but the companions ignored the sounds. They all knew time was their real enemy now, and the only weapon that would help them was speed.

They wove their way through the desolate forest, the leafless trees like giant wooden skeletons watching them pass in silence. Suddenly, a huge group of spiders sprang out of the shadows. Gameknight noticed their eyes were now red again, instead of the green he'd seen in the planets of Galacticraft.

The wolves immediately fell on the fuzzy monsters, driving them back, but the spiders had superior numbers. Hunter and Stitcher stopped and fired upon the fuzzy giants, their arrows piercing the spiders' black, hairy bodies. Spiders screeched in pain, but they were not the only ones injured; wolves yelped as well.

"Keep going," Hunter said. "The wolves and Stitcher will help me take care of the spiders."

"I'm staying too," Herder said as he drew his Ichorium sword and charged into the battle. "We'll catch up with you. RUN!"

Gameknight didn't look back. He was worried about his friends, but he knew they could take care of themselves. The *TWANG* of their bows and the growls of the wolves grew softer as they continued to sprint toward the portal that would save all of Minecraft . . . if they got there in time.

The ground suddenly shook; it felt like an earthquake, but instead of the ground just shaking, it seemed to moan as well. A bright crack split the sky overhead, letting blinding light leak through the fissure. The sky tried to seal back up over the gash, but it just grew, stretching farther toward the horizon.

"What was that?" Crafter asked.

Gameknight stumbled and fell to the ground as the surface of the Overworld lurched under his feet. The Oracle fell to one knee, groaning in pain.

"It is beginning," the old woman said. "We have little time."

The User-that-is-not-a-user stood while Crafter helped the Oracle to her feet. They all glanced upward. Gameknight's mouth went dry as he stared up at the wound spreading slowly across the sky.

"Hurry," the Oracle said, her voice getting weak.

They kept running, following Entity303 across the dying landscape. In the distance, another biome was peeking past the dead trees and gray, dried bushes, but it was still too far to identify through the gray haze.

Finally, the companions reached the edge of the decaying wasteland. It was as if a gray and dusty funeral shroud that had covered the last biome was pulled away, revealing the next biome . . . a parched desert. When they passed into the new terrain, the dry, smoldering air slammed into each of them like a punch to the chest. But the dry sands and oppressive heat were a welcome relief to the decaying stench of the Ominous Forest, and now Gamenight999 could breathe without that acidic, vile-tasting air in his mouth.

They sprinted across the desert, not bothering to stay hidden. Zombies moved about across the pale sands, their sorrowful moans adding to the clicking of the spiders that hid behind the dunes. When the zombies spotted the party of villagers and users running across the dunes, they turned and pursued, their shuffling legs moving slowly. Their angry growls alerted the other monsters in the area, drawing all the hostile mobs within earshot to their position. Soon, all the monsters in the desert seemed to be heading directly for them.

Beyond the next dune, a silvery light seemed to paint the desert with a flickering illumination. When Entity303 reached the top of the sandy hill, he stopped.

"There it is," he said, pointing at a rectangle of diamond blocks, a shining film of silver filling the opening. "I'll stay back here and keep the monsters away," Entity303 said.

"Me too," Crafter drew his sword and turned to face the approaching host of monsters. "I think I'll stay here with our new friend, Entity303." The young villager turned toward Gameknight999. "You know, he's very much like you. He started off like a griefer, just like you did, and now he's fighting to save Minecraft . . . how ironic." He patted Entity303 on the back, then nodded to the big villager. "Digger, go with them. Make sure they make it to the portal. That's all that matters now!"

"Go, child," the Oracle said, her scratchy voice soft but firm. "We will give you enough time . . . now go!"

She gripped her cane like a sword, then moved toward the first zombie. The decaying monster swiped its claws at the old woman, but she was much faster than anyone expected. She ducked, struck at the monster, then moved to its side and hit it again and again, her cane flashing bright with each attack. The monster flashed red each time it was hit until it disappeared with a pop. All of the companions stood and stared, stunned by her prowess in battle.

"GO!" she shouted, then turned and faced a spider, now with Crafter and Entity303 at her side. Behind the spider, more monsters were approaching.

"Digger, take him . . . now!" Crafter shouted.

The stocky NPC grabbed Gameknight's arm and pulled him away from the battle. They ran down the hill, heading straight for the diamond portal that shone in the darkness. Gameknight sprinted as fast as he could go, with Weaver just a pace or two ahead. Digger was a few paces behind, but the sound of his heavy boots pounding the sand was reassuring.

The sound of battle filled the air behind them, with monsters screeching out in pain and swords clashing with claws and fangs, but the User-that-is-not-a-user knew he couldn't stop or even look back. If he saw his friends in trouble, he'd want to go back and help. But that was not his job. Right now, his only task was to get Weaver through that portal.

Suddenly, the ground shook again, this time much more violently. A huge fissure opened beneath Gameknight999 and Weaver, causing the duo to stumble for a moment. Then the ground just disappeared, throwing the two of them into open air.

Dropping his sword, the User-that-is-not-a-user reached out and grabbed Weaver's wrist as they tumbled through the air. Their forward momentum carried them to the opposite side of the newly-formed ravine as they fell, hitting the far side four blocks below the top. Gameknight, fortunately, landed on a single block of stone that stuck out from the sheer wall of the ravine. The impact nearly knocked the wind from his chest, making him see stars for a moment, his head reeling. Every part of his body ached, with pain on top of pain, but he refused to loosen his grip. He held onto Weaver's hand as if the boy's life depended on it . . . and it did—the NPC was dangling over the edge.

Below, the deep fissure was slowly filling with lava. Waves of heat and ash wafted up from the liquid inferno, reminding both of them of the precariousness of their position. The only thing keeping Weaver from falling into the boiling stone was Gameknight's grip.

"Weaver, are you OK?" the User-that-is-not-a-user asked.

"I can't hold on for much longer," the boy replied.

"No, you hold on, I'll pull you up."

Using every ounce of his strength, the User-that-is-not-a-user tried to lift his friend, but the sprint through the forest and the desert, and the impact when they fell, had left him drained. He pulled harder, trying to raise the boy just enough so that he could get his hand on the edge . . . but he lacked the strength.

I can't do it, Gameknight thought. *I don't have the strength to lift him. What am I gonna do?*

"No . . . not again . . . NOT AGAIN!" a booming voice said from the other side of the fissure.

Digger was standing on the far side of the ravine, at least six blocks away . . . an impossible distance to jump in Minecraft.

"Digger, you can't make that jump . . . it's impossible," Gameknight said.

"I refuse to be too late this time!" the stocky NPC said. "I was too late to save my Topper, too late to save those villagers on Diona, and my lack of courage almost caused Tux to get hurt. I won't let it happen again. I'm not losing you, too!"

Digger grumbled something else, then started taking off his Ichorium armor. He cast the softly glowing metal aside, then dumped the contents of his inventory on the ground, everything. In the dim lighting, Gameknight couldn't quite make out everything he was doing; it seemed as if he was putting something back on, but the User-that-is-not-a-user couldn't tell for sure.

"Just hold on!" Digger shouted, then sprinted toward the edge of the crevasse.

"Digger, you can't make it . . . nooooo!"

But the big NPC didn't stop. He sprinted to the edge of the huge ravine, then leapt into the emptiness, his voice filling the air as he yelled, "FOR TOPPER!"

Slowly, gravity reached out with its relentless hand and pulled the big villager downward. Suddenly, Digger leaned forward and a pair of Elytra wings hidden behind his broad shoulders snapped open. The wings gave him enough lift to just barely make it across the chasm. He slammed into the opposite wall and slid downward, landing right next to Gameknight999.

"Digger, that was incredible," Gameknight said, but the big NPC did not reply, just reached down and grabbed Weaver's wrist. Lifting him as if he weighed nothing, Digger pulled him onto the block, then hoisted him up on top of his shoulders.

"Weaver, climb," he said.

"I can't reach the top," Weaver replied.

Digger grabbed the boy's ankles, then shoved him upward with all his strength, propelling him toward the edge of the ravine. The boy sailed into the air as if he were wearing a jet pack. He tumbled onto the sandy desert floor, safely out of the fissure. Quickly, Weaver extended a hand down for Gameknight. The ground shook again, causing the fissure to open even wider. Blocks of sand and stone fell into the river of lava that now filled the bottom of the crevasse.

"Gameknight, you're next," Digger said.

"But how will you get up?" Gameknight asked.

His friend moved close, his big green eyes filled with sadness.

"I'm not important," the big NPC replied.

"NO! I won't leave you here."

"I want my Topper back. The pain and guilt is too much; I can't bear it anymore. But if you get Weaver back into the past, then the timeline will be repaired, and Topper won't have to die. You *must* do this for me. You must get Weaver back where he belongs."

His deep voice lowered to barely a whisper. Tears flowed from his eyes.

"Please . . . I'm begging you. Bring back my Topper."

The ground shook again, this time more violently.

Gameknight sighed. "Okay."

Digger grabbed him by the waist and tossed him up onto his shoulders. The stocky NPC then shoved him up so that the User-that-is-not-a-user was standing on his shoulders.

"Gameknight, take my hand," Weaver said.

The user looked down at his friend one last time.

"Don't worry, I'll get Weaver back."

"Thank you," Digger replied. "You have always been like a brother to me. Now go!"

Digger shoved him into the air with every ounce of strength, sending him flying as he did Weaver. Gameknight landed atop Weaver in a tangle of arms and legs. Before them, the diamond portal hummed with power, a silvery light splashing down upon them.

Gameknight stood, then yanked Weaver to his feet. The ground shook again, causing more rifts to open across the Overworld, as if a giant were slashing away at the landscape with a razor-sharp knife.

"We have to go . . . now!" Gameknight exclaimed.

"What if this doesn't work?"

"Ahh . . . I don't know, but we have no choice."

The two companions moved to the portal and dove through the silvery opening, just as the Overworld groaned one more time, then fell away as if it were being eaten by some gigantic monster, the entire landscape disappearing into the void.

CHAPTER 37
THROUGH THE LOOKING GLASS

A wall of heat slammed into Gameknight999. Sweat rained down his forehead and seeped into his eyes. It stung and made it difficult to see.

"Gameknight, get up before they see you," Weaver said in a low voice.

In a flash, he realized where he was; it was the Nether, and this was the end of the Great Zombie Invasion. Jumping to his feet, he moved around behind the portal. In the distance, he could see Notch floating in the air over the Netherrack plain, the great lava ocean boiling nearby. All of the villagers were gone. A few zombie-pigmen shuffled about, searching for the thing that would change them back to their original form. Gameknight knew they would never find it, for it was their punishment for the violence they had brought down upon Minecraft.

"We need to destroy this portal before anyone spots it," Gameknight said. "But I lost my diamond pickaxe; I have nothing to destroy it with."

"I can take care of it, I think," Weaver said. He pulled the Ichorium pickaxe from his inventory and swung it with all his might. The softly glowing tool dug into the diamond blocks that ringed the portal. As soon as one block was destroyed, the shining membrane that filled the center instantly winked out.

"Keep going," Gameknight said. Weaver continued to dig, destroying each of the glacial-blue cubes until they were all destroyed.

"What should we do with the blocks?" the young boy asked.

"Well . . . you use them to help others," Gameknight said.

"What about this?" Weaver asked, holding out the Ichorium pickaxe.

"You know you can't keep it."

The young boy sighed. "I know, but you can't believe how easy it is to dig with it."

"Weaver, no one has ever seen anything like that. Keeping it will alter the timeline."

"I knowwww . . ." the boy moaned.

Holding the pick high in the air, he threw it into the lava ocean. It hit the molten stone and made a *splop* sort of sound, then sank under its glowing surface.

"You remember where the portal is located that will get you back to the Overworld from here?" Gameknight asked.

Weaver nodded.

"You know, you can't tell anyone about any of this."

"I know," Weaver replied. "Don't worry, I can keep a secret. In fact, I've been keeping an even bigger secret about what someone thinks about you for a while now. So, you see . . . I *can* keep a secret."

Gameknight was about to ask what the secret was, but the young boy raised his hand and held it in front of his friend's square face.

"Talk to the hand," he said with a smile.

Just then, there was a clap of thunder. Bolts of lightning stabbed at the landscape of the Nether; Minecraft's designer, Notch, was likely resetting some aspect of the game.

"It's safe for you to go now," Gameknight said.

"Will I see you again?" Weaver asked.

"Well . . . I don't know, for sure," Gameknight said. "My father's invention, the Digitizer, brought me here once. Maybe it will do it again."

Weaver nodded, trying to appear strong, but moisture began to form in the corners of his eyes.

"You need to take care of everyone in Smithy's village. There are lots of important people there who will be critical to the defeat of Herobrine in the future. You know I can't tell you who or why—just make sure everyone stays safe."

"I can do that, Gameknight . . . ahhh . . . I mean Smithy."

Weaver turned and started heading up the Netherrack hill to the portal that had brought them here so long ago, but then stopped. He turned and gave Gameknight one last gaze.

"I'll never forget our time together and the things you've taught me," the boy said, a tear streaming down his cheek for a moment before it evaporated in the heat of the Nether. "You can be sure I'll be watching for your return, Gameknight999. Maybe our time together isn't over . . . yet."

Then Weaver turned, sprinted up the hill, and was gone.

I hope he keeps these secrets, Gameknight thought as he watched him run from sight. *If he tells anything about their adventures, it could do incalculable damage to the timeline.*

But Gameknight knew all he could do is trust his friend and hope for the best. With a sigh, the User-that-is-not-a-user wiped tears from his eyes. He'd been through so much just to get back here. He felt as if he'd gone full circle. He'd helped to defeat Herobrine in the past *and* in the present. He'd stopped Herobrine's monster kings, and finally prevented Entity303 from destroying Minecraft. There was a feeling of completeness to his adventure. Maybe the threats to Minecraft were finally gone. A zombie pigman moaned nearby. It almost felt reassuring if all they had to worry about was zombie pigmen. He had a good feeling that Minecraft was going to be all right.

Gameknight breathed a sigh of relief and closed his eyes. He concentrated on his keyboard and imagined himself typing the word *EXIT*. Suddenly, he was surrounded by a ball of white light. It felt as if daggers of ice were stabbing at him, while at the same time he was on fire. The heat and cold grew more intense until he thought he might perish . . . and then a blanket of darkness wrapped around him, causing him to lose all sense of touch or sound or sight. It was as if he was adrift in a starless section of outer space.

Then Gameknight999 vanished from Minecraft.

CHAPTER 38

HOME

Tommy woke with a start. His head pounded, not because he'd hit it on the table when he'd been drawn into Minecraft, and not because of any effect from the Digitizer. It was likely because of all the pain and sorrow and fear and loss of this last adventure.

He thought about the last time he'd seen his friends. Digger had been standing on that lone block of stone, trapped in the ravine that was slowly crumbling apart. Gameknight had left all of his friends in that damaged timeline, each in mortal peril. Sadness swept through him as he glanced around at the safety of his cluttered basement.

"I hope you're okay, my friend," he said softly, a tear trickling down his cheek.

As he sat up, Tommy noticed his cheek was wet; he'd drooled again. He always seemed to do that when he was using the Digitizer to go into Minecraft. Using a tissue, he mopped up the moisture, then looked up at his screen.

"I have to see if they're all right. I have to see if the timeline has been fixed."

Quickly, Tommy logged back into Minecraft, then flipped the switch on the Digitizer. Instantly, a buzzing sound filled the basement. It grew louder and louder. Then the beam hit him, filling his body with the all-too-familiar feeling of fire and ice. The room seemed to spin around him, making Tommy feel dizzy. It spun faster and faster, then slowly collapsed, as if he were being sucked down a drain.

Suddenly, he was back . . . Gameknight was back in Minecraft. He'd appeared near a waterfall that streamed down from a rocky outcropping high overhead. It splashed into a small pool, the spray from the water coating his face with a fine mist.

He was definitely back.

Running to the side of the mountain, he punched the dirt blocks where he'd originally hidden his hidey-hole when he had first arrived in Minecraft. The blocks shattered, revealing torchlight from within. Gameknight smiled. He broke the other blocks and ran into the base. He found his furnace and chests right where they should have been. Throwing open the wooden box, he grabbed some iron armor, some arrows, a bow and a sword, then took off. He sprinted across the landscape toward the village he knew lay hidden behind the hills and trees.

The sun was high in the sky, but he was still worried about monsters. When he'd been in the past, the zombies and skeletons could walk about in broad daylight. That experience had him still a little nervous. Fortunately, he didn't hear any monsters nearby . . . maybe daytime wasn't monster time in this Minecraft? That would be a very good sign.

Gameknight sped across the terrain, not slowing for anything. He could feel his pulse pounding through his veins and his heart thumping in his chest. A faint whisper of fear floated about in the back of his mind. It wasn't fear of zombies or spiders. It wasn't fear of Herobrine or anyone else. It wasn't a fear of any creature he might find in Minecraft; it was a fear of whom he might *not* find.

"I hope you're OK, Digger," Gameknight said to himself. "It was wrong to leave you in the ravine. I'll never forgive myself if you were hurt . . . or worse."

He didn't want even to consider what might have happened to him.

"Hunter and Stitcher . . . last time I saw you, both of you were holding back a huge group of spiders with Herder at your side," Gameknight said as he swerved around an oak tree—a nice, normal looking oak tree, he noticed. He smiled as the smallest bit of apprehension seemed to evaporate from the looming specter of fear that had taken up residence in the back of his mind.

"And Crafter, you were holding off the monsters of the desert with Entity303 and the Oracle. I hope you're all okay."

As he dove through the diamond portal, Gameknight had thought he saw the entire world being torn apart; all of his friends would have died in that catastrophe. His blood turned cold when he imagined them suffering.

"No . . . they must be okay! I won't consider any other possibility. I put Weaver back into the past. We must have repaired the timeline."

Unless Weaver told of their adventures and changed the timeline again, he thought.

The fear in the back of his mind slowly took bites out of his courage, making his legs feel weak.

"No, I refuse to consider the *what-ifs*!" he growled.

Gameknight sprinted up a grassy hill, his nerves stretched to the limit. Crafter's village would be just on the other side. When he crested that peak, would he see what he hoped was there, or would he find death and destruction? Would he find Minecraft completely reset, and his friends converted back to just mindless pieces of code?

He slowed to a walk as he approached the top of the hill, almost afraid to peer over the peak. But he knew he had to see; he owed it to his friends. Moving to the peak, the User-that-is-not-a-user closed his eyes until he felt the east-to-west breeze on his cheeks, which meant the hill was no longer shielding him from the wind. He knew he was at the top. All he had to do was look.

Slowly, he opened his eyes and gazed down on the landscape. His heart skipped a beat.

The view below was stunning in its beauty. A tall cobblestone wall surrounded the community, a soaring stone watch tower standing guard over the village. Next to the village was Gameknight's own obsidian castle, the tall rectangular keep surrounded by circular walls.

The User-that-is-not-a-user smiled . . . so far, so good.

He sprinted down the hill and across the grassy plain, yelling at the top of his lungs.

"The User-that-is-not-a-user is here," one of the guards shouted. "Open the gates!"

The iron doors swung open as he approached. His boots thumped as he crossed the wooden bridge that spanned the deep, watery moat. Gameknight shot through the doors and began yelling.

"Crafter, Digger . . . where are you? Hunter, Stitcher, Herder . . . come quick!"

This put the village into a panic. Warriors ran to the walls, and archers filled the towers as cavalry found their mounts and assembled around the village well.

"What's going on?" Hunter yelled as she ran to him. "Are we under attack?"

A whistle pierced the air. Suddenly, Herder and his wolves appeared, the animals' eyes glowing red; they were ready for battle.

Crafter ran to him, with Stitcher at his side. Gameknight looked at all of them and breathed a sigh of relief.

"You're all okay?" the User-that-is-not-a-user asked.

"Why wouldn't we be OK?" Hunter asked.

"Where's Digger?" Gameknight asked frantically. "I don't see Digger. Where is he? Where is he?"

"I'm over here," a voice boomed from behind.

The stocky NPC emerged from the blacksmith's shop with his son, Filler, at his side. Villagers began filing out of their homes and shops, surrounding the companions, wanting to hear the discussion.

"Digger, you're okay . . . I'm so relieved. You have no idea what I've been through . . . but . . . where's Topper? I don't see Topper! Where's Topper . . . WHERE'S TOPPER?!"

Suddenly, a child shot out from behind the village well and dove at Gameknight999. The girl barreled into him, wrapping tiny arms and legs around his iron armor.

"Gameknight . . . you're home!" a young voice said.

Instantly, the User-that-is-not-a-user recognized the voice.

"Topper, it's you! Oh, I can't believe it, you're all right. I'm so happy. I'm just so happy!"

Gameknight wept tears of joy as he hugged Topper with all his strength, then scooped up her twin, Filler, and hugged them tight. He glanced at Digger and gave him a smile that stretched from ear to ear.

"I'm so glad you're all alive."

"Gameknight, what is going on?" Crafter asked. "You're acting really weird."

He carefully put the children on the ground, then turned to face his friends.

"You won't believe what happened. I went back in time to the Great Zombie Invasion. I met your great ancestor Weaver, and helped them to battle Herobrine just after the Awakening. And then a user, Entity303, messed everything up when he kidnapped Weaver and brought him into the future . . . well, I mean the present, but it already happened, so I guess it's the past, but . . . I don't know, it's very confusing. I'm sure none of you believe me. But anyways, we finally rescued Weaver and sent him back into his past. I told him to not tell anyone about this so that the timeline would remain unchanged, and it seems he kept his word."

"Well . . ." Crafter said with a smile.

"Well . . . what?" Gameknight asked.

"We believe you," Stitcher said, grinning.

"Why are you all smiling?" the User-that-is-not-a-user asked. "What's going on?"

"We believe you because Weaver . . . well, he sort of told people about it," Crafter said. "He wrote it down a hundred years ago. All of the villagers know, and have known for a long time."

"What?" Gameknight asked. "That can't be . . . none of you said anything, I mean, if you'd known, then . . ."

"Smithy be crazy, that's for sure," Hunter said with a smile, then broke out laughing.

"Smithy be crazy . . ." another villager said, followed by, "Smithy of the Two-swords be totally crazy."

The villagers laughed and patted him on the back, many of them hugging him and continuing to laugh.

"It was actually Crafter who figured it out," Stitcher said. "He found a book written by Weaver in a stronghold library. It explained the whole thing."

Gameknight turned and faced his friend. Crafter looked embarrassed and a little afraid.

"You knew?"

Crafter nodded. "I couldn't say anything and risk having you make a different decision; we couldn't damage your timeline. He cleverly hid the information in a book that I accidently found."

"How could he do that?" the User-that-is-not-a-user growled. "I told him to keep this a secret. He even told me he was good at keeping secrets, but he ended up telling it anyway."

"He wanted everyone to know what kind of hero Gameknight999 was . . . *is*. That's why he put it in the book," Crafter explained. "You can't blame him, Weaver was your biggest fan."

"I know, but . . ."

Suddenly, words scrolled through his head. *SON, IT'S TIME FOR DINNER. TELL YOUR FRIENDS GOODBYE.* It was his father texting to him through Minecraft.

"I know that look," Hunter said, her chocolate brown eyes now filled with sadness. "You have to go, don't you?"

He nodded.

"When will you come back?" Stitcher asked.

"I don't know; my dad has been telling me to use the Digitizer less. He's afraid there may be some health risks to using it a lot. I think he'll shut me down for a while, but don't worry. Nothing will keep me out of Minecraft forever."

Hunter smiled, then punched him in the arm.

"Ouch, what was that for?" Gameknight asked, rubbing his shoulder.

"Just so you won't forget about me."

"Hunter, I could never forget about any of you. You're my family, and when I . . ."

Suddenly, a bright ball of light enveloped him. Gameknight shut his eyes, trying to block the brilliant illumination, but it seemed to come from inside him. Waves of heat and chilling cold washed over him as his nerves seemed to ignite, electrifying his entire body. The light grew brighter and brighter until . . .

Tommy woke again, the puddle of drool not as large this time. He sat up and found his father standing behind him, shutting down the Digitizer. He shook his head, trying to dislodge the ache that always resided there after using his dad's invention.

"You okay?" his father asked.

Tommy nodded and smiled.

"Everything is okay now, I think."

"Good," his dad replied. "I think you've been spending a little too much time inside Minecraft recently."

"Awww . . . Daaaad." Tommy stood, knowing what was coming. "But Minecraft is so . . ."

His father raised a hand, silencing the prepared complaint; they'd had this discussion many times, and they both knew the script.

"I know you love Minecraft, so I got you something you could do that's still Minecrafty, but you won't be locked away down here in the basement."

He pulled out a book and handed it to his son. Gameknight read the title aloud:

"*Zombies Attack!*"

The cover had a picture of an NPC about to fire an enchanted bow and arrow. In the background, he saw the faint image what appeared like a terrifying zombie.

"This looks interesting," he said as he took the book from his father's hand.

"Maybe you could do a little reading . . . and maybe even some writing," his dad said. "I was thinking—you should write down these adventures you've been having, and maybe get them published."

"You think I could?" Tommy asked, a flare of excitement in his eyes.

"Why not? You could write them, and I could do the editing. I'll put your name in the book as the Technical Consultant. And when it's time to self-publish them, we'd have to do it under my name. You know how careful I always want you to be when it comes to disclosing personal information on the Internet."

"Yessss . . . Daaaad," Tommy moaned; that was his only line in that dialogue.

He inspected the book closely, then headed for the stairs.

"I think I'm gonna read this book first . . . it looks cool. Then I'll start writing out my adventures. Who knows—it might be cool to be an author."

"I wouldn't know anything about that," his father replied.

"I'm gonna read a little before dinner," Tommy said as he ran up the stairs. "Hope that's okay!"

Before leaving the basement, he glanced back at the Digitizer and thought about all the adventures he'd had through that machine, from meeting Crafter for the first time, to meeting all his other friends, to even going into outer space.

"What a ride it's been," he said softly. "I can't wait to start writing. But first, I'll do some reading."

He bolted out of the basement and headed for the sofa, the new book held firmly in his hands, ready to begin a new adventure.

MINECRAFT SEEDS

I hope you enjoyed our adventures in outer space with the Galacticraft mod. You also saw some of the Thaumcraft mod at the end of the story on planet Fronos. Both of these mods are incredible and can be downloaded to your Minecraft.

As I explained in the last couple of books, adding mods to Minecraft and getting them to work correctly has always been a challenge for me. Instead, I've learned to use Feed-The-Beast or my now-favorite, the Curse Client.

To load Thaumcraft, I found it easier to either download Feed-the-Beast, https://www.feed-the-beast.com/, and then use the DireWolf20 modpack, which worked really well on my Macbook (be sure to get your parent's permission), but you can also download the Curse Twitch Client, https://mods.curse.com/client, which is another way to run modded Minecraft. Here is a video with DireWolf20 showing how to use the newer Curse Client: https://youtu.be/lf2y1D8wMdU. Be aware, running modded Minecraft takes a lot of resources on your computer. On my PC, I can't run either the Curse Client or Feed-the-Beast, because it just gets too laggy—my PC is too old. So you may also run into issues if you try these. Please be sure to ask your parent's permission before downloading anything.

It is important to note: Galacticraft is not part of the DireWolf20 Modpack, but if you search for it in Curse Client, you'll find it in the Interplanetary Tech mudpack or the Space Astronomy mudpack. Both work really well and have the More Planets add-on, so you'll get the additional solar systems that enable you to reach Fronos and the delicious Candy Land.

Sadly, I still don't have any Minecraft seeds for you, because you need to use the mod to see the different planets. If you don't have Galacticraft, you can see numerous videos on YouTube, with your parent's permission. Here are some of my favorites:

Galacticraft Overview 1: https://youtu.be/ZY6a8YjJB04

Galacticraft Overview 2: https://youtu.be/r0aGwD919s0

Blasting off from the Overworld: https://youtu.be/ZY6a8YjJB04

Setting up a moon base and moon village: https://youtu.be/CSUIxVtNMYY

Moon Boss: https://youtu.be/CoQdA4BFlOA

Mars Boss: https://youtu.be/RdQpi1wdlxE

Planet Fronos: https://youtu.be/goGMNGLoybE

AVAILABLE NOW FROM MARK CHEVERTON AND SKY PONY PRESS

THE GAMEKNIGHT999 SERIES
The world of Minecraft comes to life in this thrilling adventure!

Gameknight999 loved Minecraft, and above all else, he loved to grief—to intentionally ruin the gaming experience for other users.

But when one of his father's inventions teleports him into the game, Gameknight is forced to live out a real-life adventure inside a digital world. What will happen if he's killed? Will he respawn? Die in real life? Stuck in the game, Gameknight discovers Minecraft's best-kept secret, something not even the game's programmers realize: the creatures within the game are alive! He will have to stay one step ahead of the sharp claws of zombies and pointed fangs of spiders, but he'll also have to learn to make friends and work as a team if he has any chance of surviving the Minecraft war his arrival has started.

With deadly Endermen, ghasts, and dragons, this action-packed trilogy introduces the heroic Gameknight999 and has proven to be a runaway publishing smash, showing that the Gameknight999 series is the perfect companion for Minecraft fans of all ages.

Invasion of the Overworld (Book One):
$9.99 paperback • 978-1-63220-711-1

Battle for the Nether (Book Two):
$9.99 paperback • 978-1-63220-712-8

Confronting the Dragon (Book Three):
$9.99 paperback • 978-1-63450-046-3

AVAILABLE NOW FROM MARK CHEVERTON AND SKY PONY PRESS

THE MYSTERY OF HEROBRINE SERIES
Gameknight999 must save his friends from an evil virus intent on destroying all of Minecraft!

Gameknight999 was sucked into the world of Minecraft when one of his father's inventions went haywire. Trapped inside the game, the former griefer learned the error of his ways, transforming into a heroic warrior and defeating powerful Endermen, ghasts, and dragons to save the world of Minecraft and his NPC friends who live in it.

Gameknight swore he'd never go inside Minecraft again. But that was before Herobrine, a malicious virus infecting the very fabric of the game, threatened to destroy the entire Overworld and escape into the real world. To outsmart an enemy much more powerful than any he's ever faced, the User-that-is-not-a-user will need to go back into the game, where real danger lies around every corner. From zombie villages and jungle temples to a secret hidden at the bottom of a deep ocean, the action-packed adventures of Gameknight999 and his friends (and, now, family) continue in this thrilling follow-up series for Minecraft fans of all ages.

Trouble in Zombie-town (Book One):
$9.99 paperback • 978-1-63450-094-4

The Jungle Temple Oracle (Book Two):
$9.99 paperback • 978-1-63450-096-8

Last Stand on the Ocean Shore (Book Three):
$9.99 paperback • 978-1-63450-098-2

AVAILABLE NOW FROM MARK CHEVERTON AND SKY PONY PRESS

HEROBRINE REBORN SERIES
Gameknight999 and his friends and family face Herobrine in the biggest showdown the Overworld has ever seen!

Gameknight999, a former Minecraft griefer, got a big dose of virtual reality when his father's invention teleported him into the game. Living out a dangerous adventure inside a digital world, he discovered that the Minecraft villagers were alive and needed his help to defeat the infamous virus, Herobrine, a diabolical enemy determined to escape into the real world.

Gameknight thought Herobrine had finally been stopped once and for all. But the virus proves to be even craftier than anyone could imagine, and his XP begins inhabiting new bodies in an effort to escape. The User-that-is-not-a-user will need the help of not only his Minecraft friends, but his own father, Monkeypants271, as well, if he has any hope of destroying the evil Herobrine once and for all.

Saving Crafter (Book One):
$9.99 paperback • 978-1-5107-0014-7

Destruction of the Overworld (Book Two):
$9.99 paperback • 978-1-5107-0015-4

Gameknight999 vs. Herobrine (Book Three):
$9.99 paperback • 978-1-5107-0010-9

AVAILABLE NOW FROM MARK CHEVERTON AND SKY PONY PRESS

HEROBRINE'S REVENGE SERIES
From beyond the digital grave, Herobrine has crafted some evil games for Gameknight999 to play!

Gameknight999, a former Minecraft griefer, got a big dose of virtual reality when his father's invention teleported him into the game. Living out a dangerous adventure inside a digital world, he trekked all over Minecraft, with the help of some villager friends, in order to finally defeat a terrible virus, Herobrine, who was trying to escape into the real world.

Gameknight thought that Herobrine was gone for good. But as one last precaution before his death, the heinous villain laid traps for the User-that-is-not-a-user that would threaten all of the Overworld, even if the virus was no longer alive. Now Gameknight is racing the clock, trying to stop Herobrine from having one last diabolical laugh.

The Phantom Virus (Book One):
$9.99 paperback • 978-1-5107-0683-5

Overworld in Flames (Book Two):
$9.99 paperback • 978-1-5107-0681-1

System Overload (Book Three):
$9.99 paperback • 978-1-5107-0682-8

AVAILABLE NOW FROM MARK CHEVERTON AND SKY PONY PRESS

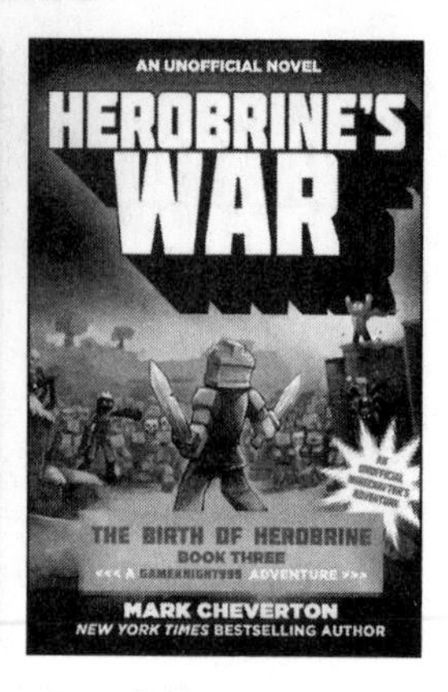

THE BIRTH OF HEROBRINE SERIES
Can Gameknight999 survive a journey one hundred years into Minecraft's past?

A freak thunderstorm strikes just as Gameknight999 is activating his father's Digitizer to re-enter Minecraft. Sparks flash across his vision as he is sucked into the game . . . and when the smoke clears he's arrived safely. But it doesn't take long to realize that things in the Overworld are very different.

The User-that-is-not-a-user realizes he's been accidentally sent a hundred years into the past, back to the time of the historic Great Zombie Invasion. None of his friends have even been born yet. But that might be the least of Gameknight999's worries, because traveling back in time also means that the evil virus Herobrine, the scourge of Minecraft, is still alive . . .

The Great Zombie Invasion (Book One):
$9.99 paperback • 978-1-5107-0994-2

Attack of the Shadow-crafters (Book Two):
$9.99 paperback • 978-1-5107-0995-9

Herobrine's War (Book Three):
$9.99 paperback • 978-1-5107-0996-7

AVAILABLE NOW FROM MARK CHEVERTON AND SKY PONY PRESS

TERRORS OF THE FOREST
The Mystery of Entity303 Book One: A Gameknight999 Adventure

Minecraft mods are covering the tracks of a mysterious new villain!

Gameknight999 reenters Minecraft to find it completely changed. Villages are larger than ever and more heavily fortified; life inside the game has become much more dangerous. Even Gameknight's old friends are acting differently, and the changes are not for the better.

Outside of Crafter's village, a strange user named Entity303 is spotted with Weaver, a young NPC Gameknight knows from Minecraft's past. He realizes that Weaver has somehow been kidnapped, and returning him to the correct time is the only way to fix things.

The User-that-is-not-a-user races to catch Entity303 and rescue his friend, but they quickly disappear into a strange portal that leads to the Twilight Forest modded version of the game. How can there be mods here in the vanilla Minecraft? Just how dangerous is this new user to Minecraft, and what are his plans for Weaver? Only Gameknight999 will be able to find out.

$9.99 paperback • 978-1-5107-1886-9

THE RISE OF THE WARLORDS

AN UNOFFICIAL INTERACTIVE MINECRAFTER'S ADVENTURE

I'm very excited about this next series, *The Rise of the Warlords.* The first book in the series is called *Zombies Attack!* (it's the same book Tommy's dad gave him at the end of this one!) As you have probably already guessed, I'm using some new characters in this series. I've been thinking about them for a long time, and have written some short stories about them. You can find *Battle with the Wither King* here: http://gameknight999.com/downloads/. These characters, like Watcher and Blaster and Planter, will bring something new and unique to my stories, and I'm really excited to have you meet them. Watcher, like some of the characters you already know, is incredible with a bow, but his eyesight is something unique and special. Planter has a great sense of compassion and a peaceful nature; I already want to hang out with her. But be careful, she can fight with her enchanted blade, named Needle, and doesn't understand the word *quit*. And I think Blaster will be a favorite. As you can imagine, Blaster really likes blowing things up, but he's also a great fighter with his two curved knives. I think you're gonna love these people . . . I know I already do.

The series is set in the Far Lands. For those you who have been playing Minecraft for a long time, you might remember the Far Lands in some of the earlier versions of the game. Maybe you were even caught in a glitch out there, finding missing chunks of land, having mountains disappear, or seeing rivers flowing to nowhere. Strange things have been known to happen there, and I thought that setting would be perfect for this new series.

Not only are there monsters galore to see in the Far Lands, I'll also be telling you about the history of this landscape. There will be some new and terribly evil villains, but also a whole new set of histories to go along with the game, like the stories of the Council of Wizards and the dreaded Warlocks. The myths about these ancient creatures will be sprinkled throughout these books. You'll learn about the great war that happened hundreds of years ago in the Far Lands between the Wizards and the Warlocks, see some of the epic structures, and find some ancient, enchanted relics, like Needle. But, more importantly, you'll see how Watcher and his friends will use the ancient relics to battle the Zombie Warlord, Tu-Kar, and his horde of monsters.

In addition to a new cast, we're trying something never before attempted with Minecraft and literature: an interactive novel that links an adventure in a book with gameplay on a Minecraft server. For the first time ever, you'll be able to read my book, then go onto the Gameknight999 Minecraft server, and play through the adventure in a custom-built adventure game.

Yes, that's right, you'll be able to explore the ancient structures, try to defeat the traps laid by your adversary, and face the monsters that Watcher and his friends will battle. Test your skill at parkour as you try to reach the top of the old church. Face the zombie general, Ro-Zar, in combat in that church—if, that is, you can survive the waves of zombies and skeletons that'll try to stop you.

Face the zombie warlord, himself, Tu-Kar, if you dare, then go to the Capitol and challenge the scariest monster of them all, Kaza. As you battle these creatures, you'll be following the storyline from the book, and seeing the fantastic structures built by the famous building team: Quadbamber (Joseph Bamber), Mr_man12 (Will Shephert), Arp97 (Adam Pugh), and Benma98 (Ben Archer). Their creations are epic; I only hope I can describe them well enough in the book so you can see them in your mind. You can see the capital above, but I'm really looking forward to seeing the Zombie Fortress, which is just being started as I'm writing this.

If you can't play on a server, do not fear; we'll also be making a version of the game that is downloadable. This version won't have all the custom-programmed monster bosses, but you'll be able to see all of the incredible structures described in the book, as well as waves and waves of monsters to battle. I think it's gonna be epic!

We'll be putting QR codes into the story, as you can see below. This will let you scan the QR code and see what we've built on the server, based on the story in the book. There are numerous free QR code readers that can be downloaded to a smart phone. Be sure to ask your parents' permission before downloading anything to your phone; you want to be careful and know where it's coming from. I tend to stick to things that actually come from the app store, just to be safe.

These QR codes will be embedded throughout the story, just to give the readers that extra bit of content to make the story come alive. Maybe we'll put a few hints or secrets on these pages to help you find hidden armor or weapons in the game, so make sure you keep checking them, as the pages will be changing over time.

This code above will take you to the ancient church where a really cool battle takes place in the game. Turn on your QR reader app on a smart phone and point it at the QR code. It will instantly take you to that page, where you can see the old church, as well as other information about the game and the Gameknight999 Minecraft Network. You can find information about the Gameknight999 Minecraft Network, as well as information about the interactive game, at www.gameknight999.com.

If you pay attention to hints in the book, you may find some extra loot in the game to help you face off against the Zombie Warlord. You can also play it with your friends, though the game gets more difficult when more users are playing.

I don't think anyone has tried anything this complicated before with Minecraft literature. We've hired programmers from all over the world to develop this custom game, and the builders are working to create the most amazing structures ever. From what I've seen so far . . . it's really cool. I think you'll really get a feel for the story and the locations when you play the game, but, more importantly, you'll taste a little of the battle that Watcher and his friends will face as they go through the adventure.

I hope you all fall in love with these new characters and the Far Lands, as I already have. Maybe you can play the online game with Monkeypants_271 and Gameknight999 (who's he?). It's gonna be awesome . . . but be prepared for some serious battles. Only the bravest Minecrafter should consider trying!

Good luck, and watch out for creepers.
Monkeypants_271

EXCERPT FROM *ZOMBIES ATTACK!*

The party moved quietly through the forest, approaching the dilapidated church from the west. They'd traveled along the road for an hour, maybe less, when they saw the tall tower of the church sticking up above the trees. When he saw the tall structure, Cutter led them off the road and approached the church from the cover of the forest, hoping to keep any unwanted eyes from seeing them too soon.

They moved from tree to tree, using the trunks to hide their presence. Watcher kept a tight hold on the rope tied around Er-Lan, keeping the monster close. The smell of the creature was terrible, and at times, Watcher had to get upwind from the monster to reduce the odor. But it did little to help.

"Everyone stay here for a minute," Blaster said.

The boy removed his black leather armor and replaced it with something colored forest green, then ran toward the edge of the forest, fading into the background. In minutes, he returned with a smile on his square face.

"I don't see any guards around the church," Blaster said. "In fact, the whole place looks deserted."

"Hmmm," Cutter said, then turned and faced his prisoner. "Where are all the zombies?"

"Er-Lan does not know," the zombie replied. "Perhaps they headed for the fortress already, but Tu-Kar had to come here and collect all the NPC prisoners. The zombie warlord might still be here with many soldiers." He turned and faced Planter and Watcher. "All must be very careful."

"Great advice," Blaster said with a mischievous grin.

"Were there any guards on the entrance to the church?" Cutter asked.

"No," Blaster replied. "But they were all sealed with cobblestone. If we are going in through the main entrance, then we'll have to dig our way through with pickaxes."

"We can't do that; everyone will hear us," Watcher said.

"You have a better idea, professor?" Cutter asked.

Watcher moved to the edge of the forest and looked up at the church and tower. It was built from stone brick, some of the cubes cracked with age, others green and mossy. Vines hung down much of the structure, giving it a sad and forgotten look. Dotting the sides of the tower were many windows, each filled with colored glass. It seemed as if a torch flickered from behind the windows, filling them with bright color. Some of the windows had iron bars across the opening, likely to keep unwanted visitors from getting in. The top of the tower was partially missing, the roof of the tower completely absent.

Surveying the structure with his keen eyes, Watcher looked for a path in without getting noticed. And then he saw it.

"Of course . . . we can jump," he said to himself.

Turning, he sped back to his friends.

"I figured out a way we can get in without being noticed," Watcher said. "We won't need to dig through any stone, and we'll be completely silent."

"Oh, really?" Cutter asked. "Tell us your magical strategy."

"Here's what I think we should do," Watcher said in a low voice. "We climb up the outside of the tower. There are iron bars we can use. We'll jump from iron bar to iron bar. We'll be able to climb much of it by using the vines."

"I like that plan," Planter said, patting her friend on the back.

Watcher beamed. He felt as if he were charged with electricity.

"What do we do with him?" Blaster asked, pointing at the zombie.

"He stays here," Cutter said. He grabbed Er-Lan and pulled him to a tree, then wrapped a rope around the prisoner and tree, tying him tight. "When we're done, we'll come back and get him, but we aren't gonna have this monster give us away in there."

"Er-Lan will stay quiet," the monster moaned. "It is not necessary to tie up this zombie."

"Be quiet!" Cutter snapped. "You're staying here."

The warrior pulled out a cloth and tied it around the zombie's mouth, making it impossible for him to speak. Er-Lan looked at Watcher and Planter, his dark eyes pleading for help.

"Don't worry, Er-Lan," Watcher said. "We'll be back for you."

"Yeah," Planter added. "It'll be okay. In no time, we'll return and set you free again."

The monster nodded as a tear slowly dripped from his eyes. Watcher could tell Er-Lan was afraid. Maybe it was fear of being tied up, or more likely of being left alone. They had formed a bond with the zombie in their short time being together, and found they had more in common than not. Er-Lan, like Watcher, felt alone in his zombie community. Being small and weak, every-one felt the monster was worthless; it was an attitude Watcher knew a lot about.

"Just be calm, Er-Lan," Watcher said. "We'll come back soon."

"How cute, the little villager trying to keep the little zombie from being afraid," Cutter said. "How pathetic."

"Be nice," Planter scolded, but Cutter had already turned his back and was heading for the church.

Watcher sighed, then followed the big NPC toward the church tower.

They sprinted across the clearing that ringed the structure, each of them glancing to the left and right, watching for monsters. Cutter was the first to reach the building. Instantly, he started climbing the vines that ran down its rocky sides.

"No, not there," Watcher said. "You can't make it to the top from that spot. Over here."

The young NPC ran around the tower until he found the spot he'd identified earlier. The vines led upward to a bar-covered window. Watcher was the first to climb, scaling the wall as if he were walking down a path. When he reached the end of the vines, Watcher climbed to the top of an iron-barred window, then sprinted forward a step and jumped out into the open air. He landed on another bar-covered window, then jumped to the next and the next, slowly rising up the side of the tower. Behind him, his friends were doing the same, Blaster and Planter following easily. It was fun, like the game they used to play as children, jumping from tree to tree in the forest, but Cutter looked uncertain and afraid, though Watcher knew the big villager would never admit it.

They moved slowly up the side of the tower, switching between the parkour jumps to climbing the vine covered walls. It was arduous work, and Watcher's muscles were soon screaming at him with fatigue. Finally, after one last terrifying leap, Watcher made it to the top of the tower, where part of the roof was completely missing. Below was an open room, with shelves of books and chests lining the wall, making the descent into the room easy.

"Look out!" Blaster shouted.

He made the leap and landed gracefully next to Watcher. Stepping on the bookshelves, he jumped down into the room and surveyed their surroundings. Planter then landed next to him and followed Blaster into the dark room.

"Come on, Cutter," Watcher said, motioning to the big warrior.

The soldier was to the last jump, but he looked nervous.

"Hurry up. Planter and Blaster are already down there. If any zombies come, they'll be in trouble. We need you . . . now!"

The warrior gave Watcher a scowl, then sprinted forward. He took one step and leaped into the air, but his foot slipped a little and he stumbled; Cutter wasn't going to make it. Instantly, Watcher dropped to his stomach. He scooted forward as far as he could, hooking his toes on the edge of the wall and extended his hand as far as he could. Cutter floated through the air, slowly getting dragged downward. They both knew if he fell from this height, he wouldn't survive.

Stretching his entire body, Watcher reached out and grabbed Cutter's wrist. Instantly, his grip started to slip; he wasn't strong enough to hold Cutter for long. Suddenly, Cutter's iron grip clamped around Watcher's wrist. It felt as if a blacksmith's anvil had just somehow been wrapped around his arm. The weight of the soldiers was too much to bear.

"I can't pull you up," Watcher said, gritting his teeth. "You have to climb."

Cutter glanced up at the boy, a look of uncertainty in his eyes. He swung his body until his boots touched the wall, then he used them to push himself up. Climbing Watcher's arm like a rope, Cutter slowly moved higher and higher until his fingers reached the edge of the stone wall. He released his crushing grip on Watcher's wrist and grabbed the edge with his other hand, then pulled himself upward. Grabbing the edge of his armor, Watcher yanked hard, helping the soldier up onto the ledge. Finally, he made it to the top and was safe.

"You two done playing around up there?" Blaster asked.

Watcher laid down on his back, breathing heavily, sweat dripping down his face. His wrist throbbed with pain, the skin red and sore.

"You okay?" Watcher asked.

Cutter stood up and glanced down at his two companions, then back to Watcher. "Why shouldn't I be okay?"

Adjusting his armor, he jumped down onto the bookshelves, then climbed down onto the chest and made his way to the floor.

"Hey archer, are you coming?" Cutter yelled.

"Yeah," Watcher sighed, then lowered his voice. "You're welcome." But of course no one heard him.

Standing, Watcher leapt down the shelves and chest until he was on the floor. Instantly, he drew his bow and notched an arrow as he sniffed the air. It smelled bad . . . really bad.

"I think there are zombies nearby," Watcher said.

"You hear or see any?" Cutter asked.

Watcher shook his head. "No, but I can smell 'em."

"I think you're imagining things," Cutter said as he drew his diamond sword. "Come on, we're going to the ground floor to look for that underground chamber."

"It would be best if we went slowly," Watcher said. "We don't want to be surprised by any monsters."

"There's nothing to be afraid of," the warrior said. "I can take care of anything in this building."

"I'm not afraid, I just think we should be cautious and think this through."

"There's time enough to think after all our friends are free," Cutter said with a sneer.

He turned and headed for the stairs, barreling down the steps two at a time, Planter and Blaster following close behind. Watcher ran after them, trying to keep up.

The stairway descended into the darkness, moving to the next floor. Cutter stopped for just an instant, but seeing only darkness, he moved to the next floor.

"We should slow down," Watcher whispered, but no one answered.

The stench of rotten flesh was getting worse.

Cutter led them to the next floor. He paused for moment, trying to peer into the darkness, but the inky blackness was impenetrable. Just as he was about to head to the next floor, the sound of something sharp scraped across the wooden floor. Everyone froze. Watcher stared into the darkness, looking for movement, but it was so dark, he couldn't see anything . . . but he knew they were there; the smell was terrible.

"Zombies," Watcher whispered. "But I can't see any of them."

No one replied.

Blaster removed his forest-green armor and put on his favorite, black, then darted off into the darkness, his leather boots hardly making a sound. Suddenly, light flared on the opposite side of the room; a torch had been placed on the ground. The shuffling of leather scraping the ground sounded off to the right, then another torch came to life. More torches appeared as Blaster darted across the center of the room.

In seconds, the entire center of the room was lit, but still no zombies. Blaster put the torches away and drew his two curved knives.

"I don't think there are any monsters here at all," the boy said.

Suddenly, a moan floated out from the far side of the room. Then another moan came from the right and left sides, almost simultaneously.

"They're along the walls," Watcher said. "I told you I could smell them."

Just then, a growling moan came from the top of the stairs, but it wasn't just one voice . . . it was many. The same sound came from the steps leading down to the next floor.

"They've sealed off the stairs," Planter said. "We have no way to escape."

Now, zombies were stepping into the circle of illumination that flickered across the room. Razor-sharp claws extended from their fingers, the dark nails reflecting the light from the torches.

"We're . . . surrounded," Planter said, her voice cracking with fear.

Watcher glanced at the monsters approaching from the right, then turned to those on the left. Zombies were standing at the top of the stairs they'd just descended and another group was slowly coming up from the lower floor.

They had nowhere to run . . . they were trapped.

Watcher drew an arrow and notched it to his string, but didn't know where to shoot. There were at least a dozen monsters in the room, if not more, and three times that many on the stairs.

It was hopeless.

He'd failed his father and sister, and now he'd led Planter, the person he cared most about in the world, to her death. Fear enveloped his body, making every nerve feel as if it were on fire. His heart pounded in his chest and his breathing was short and raspy. Looking to the left and right, Watcher tried to figure out what to do. The situation seemed impossible. This was the end, and all he could do was wait for his doom.